Into The Light

Marshall Hughes

The Revenge Series

Book 2

Copyright © 2019 Marshall Hughes
www.marshallhughes.co.uk
All rights reserved.
ISBN: 9781798245606
Imprint: Independently Published

DEDICATION

JAMIE STRUTHERS HYSLOP

&

IN MEMORY OF MY FATHER

.

CONTENTS

ACKNOWLEDGMENTS

I spent two years editing my first novel, three times, while writing the second book. Self-publishing is not an easy journey and you learn as you proceed. On many occasions, I wanted to give up but continued. Out with the Prologue, Into The Light starts where Out Of The Dark ends. Reverend Charles McIntyre inadvertently hears Jayden Scott's confession at the church just before New Year. The second book uncovers the web of lies surrounding the main protagonist. It includes first-person narratives from Jayden Edward Scott, the Reverend, Inspector Nicholas Canmore and Kristina Cooper. I did intend to wrap up the storyline. However, I went with the flow of the narrative and finished this book on a cliffhanger, so will need to write another one to complete the series, Back To The Dark.

I would like to thank several people. To the beautiful Jo Ahlberg with the philosophical imagination who inspires, excites and delights. Also, my fellow author and fantastic mentor, Jacqueline Simon Gunn, for her encouragement along this journey. To everyone on WriteStuff who put up with my book posts and the Indie Author Retweet Group (#IARTG) on Twitter who support self-published authors and share my excerpts, book marketing articles, poetry and photography. Finally, to ProWritingAid. This technological editing tool is my best friend to check the writing style, grammar, spelling, repeats, echoes, passive verbs, dialogue, pace and readability.

PROLOGUE

Three months later

My eyes flick open.

I stare into the dark space and try to make sense of the situation. The pain in my head is insufferable and my limbs, heavy. The heat is oppressive. I struggle to breathe. As my mind clears, I remember extreme fatigue followed by a floating sensation before plunging into the deep void. *He must have drugged my coffee.* As my senses become more alert, I hear a noise. It is the recognisable sound of a car engine. I am trapped in the boot of his 4x4. The plastic ties cut into my wrist and ankles with a gag in my mouth. It is claustrophobic. Perspiration covers my entire body. I panic, my heart beats faster which makes it hard to inhale and exhale because of the obstruction. I experience severe dizziness before the swirling void consumes my mind once more.

Sometime later, fresh air caresses my face. Trembling, I open my eyes only to turn away from the intense glare of the light. My kidnapper cuts the zip ties. His hand reaches out to grip my arm.

"Get out of the car," he declares. "Don't try to escape this time."

I follow his instructions.

A shiver passes through my very soul. I force myself to look at him although I am fearful of his state of mind. There is a new form of insanity surrounding this killer: delusional, psychotic, manipulative, volatile and dangerous. Despite his warning, I struggle to get away from his grasp, but he holds on tighter as we walk to the rear of the cottage. I fear death is imminent. As my assailant tries to find the lock for the key, he drops the torch. I muster the strength from my drug-induced condition and bend down. It is such a hard task. The heaviness in my limbs is like sinking into quicksand, struggling against the unbearable pressure, pulling my body into the depths of the swampy mass. I seize the opportunity, grab hold of the light and

1

crack it across his head. He flinches. His hand moves to the back of his skull. In an almost insane act of violence, I smash it over his head, again and again. As he falls to the ground, I flash the beam of light into the black abyss and try to make sense of my surroundings. I only have one thing on my mind—to escape. I rush to the car and pull on the handle. It does not open. Not sure what to do, I hear him groan as he tries to stand up. Without waiting to determine his next move, I run away from the cottage. The stones cut into my bare feet. I ignore the pain, climb over a gate and along a path which leads to the woodland. The overgrown bushes snag at my clothes and prick my skin.

He calls out my name.

I need to switch off the torch. He'll notice the light.

My eyes adjust to the dark and the moon shines through the gaping holes in the canopy. I dart through the forest, stray branches whipping past my face. No matter how fast I run, I can sense him from behind. My weary body is no longer able to function. I lose pace, stop to catch my breath and dare to look round. He is there, running like a predator hunting its prey. I have no more energy left to escape and give up, accepting my fate. I turn to confront my pursuer, drop to my knees and see the blade in his hand.

"Don't do it, Jayden. Please…"

1

JUDGEMENT DAY

"God will judge the secrets of men through Jesus Christ."
(Romans 2: 16)

New Year's Day
(03.00)

My mind is in turmoil.

It is three o'clock in the morning, several hours after the bells on New Year's Day. As a humble man of God, I sit at the front of the church and gaze up at the wooden cross behind the pulpit. I believe Jayden knows that I heard his confession. He will come soon. I saw him out the corner of my eye at the bedroom window as I made my way towards the kirk. I drop my head forward as my hands reach up to cover my face, shaking it from side to side in disbelief. I press my fingers into my temples, not sure how to process his words. Since when was my Presbyterian Church a place for confession? *How do I react to this news?* My stomach churns. *What shall I do now?* I think back to all the times that I defended his innocence. Inspector Canmore was right. Jayden Scott *is* a cold-blooded killer. *This is the ultimate act of betrayal.* I want to lash out, but the anger wells up inside, burning through my veins, finding no means of escape. *I'm such a bloody fool.* On edge, my heart beats against my chest before an icy shiver convulses through my body.

I open my mouth to speak, but nothing.

In a raspy voice, I say, "Why?"

The shock dissipates.

And then, the fury surfaces.

Unable to contain myself any longer, I shout to my God, "Is this a test? Why do you burden my life with this problem? I have only just found happiness with Jayden's mother and now this dilemma." I reach for the book on the communion table, grip it close to my chest, and whisper, "A false witness shall not be unpunished, and he that speaketh lies shall not escape."

Pacing back and forth, I recite the verse from the bible, repeatedly. I feel the inner conflict inside, tearing at my heart and troubling my soul.

"Why did you kill your own father, Jayden. Why?"

****

New Year's Day
(02.45)

I am unable to sleep. And lie in bed, thinking about my killer status. The only sound in the room is the tick-tock, tick-tock, tick-tock of the grandfather clock. It is several hours after the celebrations, quarter to three to be precise, on this fateful morning at New Year. I turn over and gaze at Kristina's delicate features. *She's adorable. I can't lose her again. This woman is the love of my life.* Just then, I hear a noise, cock my head to the side and listen. It is the front door. I get out of bed and peer through the window. The Reverend walks down the path to the church. He handled himself well, celebrating the bells, despite hearing my confession.

And now, I must confront him.

Careful not to disturb Kristina, I put on my clothes and sneak towards the bedroom door. My shoe lands on a squeaky floorboard. I turn around, stare at her, wait for some kind of reaction, but she is fast asleep. As I lift my foot, the frightful noise continues and becomes duller in pitch, creaks like an old tree trunk straining from the force of the wind. And then, silence. I push on the door with one hand as the other turns the handle, pull it open and try to avoid any other unwelcome sound. On the other side, I let out a huge sigh of relief.

Before my encounter with Charles, I gulp down a double measure of whisky for courage to face his judgement. *How much of my confession did he witness?* There is only one way to find out. I grab my winter overcoat from the stand in the hallway, ready to deal with the weather outside. As I walk towards the church, the chill in the night air is bitterly cold. My hands are numb. I breathe into them, trying to heat my fingers to open the door. I turn the looped piece of metal and enter the building through the front entrance.

I stop at the partition with the stained glass window and recall our conversation just over twenty years ago: "Remember, I'm always here for you boy. Take care of yourself and your mother." *Will you be here for me now, Charles?* My hand reaches out to push open the door. I hesitate and doubt whether this is the right decision. Everything ceases to exist at that moment. Just then, I hear his voice.

"Is that you, Jayden? Please come inside. I know you're there."

I enter the church and walk towards my adjudicator. He clutches the bible. His eyes never leave mine as I walk up the aisle.

"Charles…"

"Don't say a word. I need time to think."

He stares up at the cross, muttering words from the holy book under his breath, "Be sober, be vigilant; because your adversary the devil, as a roaring lion, walketh about, seeking whom he may devour."

I wait.

He turns.

There is a long, brutal, pause before he speaks.

"Is it true?"

"What do you mean?"

"Tell the truth," he bellows. "I listened to every word of your confession."

"What you heard is correct, Charles."

He wrings his hands together in desperation. "Why?"

"It's hard to explain. Edward… my father… he…"

"Start at the beginning. And don't lie."

"My father is an evil man. You said those words yourself."

"Yes, I recall that conversation."

"My past is not an excuse. However, I had an awful upbringing. You never knew the full extent of his violent temper. From an early age, I experienced his volatility and numerous beatings with his belt, not only towards myself but also my mother. After years of abuse, the only way I can describe how I felt was one of anger, not an exploding anger, but a cold, calculating anger, festering like an open wound that refused to heal. It lasted throughout my childhood and never left my adult life. That type of putrid anger persists, eats away, seeks revenge for everything he did to us. Does that make sense?"

He nods.

"Edward Scott deserved to die."

"Nobody deserves to die by the hand of another."

"What do you think of me now, Charles?"

His eyebrows deepen. "One of disappointment. Heavy is my heart of stone."

"You're like my real father. Please forgive my wrongdoing."

"It's not as simple as that, Jayden. You betrayed my trust and lied. I've always defended your innocence. I'm such an idiot. Now I know why you insisted he would never return. What happened? What did you do to Edward?"

"That's not important. You're happy with my mother. I made that possible."

"My happiness is irrelevant," he says. "What did you do to him?"

"It's too much of a burden for you to hear. All that matters is that he's never coming back."

"I can't deal with this situation. You're right. This is too much responsibility for a humble man of the church. You need to confess. We must contact Inspector Canmore."

"NO!" I shout. "I won't declare my guilt. I can put this right. What about my mother? Don't do this, Charles. For once in my life, I have a chance to find happiness with Kristina. Please, don't take that away. PLEASE."

He sighs. "I'm not sure what to do?"

"Find it in your heart to forgive my misdemeanour. My father caused our family so much misery. You of all people know that more than anyone. Edward had to suffer for *his* sins. That is God's will, Charles."

The Reverend walks towards the pulpit. "You must confess your crime," he says, picking up a handful of paper. He rifles through, pulls out a single sheet and hands over the script. "Read this and hope that God can forgive you."

I stare at the page.

"Stand up, recite these words and seek forgiveness for *your* sins," he bellows. "Say it like you mean every word."

If this is what it takes, then I'll do it.

With conviction, I read out the text:

Be merciful to me, O God,
because of your constant love.
Because of your great mercy
wipe away my sins!
Wash away all my evil
and make me clean from my sin!

I recognise my faults;
I am always conscious of my sins.
I have sinned against you - only against you -
and done what you consider evil.
So you are right in judging me;
you are justified in condemning me.
I have been evil from the day I was born;
from the time I was conceived, I have been sinful.

Sincerity and truth are what you require;
fill my mind with your wisdom.
Remove my sin, and I will be clean;
wash me, and I will be whiter than snow.
Let me hear the sounds of joy and gladness;
and though you have crushed me and broken me,
I will be happy once again.
Close your eyes to my sins
and wipe out all my evil.

He lets out a deep sigh. "That's enough. You say your words with sincerity."

"I say it to redeem myself, to seek forgiveness not just from Him, but also from you."

"That is not my place. It is God who decides. I will close my eyes to your sins and never speak of it again. Your confession is mine to bear for the rest of my life, for all eternity. I feel a certain degree of responsibility. I should have done more to protect you and Carolyn from your father. This is our secret, Jayden. However, you must leave my house as soon as possible. I need time to deliberate, to deal with the situation in my own way."

"I understand. It's our secret, Charles."

****

The next day, I pack the bags into the boot of the car. Anxious, I make my way back to the house to get Kristina and say goodbye to my mother and Charles. I need to leave this man alone. I am more than aware of his anguish. The pain and torment is visible on his face. I see the raging fire consuming his mind, the black smoke belching from the depths of the underworld to inflame his darkest, deepest suffering. It must be a living hell hole. A truly hellish place for a man of the church.

I meet Kristina at the front door. There is no sign of Charles or my mother. *Where is he? I need to speak to him before we depart.*

"Why do we have to leave?" she asks.

"I already told you. I have a last-minute meeting and need to work on a damage limitation advertising campaign due to a public scandal in the banking sector for one of my clients, Mr Guthrie."

"It's all very sudden."

"That's business, my darling."

"And what's wrong with the Reverend? He seems distant."

"Stop asking so many questions. I'll explain everything on our way home."

She sighs.

My mother interrupts our conversation. "Is that you packed?"

"Yes, ready to go." I appear nervous, my eyes shifting in many different directions to try and find the Reverend. "Where's Charles?"

She takes hold of my hands. "He asked me to say goodbye to you both. He's not well today. The poor man seems very ill."

"Tell the Reverend we send our love," says Kristina.

"Thank you," replies my mother. "Don't worry. I'm sure he'll be better soon."

"I'll be back in a minute. I need the toilet." I run up the stairs to the second floor and knock on the study door, hoping he is inside. "Are you there?"

"No!"

"Charles, stop being silly."

"Please go away, Jayden."

I push it open.

The Reverend sits in the chair next to the bureau. He turns his ashen face towards my direction. I move forward, kneel in front of him and attempt to take his hands. He recoils in disgust, turning his head from my gaze.

"Charles, sorry to burden you with this problem. I can't stand to see you suffer. What can I do to make this torment leave your soul?"

He looks straight into my eyes. "You must depart and never return."

"But you're my family. My life. My mentor. My friend."

"And you are now the enemy, my boy."

This is all too much. His words are brutal. I have lost his support. "I see you've made your decision."

The Reverend turns away to avoid my fixed stare.

I get up off my knees and walk towards the door, waiting for his final word. It never comes. My pulse quickens. I grab onto the bannister outside his room, trying to compose myself. I mumble under my breath, "I'm on my own."

Just then, I feel a hand on my shoulder. "I'll always be here for you, Jayden. You're not on your own. We must deal with this together."

I gasp and turn around.

"You need my depth of courage," he declares.

"Why have you changed your mind?" I say in disbelief.

"I love you like my own son. That's why I can't walk away. I'm also to blame for this mess. I need some time alone. I must find my inner strength. We'll see each other soon, I promise. Let's get your mother and Kristina."

I grip his arm. "Thank you."

He leads the way down the stairs much to my mother's delight. The Reverend stands by her side as they both wave us goodbye.

As we drive onto the main street, Kristina blurts out, "What's going on?"

"What do you mean?"

"Why is Charles so distant towards you?"

"He's not. My mother said he's unwell."

"I'm not stupid. He seems pale and withdrawn. Full of torment. Did anything happen? Tell me, Jayden."

"Why do you analyse everything all the time?"

"But…"

I raise my voice. "Stop it! You're creating something out of nothing."

She is about to say more and changes her mind. Instead, there is an icy silence on the journey to Edinburgh. I withdraw and immerse myself in my own thoughts, thinking of a plan to heal our rift. We still have to spend the rest of the vacation together. *Once I get my meeting out of the way with Mr Guthrie, we can go on another trip. Someone else could have dealt with the bank scandal. However, it was a convenient excuse to leave right away. Where shall we go? Lincoln? NO! The police information on Annabel Taylor may have arrived. The cottage, perhaps? Yes, I'll take her to Argyll. We need some time alone. After that, I have to work on Charles. I want him back in my life.*

We arrive in Edinburgh in the afternoon. I park the car in the bay at my apartment complex. I gaze over in Kristina's direction for the first time on the journey. Her body language is distant. She stares out of the window. Leaning over, I reach out my hand to caress the side of her face. There and then, I lie, to deceive the person who I want to spend the rest of my life.

"Don't worry. I'm sorry for shouting at you. Charles revealed something that not even my mother knows about. That's why he's distant at the moment. I told him to tell Carolyn."

She turns and looks with concern. "What?"

"The Reverend said this in confidence, Kristina."

"Just tell me, please."

"His past troubles him. He needed to confess his sins. Hoping someone would forgive him. It was before my father went missing. It was a long time ago."

"What happened," she asks. "Charles had nothing to do with your father's disappearance, did he?"

"No, no, no. Nothing like that."

"Thank goodness."

"He was close to a married woman. A parishioner in the village. Nobody else knows, not even her husband or my mother."

"An affair?"

I nod. "The sinful act of adultery with a neighbour's spouse. It stopped as soon as Carolyn asked for the Reverend's support. Charles insists that he's never seen her again, if you know what I mean."

"Does she still attend the church?"

"Yes."

"And you told him to tell your mother?"

"It was only a suggestion. To ease his conscience."

"That was not the right choice taking into consideration how unfaithful your father was towards your mother."

"I said that to the Reverend before we left. I told him to forget and forgive his sins and never mention it again. To allow himself some happiness with Carolyn."

Kristina nods in approval.

"You agree?"

"It was the only thing to say. I suppose we all make mistakes and your mother and Charles were not together. Although it's a surprise. I never thought he would do anything adulterous?"

"Mrs Cameron is the local florist in the village. She went through a terrible time with her husband. He got too emotionally involved with the wrong woman."

"The Reverend is a caring person. He crossed the line. It sounds as though he regrets his actions."

"He does need to forgive and forget. Please don't judge him. Charles is a good man. Don't say anything. This is an act of betrayal to even tell you."

"I won't. It has nothing to do with me, you or your mother. It's his to own. Let's not speak about his past again. Agreed?"

"Okay."

Kristina seems at ease and more responsive. The turn of events that led to my confession in the church, dealing with the aftermath of the lies and deception about the Reverend's affair is an intoxicating mix of ingredients. My senses are on high alert. I watch her every move. As my penis fills with blood, my heart quickens, excitable, and experience a tingling sensation on my skin in anticipation of the sexual act.

There is only one thing on my mind.

I shuffle closer.

"Thanks for understanding, Kristina. It's a sensitive subject."

"You should have said something sooner."

"I couldn't. I promised not to tell anyone."

My eyes focus on her lips.

She tucks a stray lock of hair behind her ear.

"At least you're loyal even if it caused tension between you and the Reverend and for us."

My gaze wanders over her curves.

"I am loyal. Too much, perhaps."

"You're a good man, Jayden."

I nod in agreement, knowing it is a lie. I am now fully erect. The somewhat pleasurable yet painful feeling in my groin is eager to enter her beautiful body.

"Let's leave the bags until later."

"Why? We may as well unpack."

"Later, Kristina."

Unable to contain myself any longer, I move forward and kiss those luscious lips in a demanding manner spurred on by the anguish, lies and deception.

"You're very intense, Jayden."

"You wouldn't have it any other way."

She laughs between our kisses.

I get out of the car, run to the other side and grab hold of Kristina's hand. With a sense of urgency in my stride, we walk towards the lift. Once on the sixth floor, I fumble with the key in the lock and go inside. I slam the door shut and trap her against the wall.

"Slow down," she insists.

"I can't. I want you and need you now."

My hands wander over her curves. I rub my pelvis into her groin. My intentions, undeniable. She responds, pulling down my zip to release my engorged penis. The tip of my shoe on either foot finds the ridge at the back, pushing each of them off my feet. She pulls down my underwear and trousers. I remove her layers of winter clothes to reveal her naked body beneath, those nipples erect due to the cold atmosphere in the apartment. I lift Kristina up and her legs wrap around my torso. Right there in the hallway, we make love against the wall. And then, I lead her to the bedroom where we spend the rest of the day in bed.

Later in the evening, I get the bags out of the car. I light a cigarette, sit inside the Noble with the door open and inhale the vapour deep into my lungs before releasing a huge plume into the night air. The after-sex-smoke helps to clear my head. I think in a more logical manner. I have already told my lovely criminologist that I have a meeting tomorrow morning. We can go to the cottage in Argyll before she returns to Lincoln. Kristina seems more at ease now that I told the lie about Charles and his affair with Mrs

Cameron. *She's so gullible. I also need the Reverend on my side. Charles made the choice to support me despite my confession. He must never find out about my other victims: Annabel Taylor, Martin Harris, Luiz Rodriguez, Raymond Cartwright and Jake Driscoe. That would destroy him and his faith in God.*

At that moment, the phone interrupts my thoughts.

I answer, waiting for Charles to speak first.

"Hello there. I promised your mother I would call to check you made it home okay."

"What a surprise. I was just thinking about you. We're fine."

"Good."

There is an awkward silence.

"Thanks for your support, Charles. It means a lot."

"We need to meet as soon as possible to clear the air once everything settles down and Kristina goes back to Lincoln."

"That's a great idea."

"I'll come to Edinburgh. That way, we'll have time on our own away from your mother."

"Perfect."

"We can see each other in a few weeks. I'll tell Carolyn I talked to you and that everything is fine. She's at a horticultural meeting with Mrs Cameron. Take care of yourself."

I try to stifle a laugh. *Mrs Cameron. How funny.* "You too, Charles."

He is the first one to hang up the phone.

That was a strain, but at least he's willing to talk. I need him on my side. Now, more than ever. I don't want to lie anymore or kill anyone else not unless it is absolutely necessary.

****

I wake up early the next day and think about my meeting at the agency. Jessica has put in place the team to deal with the crisis including the head of the bank, an independent public relations expert and our best employees within the office. Our biggest client needs to restore consumer confidence in its portfolio of brands after the economic downturn left the company in complete turmoil, relying on the taxpayer to bail it out. Mr Guthrie is now ready to rebuild the brand. It is a lucrative deal and one we are keen to represent. I must be there to lead our team and secure the contract.

I put all thoughts of work aside, roll over and spoon into her back, caressing her soft skin with my fingers. The sensation of extreme pleasure is instantaneous as my body responds. The euphoric but abnormal sexual desire for this woman is disturbing. She is like a highly addictive narcotic drug derived from the milky sap-like substance hidden inside the seedpods of the enchanting yet compulsive opium poppy. Such intoxicating beauty. She stirs, responding to my touch. I lose myself in our lovemaking, high from my drug-infused fix. For a while, we enjoy the moment, not saying a word. Kristina breaks the silence.

"What time do we leave for the cottage in Argyll?"

"When I get back from my meeting. No later than eleven."

"I'll pack my bag and be ready to go. I'm looking forward to our trip. I remember going on holiday to Glencoe when I was younger, but it's all a bit vague."

"You'll love the scenery. The landscape is stunning. We won't be able to do much hill walking at this time of the year. I checked the weather forecast. There's a thick blanket of snow over the treacherous hills. Very dangerous."

"We'll find lots of things to do to keep us occupied."

I wink over in her direction then check the clock. *Shit!* I leap out of bed. "I need to get ready," I say, grabbing a towel off the chair. "I can't be late for the meeting. This is too important."

She laughs. "It's your own fault, lover boy."

As I open the bedroom door, Kristina declares that she will cook breakfast before I finish in the shower. Once I put on my business suit, I make my way towards the kitchen. The radio plays in the background as she prepares an omelette.

I like the fact that Kristina has settled into my home. I want her in my life. She must never find out I killed my father, his mistress or the other victims. However, Marcus Hunter is sniffing about for her to do that bloody killer profile of Annabel Taylor. I must put together a plan. One that admonishes me from the whole sordid affair. Right now, I need a miracle.

"You seem very pensive?"

"Sorry, I was lost in thought about the business meeting."

Kristina hands over the cup. "Here's your coffee. Sit down. I'll finish the cooking. Do you want cheese?"

"Yes, thanks.

She smiles.

"When do you plan to go home?" I ask.

"Next week. Once we return from the cottage. I need to get ready for the start of the academic year. My students will be back soon. I also have to put together a profile for Police Scotland."

"The one for Superintendent Hunter?"

She puts the food down on the table. "Yes. I look forward to getting the information when I go home. Are you coming to Lincoln? You said you would after New Year."

I am caught off-guard. "I'm too busy. I'll organise a visit to coincide with a trip to London later in the month. Is that okay?"

"That's fine. Eat up or you'll be late."

I finish breakfast, kiss her goodbye and try to get into business mode on the drive to the agency, but my mind is in turmoil, thinking about her work, Superintendent Hunter and Annabel Taylor. *Focus on the task at hand,* I tell myself. I park the car in the bay next to the barge and head straight to the meeting room. As I have not seen Jessica Logan beforehand, I want a quick chat before we start. Everyone sits around the table, talking and drinking coffee.

"Good morning," I say with a sense of conviction, nodding in each direction. "Can you excuse us for one minute? Miss Logan, I need to talk to you."

I lead her outside the room. "Sorry, I'm late. Is everything okay?"

"Yes, Mr Scott. I have the agenda printed out and you've already looked at the brief. We're all set to go."

"Good. Let's start the meeting."

We return.

Mr Guthrie is keen to proceed.

Jessica announces the team consisting of two planners, three creatives, an online professional and a junior member from the copyright department. She continues to introduce the public relations specialist who is our client's contact. He will help to plan a favourable image for the firm alongside our advertising campaign.

"This is Stewart Bailey. He's a former marketing specialist turned public relations expert," declares Jessica.

"One of the best," replies Mr Guthrie. "Mr Bailey has an excellent track record at our bank and set up his own business about seven years ago. He's a hard worker, Mr Scott."

Stewart Bailey? He looks familiar. His name is familiar. The penny drops. *Fucking hell! Annabel Taylor's murderer, well, the main suspect anyway.* I nearly choke on my coffee and try to compose myself. "Welcome to the team, Mr Bailey," I say, shaking his hand in disbelief.

I become more restless as the meeting continues.

Mr Guthrie starts with a boring presentation outlining the challenges in the banking sector due to macro issues such as the monetary and geopolitical landscape and how technology will shape new customer trends. I switch off but continue to watch Stewart Bailey out the corner of my eye. He wears a blue business suit and a pale pink shirt, open at the neck, and appears casual yet professional. At a guess, this man is in his early forties, with grey hair pushed back from his forehead, the wrinkles appearing as faint lines across his brow. His deep-set eyes hide behind silver-framed glasses perching on top of a button nose with a high cleft, thin upper and protruding lower lip. When he talks, he has a habit of biting his top lip, then continues for a while, only to repeat the same ritual. It is very distracting. He must be good at his job or Mr Guthrie would not recommend him. That old dog is a shrewd banker with an entourage of experts to keep the bank afloat amidst the economic crisis.

I turn my attention towards Jessica who continues to go over the client brief. We agree that the advertising campaign and the public relations exercise should focus on a customer-centric strategy through personalisation of the consumer experience, rewarding loyalty and the simplification of the banking process through technological developments. With this in mind, I ask the planners and creative teams to generate ideas around this concept. The online specialist can focus on some digital strategies for the next meeting. Everyone leaves the room. Mr Guthrie appears content with the outcome.

"Nice to see you, Mr Scott," he declares. "It's always a pleasure doing business with you."

"Likewise. We'll design some exciting campaigns and work with your marketing department and PR consultant. You'll have the final decision on what you think is the best advertising strategy to meet your objectives."

He shakes my hand. "I look forward to that very much. Good to see you again, but I need to go. My day is full of back-to-back meetings. Get to know my public relations expert. He knows all aspects of our business, don't you, Mr Bailey?"

"I certainly do," he replies.

As Stewart Bailey puts the papers in his briefcase, I say, "Can I have a quick word with you before you leave?"

He nods.

"Would you like me to stay, Mr Scott?" asks Jessica.

"No, I can deal with it from here. Catch up with you later."

She leaves the room. "I'll be in my office."

I turn my attention towards Stewart Bailey and gaze at him for a few moments. "Please don't take this the wrong way. I need to ask you a question because I remember..."

"Remember what?" he says in a defending tone.

"Are you the person accused of murdering that woman?"

He takes a sharp intake of breath before he continues. "I see you're a man that gets straight to the point. The case never made it to court. I had nothing to do with her death. Let me reassure you, my arrest was all a misunderstanding."

I know how you feel. You had DCI Marcus Hunter on your back. I had Inspector Canmore on mine. The only difference is that you're innocent. I'm the guilty one.

He continues. "The evidence was circumstantial. Mr Guthrie offered support throughout the entire case. It was a long time ago. That episode is part of my past. I have an impressive track record if you would like to see my credentials?"

"Yes, please send the information to Miss Logan. We can keep it on file."

He nods. "I hope this misunderstanding will not ruin our professional association on this deal?"

I hesitate. "Of course not."

"Thank you."

"We'll talk again," I say, shaking his hand.

"Goodbye."

Once he leaves, I open the balcony door next to the meeting room and light a cigarette. Looking out across the quayside, I inhale the smoke deep into my lungs before letting out a huge sigh of relief. *Jesus Christ! You couldn't make up my life at the moment. It's just bizarre. Why him of all people? Why now? Is there some kind of reason?*

I stub it out and go to find Jessica Logan. She appears enthusiastic about the business deal. Not giving a shit one way or another, I tell her that I am going to the cottage for a week. Miss Logan is more than happy to run the agency in my absence. I also inform her Stewart Bailey will send his business background and to keep it on file. *I want to get to know you better, Mr Bailey. After all, we have a lot in common. I am the one who killed your ex-lover, Annabel Taylor.* Still reeling from the unexpected encounter, I leave the office and make my way to the flat, back to normality with my beautiful criminologist. I park the car and wait for the lift to come down to the ground floor. It seems to take forever. Finally, it arrives. I look forward to our trip to Glencoe, away from all this nonsense. The unpredictable nature of events over the last few days is out with my control. At least we can spend the rest of the holiday alone with no more interruptions.

On the way up in the lift, I daydream about her body and smile. The doors open. My face changes. I am not sure how to react. My jaw slackens, mouth open, eyes wide, staring at my nemesis. I stop breathing for a second, frozen to the spot, trying to comprehend the situation. I am about to say something but unable to find the right words and glare at him with a burning hatred in my eyes.

He speaks first.

"I thought I might have missed you, Mr Scott."

With a sense of utter confusion as to why he is at my apartment, my thoughts are incomprehensible. *I need to pull myself together and deal with the situation.* They both stand at the door of the flat, stare in my direction, waiting for an answer. I snap out of my confusion, clear my throat and regain my composure.

"How can I help you, Inspector Canmore?"

"It's been a while since we last spoke. Just a quick visit to update you on your father's case. I told Dr Cooper that we have the resources in place to restart the investigation."

I stare at Kristina. She is pale, her gaze never leaving mine.

"You already mentioned that before at my father's memorial. Why another visit, Inspector Canmore?"

"My superior officer, who is now DCI Grace McFarlane, has given the go ahead to search the area in Argyll over the next few months, weather permitting of course."

With a smug grin on his face, he waits for my reaction.

"Do what you must but stay away from my family."

"Is that a threat, Mr Scott?"

I barge past him, take Kristina's arm and lead her into the flat. I turn and face my adversary. "Goodbye, Inspector Canmore. Keep us updated about your investigation. However, you won't find anything because there's nothing to find."

"I'll keep you informed. Good day, Mr Scott."

On that note, I slam the door.

I feel angry and want to lash out at the nearest available object. Instead, I stride into the living area with Kristina following behind. I take the lid off the decanter and pour myself a large whisky, open the balcony, switch on the overhead heaters and light a cigarette, oblivious to the biting wind. After several moments, I am ready to look her straight in the eye.

"Are you okay?" she asks. "That was intense."

"I'm fine. This is what I have to deal with, Kristina. What did he say?"

"Not much. He arrived just before you."

"Don't tell that man anything."

"Why is he so adamant you're guilty, Jayden?"

With a look of disappointment on my face, I reply, "Why are you even asking that question? If you don't believe what I've told you, you may as well go home. GO! Get out of my sight."

"Don't you ever speak to me like that again," she declares.

I turn around, stare out over the Firth of Forth and hear her footsteps on the parquet floor as she leaves the living area. I gulp down the drink and pour another. *This is a fucking nightmare. I am powerless. First the Reverend, then Stewart Bailey and now Inspector Canmore. How much worse can it get? And, she's invading my space. I need time to think alone about a plan of action to deal with these unexpected turns of events. It's all a mess in my mind.* I decide to go for a walk and clear my head. Our trip will have to wait, assuming she is still here when I return. Right now, I do not care about anything but my own survival. I grab my winter overcoat off the stand and proceed to the front door.

I hear her voice. "Don't leave, Jayden. If you go, I won't be here when you get back. We have to talk. It's your choice."

I come to my senses and know there is no choice. I need to stay. She is my world. I turn around, take off my coat and walk back into the flat.

****

The following day, we head off to the cottage. Much to my delight, our chat cleared the air. I told her everything about the devious Inspector Canmore. She believed my version of events. Unbeknownst to Kristina, this beautiful criminologist is now my partner in crime. Finally, we can spend time alone, away from all the mayhem of the last few days. I want to meet with Charles on my return and will deal with Inspector Canmore in my own time. That modern-day Macduff is a dead man. One way or another, he will die, but not by my own hand. I have something more appropriate in mind for his death. Once Kristina returns to Lincoln, I will fine tune my plan in more detail. Halfway through our journey, we stop at a traditional tavern overlooking the shores of Loch Long. I park the Noble and turn towards Kristina. She appears deep in thought.

"Are you okay? What are you thinking about?"

"My work. I have a lot to do when I get back. I've been so embroiled in your life, I have forgotten about my own."

"Relax and enjoy our holiday. It will be the first of many. Sorry about your encounter with Inspector Canmore. Let's forget about his visit and have a good time together. Agreed?"

"Okay."

"Shall we have something to eat? This is a beautiful place, just like you, my darling," I say in a playful voice.

She laughs. "Your chat-up lines are appalling."

I run a finger down the side of her cheek. "That's better. I love to see you smile. No more thoughts about work or anything else until you return home."

"You're right."

We enter the tavern, the atmosphere thick with heat from the open fire. I go to the toilet and let Kristina order the drinks, deciding on a local beer for a change. On the way back, I see the barman flirt with my woman. She pays the money and returns to her seat. I tell the bastard to back off, staring at him while I sit down. *Fucking asshole.* We look at the menu and decide on some braised venison, vegetables and bread.

"You order, if you like," I declare.

I watch the nervous barman as he tries to avoid my eye contact. He takes the menus and scuttles out of the pub towards the kitchen. With a sense of satisfaction at the outcome, I lean over and take hold of her hands across the table.

"I love being with you, Kristina. I want this trip to be a special one for both of us, creating memories to remember in the future."

"You're very serious, Jayden. We've only known each other for a short time."

"You must realise there's a connection between us. It's fate. We were always meant to be together."

"I'm aware of our connection but we need to slow down."

"No! Life is too short. Don't deny how you feel, Kristina."

"I won't," she declares. "What's our plans for the rest of the week? Do you have anything in mind?"

"Plenty of relaxation. Just the two of us."

She rolls her eyes. "Sounds intriguing."

A waitress interrupts our intimate moment. The hearty venison steaks include root vegetables and a red wine sauce with crusty bread. It is delicious. I want another drink but decide to wait until we get home. I will have a whisky once we sort out the cottage. I pay the bill, leave the pub and relax for the rest of the journey. Kristina enjoys the view while I concentrate on my driving. I like the silence. Alone with my own thoughts. *As soon as she leaves for Lincoln, I'll put my plan into action to rid this world of Inspector Canmore. I can't let that search go ahead. When Kristina fell asleep last night, I watched a documentary on how to locate a buried body. It's difficult, but not impossible. After such a long time, the scent of death is not as strong. And the atrocious Scottish weather is in my favour. According to expert opinion, rain carries away the smell through the soil and the sniffer dogs might be way off track. I assume his sidekick Sergeant Murray and his mutts are part of the new search. How else would they find Edward Scott? Although important, this is not at the top of my agenda. Reverend McIntyre is first on my list and dealing with Kristina's reaction to her criminal profiling case when she finds out the connection between my father and Annabel Taylor. After that, I can focus on Stewart Bailey and Inspector Canmore. In the meantime, I hope to enjoy our trip. It doesn't bother me anymore that my father's dead body is near the cottage. At first it did, but now his corpse is part of the landscape. Left to rot for seven years, his lifeless skeleton is devoid of substance, the internal organs devoured by bacterial decomposition, insects and maggots. That is what he deserved.*

As I drive through the valley, I am more upbeat and back in control for the first time since New Year. I glance over at Kristina and notice she has fallen asleep. I stop in the layby near the cottage and have a cigarette. The winter daylight starts to fade. I stare in awe at the mountain range, thin rays of light from the sun filter through the clouds, reflecting off the snow-capped peaks, turning the surface a bone-like shade of white. It is alluring yet treacherous all at the same time. *This is very peaceful. If we do any hiking, it needs to be at ground level.* I walk to the edge of the layby, flick the cigarette into the boggy marsh, reminiscing about the fox I hurled into the depths of the swampy mass. *Interfering bastard, scratching at my father's grave until I beat it to death with the shovel.*

A voice interrupts my thoughts. "Jayden, what are you doing?"

"I'm just coming." The harsh winter weather is severe. I dash back to the car. "I stopped for a cigarette. How are you after your sleep?"

"Much better, thanks. Are we nearly there?"

Shivering, I say, "About ten miles along this road. I warn you now, the cottage is cold at this time of year. I'll light the fire as soon as we reach the house. Tomorrow, we can take a trip to the local village and stock up the larder."

"Good idea."

I turn on the engine, turn up the thermostat to full blast and drive through the winding road which leads to the heart of the glen. Before long, we arrive at the whitewashed cottage.

"It looks beautiful, Jayden."

"You'll love it here. Come on, let's get the bags out of the car. You unpack. I'll fix the heating."

"Deal."

I open the front door and the damp smell attacks the senses, my nose wrinkling in disgust at the unpleasant aroma. *It's nothing a good fire won't sort out.* My fingers find the light switch. We enter the cottage and stand in the hallway, shivering. As we exhale, water vapour from our breath manifests into tiny droplets of ice, floating like a burst of smoke into the air. I kiss her mouth and feel the cold on the tip of her nose.

"You're right. It's freezing," says Kristina.

I laugh. "I warned you. There's no quick fix until we light the fire and stoke up the oven."

She groans.

"Leave the bags. Come into the kitchen. Better still, let's have a drink to warm up."

I pour two large measures of whisky, light the candles and stove, sort the fire and several hours later, the bitter atmosphere starts to heat up. We keep on our winter coats, hat, gloves and scarf. As the night progresses, we peel off each layer.

"Better?" I ask.

"Much better," she replies.

"We can leave the unpacking until tomorrow. It will still be cold upstairs. It takes a while for the heat from the fire to circulate through the radiators. Shall we settle in the living room for the rest of the evening?"

"That would be nice."

I pour us another drink. We talk until the early hours of the morning, avoiding any discussion about the recent turn of events. The heat, whisky and glow from the flames are a seductive cocktail of ingredients. With every little touch, I see her pupils dilate, showing a subtle yet meaningful signal of her sexual desire. The outcome is inevitable, our intimacy relentless. The rest of the vacation seems to pass by in an instant. We spend our time resting, read, eat, walk and make love, shutting out any unwanted interference from the outside world. Everything is fine until the last day. We wake up before midday. I prepare breakfast when Kristina receives a call. She always puts it on speaker phone. I listen to the conversation from the living room drift into the kitchen.

"Hello. This is Kristina Cooper."

"Dr Cooper. This is Superintendent Marcus Hunter. I've been trying to get in touch with you for several days, but it keeps going straight to your answer message."

"There's not much of a signal. We're on holiday at the moment."

"Sorry to interrupt. Shall I call back at a more convenient time?"

"It's fine. How can I help?"

"I sent the box file to your address in Lincoln. Another one will follow soon with more in-depth information on the case."

"Thanks. I'll get it tomorrow when I return home. It might be a while before I read the material. I need to focus on my teaching preparation first."

"There's no hurry. However, I'm keen to get your expert opinion. I must emphasise Annabel Taylor's ex-partner, Stewart Bailey, is the prime suspect. Due to a technical error, his case never made it to court. Mr Bailey was in the Tollcross area that night. We have the information on CCTV footage. Keep that in mind."

"Please don't include too much detail about him at the moment. It will bias my analysis."

"In that case, I'll send the other box file in due course. Have a wonderful time, Dr Cooper."

"Thank you. I'll speak to you soon. Goodbye."

She disconnects the call.

"Kristina, come and get breakfast. It's ready," I shout.

Well, well, well. Stewart Bailey. At least he didn't mention my father, not yet anyway. What kind of profile will she conclude from the box file of information? I wonder if it will fit my characteristics? Let's see how clever you are Dr Cooper. And you, Stewart Bailey, are a convenient scapegoat. One way or another, I aim to set you up, but this time your guilt will be irrefutable.

2

CRIMINAL PROFILE

"Only you can control your future."
(Theodor Seuss Geisel)

I feel out of control.

But now, my criminologist mind has time and space to reflect. I gaze out of the window on the aeroplane and consider the events over the last few months. From the flowers to my keynote speech, the moment we met in the Balmoral Hotel at the whisky bar to his opening of the London agency, New Year, the Reverend's strange behaviour, Inspector Canmore's allegations and our visit to the cottage. I seem to be riding on a tidal wave of emotion with no control over its potential, destructive force. Jayden Scott is enticing and at the same time, elusive. I understand some of his past through my discussion with Jacqueline Hayes, the Reverend, his mother, and of course, Inspector Nicholas Canmore. Out with that, I have no more information about my lover. My analytical mind races out of control, scared to leave anything to chance. Thoughts that may not even have any logical reason. I take my diary out of my bag, find a blank page at the end of the book, and write down the key points.

How did Jayden know where I was staying in Edinburgh when I gave my keynote speech?

Why did he behave in the way he did after we went to see Macbeth? Why did he treat me like a whore?

What is wrong with Reverend McIntyre?

Did Charles have an affair or is there something else?

Why did we have to leave the manse early? Work? Really?

And, why is he so intense?

I ponder over my own questions. *I once read that control is about certainty and analysis to try and solve that uncertainty. Perhaps I'm being over-analytical? A relationship is nothing if it's not based on trust. Why do I doubt him? I'll ask him about my concerns when I phone later on tonight. Until then, I need to put it to the back of my mind.*

The flight attendant interrupts my thoughts. "Dr Cooper, here's a complimentary bottle of champagne for flying business class."

"Thank you."

She puts it down on the table and fills up the flute. "A three-course lunch is also available. I will bring the food. Can I get you anything else?"

"No. This is lovely, thanks."

I take a sip of champagne and return to inquisition mode, dismiss my advice to ask Jayden about my concerns and attempt to answer my own questions.

"How did he know where I was staying?" I mumble to myself.

I wrack my brains to recall if I told anyone about the Balmoral Hotel. *No, only my parents.* Just then, I remember the night out for my colleague's birthday in Lincoln. Therefore, several people at my work knew as well as the administrator within our department who booked the accommodation. I write down the names and will make a point to ask if anyone inquired about my whereabouts. I stare at the second question about our trip to the theatre to see Macbeth. *Is that how he treated his ex-lovers? Encounters with prostitutes, perhaps?* I take a large mouthful of champagne and another. *At the Reverend's house after the theatre, Jayden seemed oblivious to everything around him and the consequences of his actions. Why did he behave in such a manner?* Unable to answer my question, I give up. *I'll leave that for now. What about Reverend McIntyre and his affair?* I recall his drastic change in attitude and appearance. It happened almost overnight not long after the celebrations. Did something happen at the church on New Year's Eve? Why did Jayden not return with Charles? My head hurts thinking about the situation but continue. *And what about Jayden's explanation on the way back to Edinburgh about the Reverend's alleged affair with a married parishioner? I will talk to Charles, informally, to see his reaction.* I write down one final point and underline the words in bold print.

INSPECTOR NICHOLAS CANMORE

Why does he assume Jayden is guilty of his father's disappearance? And why does he think Edward Scott's remains are in Argyll? I remember the disappointment on Jayden's face when I questioned him and his response to my outburst. *If you don't believe me, you may as well go home. GO! Get out of my sight.* He commands such loyalty, but I need answers to these questions. I have so many doubts. *The hurt, I can't bear the pain. No, not again. Not after my divorce.*

I slam the diary shut.

And bend my head as my thumb and index finger massage the muscles on my forehead, releasing the tension. "What a stress," I say to myself.

I catch sight of the attendant walking up the aisle. She looks at the half-empty bottle of champagne. "Here's your lunch. Are you okay?"

"Yes, I'm fine. Thank you."

She raises an eyebrow and leaves the tray. I eat some of the meal and pour another drink. For the first time on the flight, I relax, and conclude that all this analytical deconstruction is pointless. However, I need to pursue it further.

I open the diary and write a plan of action.

Ask colleagues to see if there were any inquiries about my contact details for the conference.

Talk to Jayden about his past. Get to know him better.

Phone Charles for a casual chat to thank him for his hospitality at New Year and find out what is wrong.

Talk to Inspector Canmore?

The last point, I am not sure about so leave for now. Jayden seemed very relaxed at the cottage. *Surely, he would not take me there if he had done something to his father?* The more I think about the possibility, the more absurd it appears. It does not make any sense. He is right, that policeman is a lunatic, obsessed with finding evidence that does not exist. We will have to deal with the official search together, if and when it takes place. More coherent, I somehow justify the outcome in my mind and look forward to time on my own before I go back to work. The previous few months have been a roller-coaster ride of emotion: frustration, excitement, disappointment and now, I am too reflective and analytical for my own good. *This is how my mind works. That's the way I process information. It's my job.* As a distraction, I read a magazine and finish the bottle of champagne. The steward makes the announcement to fasten our seat belts as the plane prepares to land. I listen out for the familiar sound to unfold the wheels under the body of the aircraft but there is a screeching sound that never seems to end. I turn towards the passenger on the other side of the aisle. Mouth agape, her ageing eyes focus on mine for reassurance. Not knowing if there is a problem, I shrug my shoulders. The deafening noise continues until it dies out and ceases to exist. There is an eerie silence and it starts again. I cover my ears with my hands until the noise stops.

There is an announcement:

This is the captain. Please do not panic. We have a serious malfunction with the equipment on the plane and need to make an emergency landing. On my instruction, assume the brace position. Lean forward with your hands on top of your head and your elbows against your thighs. Ensure your feet are flat on the floor. I reiterate, please do not panic.

I do just that and struggle to control the fear welling up inside. The pounding of my heart threatens to burst through my chest. Heavy breaths change to short raspy gasps as I search for the mobile in my bag. I am just about to text my parents and change my mind. *Don't call. They will worry too much. I'll be fine. I'm not going to die on this plane.* I clutch hold of the phone with trembling hands and manage to spell out the right words to send to Jayden.

There is a technical fault with the aeroplane. It has to make an emergency landing. I wish you were here.

There are cries of help from some passengers. The flight attendants try to calm the situation. However, the atmosphere in the cabin is out of control. The plane tips to the side. It continues to circle the airport below, again and again. The elderly woman on the other side of the aisle unclips her seatbelt and sits in the next seat.

"I hope you don't mind," she whispers.

"Of course not," I reply. "We'll be fine."

She slides her hand into mine. "I'm meeting my husband from this plane if…"

"You'll still meet him."

"I had a bad premonition about this trip earlier today. I seem to have some sort of sixth sense."

"Your intuition should tell you it will be all right."

"I'm not sure. Not this time."

The text alert on my phone goes off.

What the hell is happening? Are you okay? I'll call you. I left for East Midlands in my car. It's the quickest option at the moment. I'll be there in over four hours. Pick up if you have a connection.

The altitude of the plane must be low enough to receive a signal because he calls my mobile. I let go of the old woman's hand to answer the phone.

"Kristina, are you okay?"

"What did you say?"

"ARE YOU OKAY?"

"Yes, yes, I'm fine."

"What's wrong?"

"There's a problem with the landing equipment. What does that mean, Jayden?"

"I'm not sure."

"Why does the plane keep circling the airport?"

"It's getting ready to land."

Another announcement interrupts our conversation:

All flight attendants, please return to your seats. Everyone must assume the brace position. I will land the aeroplane without any equipment. They have failed to extend.

I squeeze my companion's hand for the last time before the descent. "Be brave."

"You too," she says with tears in her eyes.

"Kristina, you stay on this phone. Do you hear me? Kristina…"

I whisper into the device. "I hear you."

"For fuck sake!" he shouts. "It must be the wheels. He's going to land the plane with no fucking wheels."

"Jayden, I'm scared."

"Remain strong. He *will* land the plane and it *will* all be fine."

As it descends to the airport, the aircraft almost appears to grind to a halt, hovering in the turbulent wind, adding to the drama as it sways back and forth towards the runway. I wait for the touchdown. It never seems to come. All of a sudden, there is a massive jolt, followed by the most horrendous noise as the metal makes contact with the tarmac. I envisage sparks flying from the underbelly of the plane. Screaming voices echo throughout the aircraft. The cabin fills with the stench of hot-metal fumes, releasing the oxygen masks. I grab one, pull it over my companion's head and put on my own before crouching back down into the brace position. Jayden's voice sounds like an echo in the distance, shouting, although I have no idea where it comes from. I have lost my phone. The old woman grabs hold of my hand. I squeeze it tight, praying for the plane to stop. The screeching continues. As the aircraft veers off to the right, the noise subsides and comes to a halt. The doors open. Through the haze, the flight attendants release the inflatable chutes. I dare to peer out of the window, see only dense smoke and hear the wailing noise of sirens from all directions.

Still gripping onto my hand, she declares, "We're alive."

I reach over and slip off her mask.

And take off my own. "What a relief!"

The lady reaches over and wraps her bony arms around my neck. "Thank you, my dear."

I find my phone under the chair. It is out of charge. I put it into my bag. We leave our seat, follow the lights on the ground to the door and slide down the inflatable. At last, we are free from the plane. I lose my companion in all the commotion. There must be at least one hundred and fifty passengers on the tarmac. The medics take many of the people away by ambulance, some receive treatment on the runway and most accept emergency foil blankets. I wrap it around my body, shivering in the cold weather. Buses arrive to take us to safety. We have hot drinks and await the arrival of our luggage. I assure the staff that someone is picking me up. I spot the woman with her husband, walking arm in arm towards the exit and rush over, tapping her on the shoulder. She appears startled but relieved when she sees my face.

"This is the young lady that took care of me on the plane," she says to her companion.

He shakes my hand. "Thank you very much."

"My pleasure." I look towards his wife and say, "How are you?"

"Tired. Exhausted."

I find my purse in my bag and take out a card. "I feel the same. Please get in touch once everything settles down."

"Definitely. I need to thank you for all your help, my dear. We stay in Lincoln. Do you?"

"Yes, close to the marina."

"Wonderful," she says. "Is someone coming to meet you? I don't want to leave you alone."

"My partner is on his way."

"The man who phoned on the plane?"

"Yes, he's travelling from Edinburgh in his car."

She smiles. "Young love."

I nod in agreement. "What's your name?"

"Clarissa Evans."

"Kristina Cooper."

We shake hands.

I bid her farewell.

"Goodbye, my dear."

"Take good care of yourself."

I find a secluded spot at the back of the room, lean against my case, sit on the floor and lose all concept of time. The hours seem to tick by at a slow pace. As the area empties, I see someone talking to a member of the aftercare team. A figure runs over in my direction. It takes a moment to recognise him. He bends down, stroking my face with his fingers.

"Kristina, my beautiful girl. I thought I had lost you."

I wrap my arms around his neck. "Jayden. How did you get here so fast?"

"I drove like a maniac down the motorway. You'll be okay. I'm here now."

He takes my luggage and grasps hold of my hand. We make our way through the terminal. Once outside, the air is fresh and cool in contrast to the suffocating atmosphere inside the airport. For the first time since the disaster, I become more coherent, the disorientation dissipating with each passing moment.

"Are you sure you're okay?"

"Much better. The last few hours are a blur."

"You're in shock. It will pass."

"I hope so. I'm glad you came."

"There was never any choice. You are my life."

"I know."

"Come on. Let's get you home."

"I need to contact my parents."

"I'll deal with that later."

Jayden bundles the bags into the boot of the Noble. He drives to

Lincoln. Once inside the flat, we settle down. I experience a pang of guilt. *He's so loyal. Why do I even question his behaviour?* I cuddle into him on the sofa and fall asleep.

****

I wake up the next day in a state of confusion until the events come flooding back into my mind. It is a miracle that I am still alive. I turn over. Jayden is not there. I cock my head to the side and hear voices drifting from the other room. I drag myself out of bed, take the robe off the peg on the door, wrap it around my body, stand for a few minutes and gaze at my reflection in the mirror. My face appears dull and lifeless. However, I notice red blemishes above my cheekbone. I press one, apply pressure with my finger, trying to make it disappear but it returns. I give up, leave the bedroom and walk towards the sound of voices. *It must be my parents. I'm not sure if I have the strength to deal with my mother. She always has an opinion on something. I wonder what advice she has today?*

I open the door.

Marion rushes forward. "Kristina. Thank goodness you're okay." She wraps her arms around my body, only to pull back, staring at the blotches. "You look awful. There's a rash on your face. Come and sit down. Tell us everything."

I sit next to Jayden. "I… I don't want to talk about the accident."

She ignores my comment. "The emergency landing is on every channel of the news. It must have been horrendous."

"It was very frightening."

"Leave her alone," insists my father.

"I told Jayden about the crash last night. Did he not tell you?"

"He did."

"But…" she replies.

My father interrupts. "Stop it, Marion. Kristina will speak to us in more detail when she's ready."

"If you insist, William."

"She must deal with the trauma in her own way *and* in her own time."

There is an awkward silence until the doorbell rings.

"Jayden, can you go? I'm not dressed."

"Of course."

He leaves the room.

I address my mother. "We'll meet up soon and talk about my experience in more detail. Okay?"

"You do what you feel is best. Remember, we're here for you, darling."

"I know." I change the subject. "What do you think of my partner?"

"He seems a lovely young man," declares my father.

"Jayden is extremely polite. You're a lucky woman. He adores you unlike your last disastrous relationship," says my mother.

My father gives her a sideward glance and sighs.

"What have I said now, William?"

"Nothing, Marion."

Jayden opens the door. "Kristina, I signed for a package."

"Thank you."

He hands over a large parcel.

I knit my brow together and try to figure out the content. I remember. It is the box file from Superintendent Marcus Hunter.

"Open the package. What's inside?" asks my mother.

"I think it's work-related. I'll do it later."

"Your life always revolves around your job. Take time off to recuperate. I can phone the university."

I interrupt. "There's no need. I must keep busy."

"If you insist. I'm only trying to help."

"Please leave me alone. Do you mind? I feel really tired. Can we meet up next week?"

She sighs.

"We need to go anyway," declares my father.

"I'm not being rude. I need time to come to terms with the accident."

He takes control. "I'll take you to lunch, Marion. Let's leave them for now."

She agrees but is not keen to go. We see them to the door and say our goodbyes. *My mother is so damn persistent and opinionated. I wonder what she really thinks about Jayden? No doubt she'll say in due course. He's been very supportive. Why did I question his behaviour? I'm too analytical for my own good.*

He wraps his arms around my waist. "Are you okay?"

"I was thinking about my mother."

"She's quite a domineering character."

I laugh. "What an understatement."

He kisses my lips, pressing his body into mine. "I want you."

"Please don't."

Jayden's hands continue to wander over my curves, his intent undeniable.

"Stop! It's not the right moment. I'm too exhausted and need time on my own. That's how I deal with an upset in my life."

He steps back.

"Are you sure?"

"Yes."

"I understand. Listen, I can go to London until the end of the week. I have work to do at the agency on the perfume brand. It will give you time for yourself. I will visit you on my way back to Edinburgh."

"You don't mind?"

"No, I realise you need to be on your own."

"It's how I cope."

"Shall I make us something to eat first?"

I nod. "Thank you for your support, Jayden. I appreciate the effort."

He kisses my forehead. "I know you do."

After lunch, he leaves the flat and plans to stay in London for the next three days. I breathe a sigh of relief and welcome the solitude. I call my Head of Department, Professor Johnson, and tell him about the accident and agree to take time off work. Not much. Just enough to recuperate. I also phone and ask several people to see if there were any enquiries about my stay at the Balmoral Hotel. Nothing. *How did Jayden track me down?* I scratch my head. At that moment, I remember the woman we met on the night out in Lincoln. *What's her name? Did she have anything to do with Jayden? She seems his type. Samantha? Band? No! Think! Bank? Samantha Banks!* I search her name on the internet. Mouth agape, I see her connection to a business called Insightful Solutions. It is a company who deal in overt and covert surveillance. Surely not? Is this a coincidence? Am I paranoid?

I decide to ask him later.

I pick up my diary, read the notes I jotted down on the plane, dismiss Samantha Banks for now, and focus my attention on Reverend Charles McIntyre and his alleged affair. I press on the number in my contacts list and wait for an answer.

"Hello."

"Charles, it's Kristina Cooper. How are you?"

"I'm fine," he says, warily. "Is everything okay?"

"Yes."

"Where's Jayden?"

I say nothing about the plane incident.

"He's gone to the London agency."

"Always working, my boy."

"That's true. I phoned to check up on you."

He laughs. "Why? What have I done?"

I chuckle at his joke.

"Check up on what?"

"I need to understand why we had to leave early?"

"Jayden went back to Edinburgh for an emergency meeting."

"Did anything else happen?"

"No, everything is fine, Kristina. We arranged to meet once Jayden returns from his trip next week. I spoke to him yesterday."

"Oh, that will be nice." I change the subject and say nothing about Mrs Cameron. "How's Carolyn?"

"She's fine. It's a busy time of year. We're both helping the elderly and poorer families in our community through the winter."

"You're such caring individuals."

"It's my job and my life."

"I'm glad you sound better today. We were worried about you."

"There's no need. I do appear lighter in spirit, thank you."

"What a relief."

"Honestly, I'm fine."

"I have to go and do my work."

"Nice to speak to you, Kristina."

"And you, Charles."

"Goodbye, my child."

I hang up the phone.

Everything seems fine. I never had the courage to ask about the affair. It was a long time ago and a private matter. Anyhow, it was well before the Reverend got together with Carolyn Scott. It is none of my business. He is meeting Jayden soon, so everything must be okay. I score a line through the note in my diary.

As the day progresses, I sort out my teaching to avoid dealing with the traumatic experience. However, what I try to ignore in my conscious life, pursues my subconscious mind when I am asleep. Since the crash, the focus of my nightmares include terrifying scenes of the emergency landing. The horrendous screeching noise of metal bursts my eardrums. In a state of confusion, I frantically search the smoke-filled cabin but find no means of escape. My fate rests in the hands of the suffocating tendrils of smoke, the dancing vapour wrapping itself around my throat. I gasp for air. With each inhalation, I threaten to pass out, and then, I wake up.

As such, I tire during the day, although I still try to concentrate on my work. Right now, the package containing the box file is a distraction. I glance over, wondering what secrets it holds inside. I am about to open the parcel when the phone rings. It is seven thirty. *Who is it? Jayden arranged to talk at ten? My mother, perhaps?* I do not recognise the number but decide to answer.

"Kristina Cooper?"

"Yes."

"It's Clarissa Evans. How are you, my dear?"

"I'm fine and glad you took the time to call."

"I wanted to phone and thank you for all your help. You were my rock in times of uncertainty. Such control for someone so young. It has helped me deal with the trauma."

I'm not in control now. "My pleasure."

"How are you coping?"

I stammer. "You know...to be honest...not too well. I experience horrendous flashbacks and find it hard to concentrate on my work. I seem to be shutting out the dreadful ordeal. It could be post-traumatic stress, perhaps?"

"That's not too good. I've read that sharing a difficult experience helps with recovery. You must fight your way through the bad times to keep your sanity, my dear."

We talk for hours, reliving every single detail during and after the crash. She is the one who takes control. Clarissa is a shining light in the face of my denial. She radiates positive energy to counteract my negative thoughts. That night, and much to my relief, the dreams are listless in nature, having no power left to attack. I sleep with no fear from the deadly tendrils of vapour.

The next morning, I wake up much more alert, ready to tackle the day ahead. During the discussion with Clarissa, calls and texts to my mobile phone from Jayden kept interrupting the moment, the annoying notifications going off during our conversation. Unable to face reading them the previous night, I decide to look at the messages before calling him.

It is insane.

There are ten texts.

I see you are busy with another call. I will try again later.

Who are you speaking to?

Did we not arrange to talk at ten?

Contact me when you're finished.

What's going on?

Is it someone else? A man?

Phone when you're free.

I'm worried about you.

I give up.

Good night.

He is so intense, possessive and commands such loyalty.
I dial the number.
Jayden answers straight away.
In a curt tone, he says, "Are you okay?"
"Much better."
"What happened last night? I called and text you. Your phone was engaged for hours. Who did you speak to for so long?"
"There's no need to worry. It was the lady from the plane. Clarissa Evans."
"And…"

"We talked about our experience."

"Why did you not talk to me about the crash?"

"She was there at the right time and understands my situation. It's such a relief. I feel much better."

He sighs. "I suppose that's all that matters. I'm driving back to Edinburgh in two days' time. Shall I still come to Lincoln?"

"I'm not sure."

"What's wrong?"

I pause. "Do you know a woman called Samantha Banks?"

"Who?"

"She deals in overt and covert surveillance."

"What are you talking about?"

I blurt out. "How did you know I was staying at the Balmoral Hotel when I gave my keynote speech?"

"You think I paid someone to follow you?"

"Maybe…"

He laughs.

"What's so funny?"

"I phoned your university and asked."

"Who?"

"I have no idea."

I must sound like a right idiot.

"I'm sorry, Jayden."

"Are you alright?"

"Not really."

"I can't think straight."

"Shall I come back and see you or not?"

"I suppose so."

"I've missed you. I never wanted to leave in the first place."

"I needed time on my own."

"As long as it helps. And, no more nonsense about surveillance."

"Sorry."

"I must go. I have a meeting in five minutes. I'll text you when I leave London."

"See you in a few days."

He hangs up the phone.

That was a strain.

It rings, again.

"Is everything okay, Jayden?"

"I forgot to say, I adore you, Kristina Cooper."

"Likewise, Jayden Scott."

Not saying another word, he disconnects the call.

I smile to myself. *He's very unpredictable!* I turn my attention towards the package containing the box file. I go to the kitchen and pick up a knife from the rack. The sharp blade pierces the strip of brown tape. I slide it along the indent, pull it off, take out the box and lift off the lid to reveal the deadly information inside.

****

I gaze out of the window. The day ends as night commences. The heavy oppressiveness of the winter light fades like that of life and death itself. I turn on the lamp and study the photographs. Annabel Taylor lies in a pool of her own blood in the street outside her flat. There are close-up photos of the crime scene, the contents of her bag and naked corpse on the mortuary slab, revealing the deep yet precision-cut slit on her neck. I pick up the pages of notes from the Lothian and Borders police report and sift through the information, reading about her background. I think back to my criminal profile training. It is necessary to familiarise oneself with this material to understand not only the murder victim but it may also provide small clues to the perpetrator's motive, social circle and nature of the relationship with the victim, if any.

I read the material until I have a clear picture of the victim's life. Hours later, I make a cup of coffee and sit down on the sofa, thinking about the key pieces of information. The documents reveal that Annabel Taylor was born in Edinburgh at the Royal Infirmary in the heart of the city. She was an intelligent, clever woman. Miss Taylor stayed there all her life and obtained a finance degree to become a Business Development Manager in the banking sector. This is where the victim met Stewart Bailey. They lived together for five years in his apartment at Tollcross. She moved out and bought a one-bedroom flat in the same area, living alone until her death. Annabel Taylor also took out an injunction to stop the harassment from her ex-partner.

I take a sip of coffee, pick up the file and read about her physical attributes. At the time of her murder she is thirty-six years old, 5 feet

8 inches tall with a slim build. The autopsy report reveals digested food contents in her stomach from lunch, low levels of alcohol in her bloodstream, no narcotics, prescription drugs or any other harmful substances. The slit across her throat is quick and clean from a sharp blade with a serrated edge. The killer put a lot of effort into planning her death, there is no doubt, and left no trace or evidence at the crime scene. The light area of skin indicates that she had a ring on her finger stolen on the night of her murder. A keepsake, perhaps? The police report also states that someone removed her purse and mobile phone.

I ponder over the information.

Did the murderer try to make it appear like a robbery? Maybe it was theft. However, it seems too personal because the perpetrator took time to remove her ring. I review the information, again, from the officer at the murder scene. He recalls the scenario as one of chaos. I scrutinise the photos of the poor woman who found Annabel Taylor dying in the street. The report describes her role in gruesome detail as she tried to stop the flow of blood from the victim's neck. The last image shows the lady sitting by the dead body with a blank expression on her face, numb, holding out her hands, staring at the blood.

I shudder.

And place the coffee on the table. I delve deeper into the box file. My fingers rest upon a plastic case. I lift it out, stare at the writing on the front cover and there in bold capital letters states: **CCTV FOOTAGE**. My heart quickens. I remove the folder and load the disk into the side of my laptop. It seems to take forever to read the old format.

The play button appears on my screen.

I click on the link and sit down, tap my fingers on the table, waiting for the images to appear. I watch with interest. At twenty past seven the scene focuses on Stewart Bailey. I recognise him from the photographs in the file. He enters the bar with a friend and leaves an hour later, disappearing out of sight from the main cameras. At ten past eight, Annabel Taylor walks up the street with an air of confidence in her stride. To see this lady alive rather than the ghost-like figure on the mortuary slab takes my breath away, the lifeless woman suddenly appearing on the screen. Miss Taylor pushes open the door and strolls into the pub. She comes back out five minutes later with a drink in her hand, sits on the seat outside the bar and lights a cigarette, searching for somebody in all directions. *Who is she waiting on?* I pause the footage.

My attention turns towards the material on the table. I search for additional information. *Her ex-lover Stewart Bailey was in the area that night, but did she wait for him or someone else?* No matter how much I read, there is no further intelligence on her love life. Just then, I remember saying to Superintendent Hunter not to send any extra detail. *Bloody idiot. I will now need to wait for the next box file.* I watch more of the footage.

With interest, I stare at the screen as Annabel Taylor finishes her drink and crosses the main road only to disappear down a side street, her fate lost to the surveillance cameras. I continue to observe the material to see if anyone follows, but nothing. *What on earth happened? Who would commit such a heinous crime? I suppose that is why I'm here, to profile her killer.*

I peer closer.

At that moment, I notice someone inside the café on the other side of the street stand up to leave. I zoom in on the picture. The silhouette is almost unrecognisable yet distinctive. *It's definitely a man.* The figure wears a baseball cap to obscure his facial features and puts on a pair of gloves. I rewind, zoom out and see Annabel Taylor cross the road. As she disappears around the corner, I watch with anticipation to determine if the mysterious person in black leaves the coffee shop, but no, he never appears. *Is that her killer? Where did he go? Out of a back entrance, perhaps? Am I making this up to fit the narrative? That man could be anyone.* Deep in thought, my heart skips a beat at the sudden shrill of the phone, piercing through the silent atmosphere like an unwelcome force.

I hesitate.

It goes to my answer service.

"Kristina, it's Jayden. This is to let you know I plan to leave London in the morning. I should be with you by midday. Call later or ring tomorrow."

I'll leave it for now. I'm too exhausted. At least his message has put an end to my wandering mind. I notice the time. It is after nine o'clock. I make a quick meal and pour a glass of wine. *Just what I need. This will be a hard profile to figure out. However, this is only the start.* I pick up the glass, head towards the bathroom, light a few candles and run the bath. *I have to wind down.* Once inside, the hot water relieves the tension. I try to switch off from my analytical mind and lose myself in the tranquility of the moment, happy, thinking for the first time in ages to the man in my life. *I'm so lucky to have met him.* I lay any reservations aside and look forward to our next encounter.

The next day, the noise shrills through the air at ten o'clock. Half asleep, I reach over to the bedside table. My fumbling fingers grasp hold of the phone from the charger stand.

"Hello…" I say in a sleepy voice.

"Hey, have you just woken up?"

"No."

He laughs.

"I left early. I'll be with you in less than an hour."

"What? I'm so disorganised and still in bed."

"Stay there. See you soon."

I experience a flutter of desire. "If you insist. You're the boss."

"I am, indeed, Dr Cooper."

"Let yourself in the flat. I realise it's a cliché. There's a spare key under the flower pot outside the door."

He laughs, again. "You're not very practical for someone with a criminologist background, are you?"

"Nope!"

"See you shortly, Kristina."

I wait for him to arrive.

Sure enough, the key turns in the lock an hour later.

He heads straight towards my bedroom.

Without a word, we look at each other. His breathing is heavy as he undresses, his stare full of lust, never leaving mine. My heart races in anticipation. I pull back the covers to reveal my naked body, inviting him to take what he already knows he owns. Our lovemaking is intense, passionate and takes us both to extreme heights of pleasure. We fall asleep in each other's arms and wake up later in the day.

He caresses my face. "You're beautiful."

"Thank you."

"Never leave, Kristina. Promise."

"Why would I do that? Stop being silly."

"I need you to say the word."

"I promise, Jayden."

"Good."

"Are you okay?"

"Yes. I just never want to lose you."

"You won't. That's another promise."

He laughs and changes the subject. "I'm starving. Shall we order something to eat and have a lazy night? I have to leave in the morning."

"Sounds perfect."

He finds one of the most expensive Japanese restaurants in Lincoln and orders a tantalising spread of eastern delights. We both force ourselves out of bed before the food arrives.

KNOCK, KNOCK, KNOCK!

As we rush to get ourselves dressed, he says, "You get the plates, cutlery and wine. Take it through to the sitting room. I'll go to the door."

I listen to him speak to the delivery man, and then, silence. I lift up the bottle of wine, gather up the dishes and look forward to our meal. Kicking open the door with my foot, I enter the room and see him stare at the images of Annabel Taylor, fixating on her naked body on the mortuary slab, the two bags of food still dangling from each hand. I put everything down on the table in the corner and say, "Jayden, I'm sorry about the file. I forgot it was there."

He turns, looks at my face, and shakes his head like he is trying to comprehend the situation. "I never expected to see... photographs... of... a dead woman."

I rush over, gather up all the information and dump it in the box file. "Sorry, it's horrible."

He composes himself, takes a deep breath and says, "It's shocking but fascinatingly gruesome."

"That's one way to describe the situation. My work is a bit of an oxymoron, I suppose, which is why I have such an interest in my job," I say, closing the lid.

"Interesting," he declares. "Come on, let's eat. It's been a long day."

Jayden is quiet for a while. He appears to relax the more we eat and drink.

"Better?" I ask.

"Yes," he says. "Is that your profile case?"

I nod. "I'm sifting through the reports at the moment."

"What have you learned so far?"

"That information is confidential, Jayden. A missionary killer, perhaps? Who planned this murder, I'm not sure? I don't have all the evidence to establish such a judgement at this early stage of the investigation."

"Who is she?"

"Let's not talk about my work. We've had such a lovely time."

"What's…"

"It's private. Change the subject."

"Okay, okay."

We finish our food in silence, head to bed and watch a movie until we both fall asleep. In the morning, my inquisitive man seems back to normal. We make love before he leaves. There is not the hunger or depth of passion like the previous day, but it is still intimate. I kiss Jayden goodbye at the front door, not wanting him to leave. *I will miss his company. I plan to visit Edinburgh for a long weekend in a few weeks' time.* I hear him speak to someone on the stairs before he leaves the building and lean over the bannister. *It's the postman.* The young man carries a parcel in his hand.

"Good morning, Miss Cooper. You must sign for the package."

It must be the other box file.

Once I scrawl my signature on the hand-held device, he says, "Thank you. Have a great day."

Rushing into the flat, I head straight for the kitchen to get a knife, split open the tape, pull out the box and take off the lid, excited about the information inside. Most if it duplicates the material I already have. With a sense of disappointment, I scan the pages, seeking new evidence. And there, right before my eyes at the bottom of the page on some random report, the detail I need to continue the investigation.

My heart quickens.

I read the text.

"Annabel Taylor had an extramarital affair with Edward Scott who disappeared a week before her murder, husband of Carolyn Scott and father to Jayden Edward Scott. Nicholas Canmore is the officer in charge of his disappearance."

3

WEB OF LIES

"What a tangled web we weave, when first we practice to deceive."
(Walter Scott)

I drive up the monotonous A1 motorway and think about our amazing lovemaking the previous night, the smell of Kristina's beautiful body still lingers, her scent, unmistakable. *She can never leave, no matter what the outcome of this tangled web of lies.* And what a bonus to see the stone dead remains of Annabel Taylor on the mortuary table. My groin stirs, thinking about both women. However, I need to focus on the task at hand. I am due to meet Reverend McIntyre tomorrow in Edinburgh to convince him I repent my sins. *What will he say and how will he react to the knowledge of my secret? I wonder if he has found his own inner strength to deal with the situation. Poor bastard. Why did he have to witness my confession?*

I let out a huge sigh.

There are too many issues. It is necessary to sort out each of these dilemmas, tie up the loose ends, one at a time. For once, I am not sure where to start. Noticing the sign, I stop at a service station to get a coffee, sit in the Noble, light a cigarette and contemplate a plan of action. I take out a pen and a spare piece of paper from my briefcase and jot down my agenda over the next few weeks.

(1) Lunch with Reverend McIntyre.

(2) Stewart Bailey, you are my scapegoat in the Annabel Taylor murder. I still have that stupid cow's ring. Set him up, frame the bastard and make sure there's no doubt who is the 'guilty' party.

(3) Inspector Canmore. He is a dead man. When? How? Where? Who? Not by my blade but the hand of another. Dark Web? Hitman? Keep it underground?

(4) Superintendent Marcus Hunter. That policeman is an idiot. Don't even worry about him!

(5) My beautiful criminologist. Once I plant the evidence, there will be no doubt that Stewart Bailey is the guilty party in the Annabel Taylor murder and no need for a profile to emerge.

Content with my plan, I have another cigarette, blowing the smoke out of the window. My mind wanders back to Kristina. She is clever to make the connection to Samantha Banks. However, my criminologist will never find out the truth about the covert surveillance. Her inquisitive nature initiates a reaction. Every time I think of Kristina, my body responds. I have no control over my insatiable desire. Just then, I hear a voice.

"Hey, you got a light?"

I peer out of the open window.

A woman leans against the door, bending down with her cleavage bulging out of a tight dress, holds a cigarette between her fingers, the claw-like talons painted a deep shade of blood red to complement her full lips.

I light the cigarette.

"Thanks. Do you want anything else?" She points. "I have a hotel room over there, lover boy."

It is a tempting proposition due to my state of arousal.

At that moment, my phone rings.

It's Kristina.

"Piss off," I say, pressing the button to wind up the window. I see the hooker walk away in search of other prey in the car park. I slide the icon along the screen, eager to answer her call.

"How's my favourite criminologist?"

"… She's okay…"

There is an awkward silence.

I wait.

"Jayden, we need to talk."

"It's fine. I stopped for a coffee, anyway."

She stammers. "Well…"

"What is it, Kristina?"

"I have to ask you something."

"Yes?"

"I'll get straight to the point," she says with conviction. "I've just read that Edward Scott had an extramarital affair with Annabel Taylor."

"Who?"

"My murder victim. She had a relationship with your father. Did you know about this information?"

Fuck! "No. However, Inspector Canmore mentioned the details of an affair. I had no idea she was the same person as your profiling case."

"Are you certain?"

"Of course, I'm sure. Why the hell are you asking?"

"Because of the way you reacted the other night in my flat to the crime scene evidence as well as your persistent questions."

"Wait a minute. Anyone would react like that if they saw those gruesome photographs."

She sighs. "First, there's the accusation from Inspector Canmore about your involvement in your father's disappearance and now this connection between Annabel Taylor and Edward Scott. It must link the two deaths to the same person."

"I don't know. I'm not an expert, Kristina. Why can't you ask that policeman in charge of the homicide? What's his name?"

"Superintendent Marcus Hunter."

"Does he not have more information about the case? If my memory is correct, the police arrested someone for Annabel Taylor's murder."

"It never went to court."

"What are you implying, Dr Cooper?"

"I'm not implying anything."

"Yes, you are. I'm not stupid."

"I need time alone to think."

"Don't go, please."

She hangs up the phone.

I call back but receive no answer.

And light another cigarette, mumbling, "This is not good." I inhale a deep breath of smoke, exhale and pull the keys out of the ignition, get out of the car and march over to the woman, grasp hold of her arm and say, "Two hundred for a quick fuck." We go to her hotel room. She undresses while I put on a condom. I take her from behind. A multitude of emotions battle each other for supremacy between my mind, body and soul. The thrill to be back where I belong with a hooker is exhilarating, the physical pleasure undeniable, and the guilt about betraying Kristina, toxic but intoxicating. It is exciting, cold yet functional. As I close my eyes and focus on the sensation, Kristina Cooper is never far from my thoughts, her accusatory tone fuelling my desire. I use this woman's body for my own gratification. Once it is over, I throw the money on the bed and leave the hotel.

I get back into the Noble and drive to Edinburgh with a sense of satisfaction and frustration. *Why did Kristina force me into that sexual encounter? Why is she so untrustworthy? Forget her, for now. I have other issues to deal with like Reverend McIntyre, Stewart Bailey and Inspector Canmore.* Once inside my flat, I unpack, open my favourite bottle of whisky and drink too much, relishing over Kristina's accusatory phone call as a reminder of the exhilarating moment my blade cut Annabel Taylor's throat. *You'll see I'm innocent once I frame that Bailey fucker,* I think to myself, just before I fall asleep.

I wake up in the morning and catch sight of the empty bottle on the bedside table. My stomach lurches, the stale stench of alcohol lingering in my mouth. *I need to call the office today and also meet up with Charles for lunch.* I check my phone. There are no missed calls or texts from Kristina. *Leave her alone to think. She'll eventually realise I'm innocent.* I get out of bed and head towards the bathroom. Once in the shower, I stay there for ages, washing away the smell of the dirty whore from the service station. I also clean my teeth with rigour to get rid of the taste of drink in my mouth. Feeling more alert, I stare into the mirror. *Better, much better.* I wrap the towel around my waist and call Jessica Logan. She says everything in the agency is fine. Miss Logan received Stewart Bailey's information. I ask her to send the document and turn on my computer.

I click on the file.

He has an impressive track record, working his way up through the hierarchy in the bank until he left seven years ago to deal with the court case. He set up his own public relations agency, Bailey Communications, not far from his home residence. He is forty-eight, twelve years older than Annabel Taylor at the time of her death and lives in a flat near Tollcross, not that far from his ex-lover. I input his number on my phone. *I might arrange to see him to discuss Mr Guthrie's brief before the end of the week, get to know him better, before finalising my scapegoat plan.* Right now, I need to go to the George Hotel and meet the Reverend where my father's memorial took place almost three months ago. Charles sent a text to say he is on the train. *The hotel will bring back a few memories about Inspector Canmore reopening the case, fiddling with Edward Scott's ring in front of my face. That's my fucking keepsake and I want it back, you bastard! I must calm down and find a compromise with the Reverend first, next, Stewart Bailey and then, focus all of my anger towards that modern-day Macduff.*

I dress, stare at the reflection in the mirror and thank myself for my advice. With a sly grin, I splash on some favourite cologne, find my overcoat, and head to the car park. I press down on the key, hesitate, pondering over my mode of transport. *I'll need a drink to deal with this situation, that's for sure. Leave the vehicle at home.*

Instead, I call a taxi.

Feeling apprehensive, I give the driver the destination and stare out of the window, contemplating how the Reverend will react. I dread the encounter, pay the driver and walk through the door to the hotel. The nervous anticipation is all too evident. I run my tongue around the inside of my mouth, trying to generate some kind of moisture to alleviate the dehydration. I follow the signs to the bathroom and turn on the water fountain. The first gulp of cool liquid moistens my dry lips, the next eases the dehydration and finally, the short bursts of fluid satisfy my thirst. I let out a huge sigh, clear my throat and feel ready to confront my adjudicator.

I go into the lounge. The Reverend sits at the bar drinking a glass of whisky. He waves over in my direction. As I walk towards him, I stare at his features and try to read his mood. *What's he thinking?* His eyes squint, watching my every move. With an unexpected gesture, he stands up and lays his hand on my shoulder. "Good to see you, my boy."

"You too, Charles."

"Sit down. I'll get you a drink." He calls over to the bartender. "Double measure of Black Bottle whisky, please."

My stomach churns.

The Reverend gets up off the barstool. "Let's find somewhere more private." He leads us to a corner table. "That's better."

I take a small sip of the blended malt, waiting for him to start the conversation.

"Your mother sends her love."

"Thank you. I'll call her later."

We both speak at the same moment. "Charles…" "Jayden…"

He laughs.

It breaks the ice.

I proceed. "How are you today?"

"Fine. I've had time to think. I'm to blame for this mess."

"No, you're not."

"Listen, my boy. I knew what was going on. I'm the one that never intervened and let you both leave the village with that man. I turned a blind eye."

"Stop being too hard on yourself."

"I'm not."

"What do we do now?"

"Nothing. Edward Scott is dead. I don't want to know what you did to your father. Forget the man existed. Will they ever find him, Jayden?"

I take a drink and look over the rim of the glass.

"What is it?" he asks.

"There's one problem. Inspector Canmore is reopening the case."

"What? After all this time?"

"He's convinced that I buried my father somewhere in Argyll. Remember, Marcus Hunter called off the search. We received a letter of apology."

"How could I forget?"

"That lunatic, Canmore, has the permission and resources in place to examine the area, again."

Charles groans.

"Will he find anything, Jayden?"

"Yes, if he looks hard enough."

The Reverend's hand reaches up to his forehead, his fingers massaging his brow. "Did you move your father's body to the cottage when you met your friends on your twenty-third birthday?" He frowns and says, "Don't answer that question."

"It's the truth. Those bloody dogs may find him this time."

He gulps down the remains of the whisky. "This is a nightmare." He calls out to the bartender. "Two more double malts, please."

"Are you sure that's a good idea? We need to keep a clear head."

"This is the best thing for us right now. I want another drink."

"Take it easy, Charles."

He nods.

"There's just one more issue. Kristina knows about the search. She was at my flat when Inspector Canmore announced the news although I have known about this since my father's memorial."

"What did Kristina say?"

"We spoke. She believes my version of events."

I better not tell him I took her to the cottage after New Year. It's a step too far. I don't have to tell him everything. Only the basics.

"We must keep it that way," he replies. "I'll write a letter of complaint to Police Scotland about the constant harassment from Inspector Canmore. Let's hope they discover nothing."

"That's all we can do. I watched a documentary about how hard it is to find a buried body. It's not as easy as it sounds. Rainwater carries the scent of death away from the actual burial spot, especially from high to low ground."

He interrupts. "STOP! You say it as a matter of fact, devoid of any kind of emotion or guilt."

"That's the way I feel. After years of abuse, I don't have any guilt but I do repent, Charles. I said it all in my speech in the early hours of the morning on New Year's day at the church. I begged HIM for forgiveness to close HIS eyes to my sins and wipe out all MY evil."

He sighs. "I know you did."

"What do we do now?"

"Pray that he never finds Edward Scott's corpse. When does the search take place?"

"I'm not sure? When the weather is more favourable. It's nearly the end of January. I suspect in a few months."

"That gives us time to make a complaint. Shall I deal directly with Inspector Canmore?"

"No! He mentioned a superior officer. What's her name? Grace someone. McFarlane. DCI Grace McFarlane."

"Perhaps I could at least get the search delayed if I complain enough."

"It's doubtful."

He shrugs his shoulders and changes the subject. "How's Dr Cooper? Your mother mentioned about the plane crash. Marion called with all the details."

"She's fine and has taken time off work to recover."

"Good. Kristina mentioned nothing about her ordeal the other day when she phoned."

"She called you?"

"Yes."

"What about?"

"It was a strange conversation. Kristina seemed more interested in my health than her own. She kept asking if I was all right?"

Bloody hell. Did she ask about my lie about his alleged affair with Mrs Cameron? "Anything else?"

"She had something on her mind."

I reassure him. "Kristina was concerned about your health after our abrupt departure from the house. She wanted to know why you were upset."

He leans forward. "You must always protect her, Jayden. If this goes wrong, you have to leave her alone. Promise?"

I'll never leave Kristina. "I promise."

"Never cause her any harm. She deserves better."

"I agree."

"Thank you. Let's have another whisky and eat. After that, I need to get my train." He checks his watch. "I arranged for a taxi to come back in two hours."

We have lunch and several more drinks. We talk about anything and everything to avoid the dilemma we both have to face. *I hate lying to Charles. He's a good man and wants to help. Silly bastard! Better to have him on my side than an enemy. I don't want to deal with the Reverend on top of everything else.*

****

I spend the next few days catching up with work at the office. Our team has the brief underway and Jessica liaises with Stewart Bailey on a television advertising campaign to reposition the bank. They focus on consumer benefits with a 'feel-good' message: caring, sharing, people, a strong sense of community, technology, mobile applications and money transfers. The employees put the storyboards together ready to make a choice for the spring launch. I am happy with the progress. What about my own plans? I will deal with Stewart Bailey later, but for now, I contact Kristina. The call goes straight to her answer phone and leave no message. *It's not a bad thing. She must still be working on the information about my father and Annabel Taylor. Besides, I need time alone to consider my dilemma about Stewart Bailey and Nicholas Canmore. Kristina will soon find out I'm innocent.*

First, I turn my attention towards my plan for Inspector Canmore. And leave the office early to buy a new mobile, SIM card and pay by cash. This phone has one purpose and one purpose only: to approach a hitman on the Dark Web and set up an email account under a false identity. As I drive back to the flat, I think about my plan of action. *I have limited knowledge. I need to do some research and download a server to mask my IP address, and then, I can contact someone on the dark side of the internet.* Once inside the apartment, I put on the heating, light the fire, and turn on my laptop. I watch a few online tutorials on how to access the Dark Web. *It's very interesting, almost too easy. I suppose it's legal until you access illegal content.* I follow the instructions for the Tor browser to allow one to communicate annonymously.

As it infiltrates my machine, I light a cigarette and wait.

What and who will I find? I'm a lone wolf with regards to hunting and killing my prey with no dependency on anyone. How much will it cost in bitcoin to hire a hitman? I imagine it's very expensive. Perhaps I should just kill him myself? However, the police know my modus operandi through the Annabel Taylor murder. I could buy a gun and shoot the bastard but what about an alibi? No! I need to be somewhere else when the murder takes place so there is no doubt of my innocence.

In the meantime, I read about the Dark Web. It is five hundred times larger than the worldwide web and The Onion Router is a government initiative for operatives to communicate with each other. I refer to an article with interest:

Created by the US Government

"In the mid-1990s, US military researchers created a technology that allowed intelligence operatives to exchange information completely anonymously. They called it 'Tor', which stands for 'The Onion Router'.

As part of their strategy for secrecy, they released Tor into the public domain for anyone to use. Their reasoning was simple: the more people using the system, the harder it would be to separate the government's own messages from the general noise. You can't be anonymous on your own.

Tor spread widely and today is a critical part of the so-called 'dark web': a network of untraceable online activity and hidden websites, of which Tor hosts approximately 30,000. And that anonymity has attracted a huge range of people; all who want to keep their activities hidden."

The programme download on my computer interrupts my reading and spurs into action, opening the Tor server on my desktop. I check the security settings and put it to the greatest level of anonymity, realising it will run slower than normal, but with the highest security to mask my illegal activity. I access the hidden Wiki page, eager to scan the content. *What am I searching for? Guns, hitmen, transaction information?* My heartbeat quickens. The elation, evident. I penetrate the sinister side of the internet and create a fake email account under the name of Edward Cooper on my laptop. I smile at my choice of identity and read up about encryption, setting up a private and public key, ready to interact with dubious characters on the Dark Web. *This is unbelievably exciting.* My body responds to the adrenalin rush surging through my veins. Unable to stand it any longer, I have a shower, relieve myself, order food and settle down to investigate the darker side of human nature.

I take a large mouthful of whisky, open the browser and type in the word "guns". My eyes scan down the recommended links and focus on a site selling an arsenal of different firearms. The name of the person is SocialMisfit from Nottingham. I click on the link and it connects straight to the website. *Whoah!* There are photographs of each type of gun, ranging from handguns, revolvers, rifles and shotguns. I imagine how Inspector Canmore might end the last few moments of his life. Close range with a handgun or long range with a rifle? *Long range would be better. Less chance of being caught.* The cost is one bitcoin (just under three thousand pounds). My mind shifts back to the two people I murdered at point-blank range—Raymond Cartwright and Jake Driscoe. I shudder, remembering the intense situation where I nearly got killed. *There will be no room for error. I need someone to plan the fine detail.* I send a message to SocialMisfit through the contact details on the website, leave my email address, public and private keys and wait for a response.

In the meantime, I call Kristina.

There is still no reply.

Fuck you!
I throw the phone on the couch, light a cigarette and open the doors to the balcony. It is too cold outside. *No thanks!* Instead, I pour a measure of whisky and sit in front of the fire, inhaling the smoke deep into my lungs. I stare into the depths of the fiery flames. *What a bloody mess, but I can sort it out. Charles is on my side and Stewart Bailey will be my scapegoat in the Annabel Taylor murder. Kristina will return and Inspector Canmore dies, one way or another. The search in Argyll may never happen and we can live in peace, away from all this drama.*

The single beep on my phone interrupts my thoughts. *It's a text message from Kristina.* I stub out the cigarette and read it with interest.

I'm sorry, Jayden. I can't speak at the moment. There's too much on my mind. I am also very busy at work. It's not that I don't believe you. I need to go through the evidence and sort this out alone. I miss you.

I reply.

Then stop this nonsense.

She responds.

You're very condescending.

The conversation continues.

Talk to me, Kristina. Call my mobile.

I can't. I told you. I require time on my own.

Why? Stop being analytical. Please phone.

I wait. There is no more correspondence. It is a relief. I must focus on the task at hand. I light another cigarette, search the web for further material, click on a few "contract killers for hire" surprised by the open nature of the information:

I am the perfect contract killer (ex-military) to take care of your problem, making my services better than any other assassin. Pay enough bitcoin and I can do the job.

We know nothing about each other and will never meet. This service is confidential. I am a cold-blooded killer and the desired victim just disappears.

We are a team of four contract killers operating in the US, Canada and EU. Bitcoin required upfront. Termination guaranteed in one to three weeks of payment.

Shoot To Kill. Dead and Gone. Innocence no Guilt.

I like the last person. It's straight to the point but has no further information available. Strange? How do you get in touch? Just then, I hear the familiar tone of an email in Edward Cooper's inbox. I close the content and click on the mail. There is a response from SocialMisfit. However, there is an encryption code. It makes no sense. I type in my password and the message appears.

How can I help you, Edward? Are you interested in purchasing a gun?

Just browsing the Dark Web to see what is available.

I have a good choice. Is it for personal use? Leisure? Hunting? Protection?

Not sure yet?

What does that mean? You must know why you need a gun? I am here to satisfy your needs. If I don't have one in stock, I can acquire it for you. I provide a professional service to meet all of my customers' requirements.

You're very efficient. It's for a personal project.

What kind of project?

The situation is complicated.

How complicated?

Very complicated. I don't just need a gun, I need someone to pull the trigger.

At least you're honest and get straight to the point. That's not my area of expertise, Edward. I only sell the goddam firearms.

I understand. If you know anyone, give me a shout. I'm willing to pay a large amount of money for this transaction to take place.

Sorry, I can't help you.

No problem.

I wait, giving him time to contemplate the offer.

How much bitcoin?

Seven.

That's only £20,000.

Correct.

Let me think about the offer, Edward. I'll contact you in a few hours.

Speak soon, SocialMisfit.

Perhaps.

I look at the time. It is just before midnight. Deep down, I know he will get back in touch to help rid this world of that interfering bastard. This operator must have good contacts on the Dark Web. *I'll wait to see how much more bitcoin he decides upon to seal the deal.* I check my safe and count out more than £50,000 in spare cash. I always keep money aside in case of an emergency. This is such an occasion. *I'll increase the amount if necessary. I can tell by his tone he's a businessman, eager to make money. Let's see if he gets in touch tonight?* I wait for hours, pace back and forth, listening out for the sound of the email, but it never arrives, not in my conscious state of mind. I relax and sit in front of the fire, battling against the drowsy atmosphere, eyes heavy with sleepiness, my head falling down and jerking up until I succumb to the realms of sleep. Sometime later, I hear a familiar voice. *Wake up! You have a message. Get up!*

My eyes flick open.

I shout out, "WHO'S THERE?"

Silence.

I look around the room. The more I assess my situation, the confusion in my mind regains some kind of clarity. I laugh at my reaction to the mysterious messenger. *It was my voice. Silly bastard!* I sit up, loosen the muscles in my neck, stiff from an awkward sleeping position and check the laptop. Right enough, there is an email from SocialMisfit. I type in the password to unlock the message.

I have a contact in mind that suits your requirements. For my service, this will cost seven bitcoin and a further eighteen for the contract killer. Go to my website and click on the SocialMisfit logo in the right-hand corner of the screen. It takes you deeper into the Dark Web. From there, scroll to the bottom of the page and access the word "secret" and connect to my contact Shoot To Kill. Let me know if you want to continue. The money transfer needs to be finalised before we proceed. I'll act as a middleman and deal with you to complete the transaction.

I go to his website and follow the instructions. *So, this is the infamous onion layer to access the Dark Web, delving further into the darker aspect of the criminal mind and the sinister trade in illegal activities.* Right enough, it connects with Shoot To Kill. I'm sure it is the same person I viewed earlier. This site has a lot more detail, stating that he does not take out children, politicians and high-profile celebrities. It even has testimonials from satisfied 'customers'. I calculate the cost. Twenty thousand for SocialMisfit and fifty thousand for the contract killer. *Just within my budget.* I reply with one sentence and wait for a response.

Get in touch soon to seal the transaction.

Despite the early hour and much to my surprise, there is an immediate response.

I'm based in Nottingham. Once I receive the details and payment, the deal is secure. We require at least a month to fine-tune the plan.

That's too long. I need it done within the next two to three weeks.

Perhaps. I will get back to you on that one. We may require more money.

There is no more money SocialMisfit. Take it or leave it?

I'll be in touch soon.

Thanks.

With a heavy sensation in my limbs, I go to bed for another few hours' sleep. As I nod off, I envisage a long range bullet travelling at supersonic speed until it finds its target, straight through his goddam head. *Your life is coming to a ghastly end, Inspector Canmore.*

****

I get up several hours later, content with my progress. I check the phone. There are no texts or calls from my criminologist. *I miss her so much. I decide to forget about Inspector Canmore for now and focus all of my efforts on Stewart Bailey. It's a priority. I want Kristina back in my life, sooner rather than later. I need to put a stop to the killer profile for the Annabel Taylor murder. She's a clever woman. With more time, my beautiful criminologist will fathom it out. That would be a disaster.* I gaze out of the window. Even on the coldest of winter days, the sun permeates through the frosty haze, the rays of light elevate my soul, bringing some kind of hope to my precarious situation. *Focus on the Bailey plan. Nothing must go wrong.*

I get ready for work and keep busy over the next few days. In the evening, I follow Stewart Bailey from his office in Tollcross to determine his routine. He is a creature of habit and meets the same friend at a local pub before walking the short distance to his flat. *Perfect. I must set him up so there's no doubt about his involvement in the murder of his ex-lover.* Bailey lives on the top floor of an old Victorian tenement block comprising of eight flats, each with a front-facing balcony. To gain entry to the building, there is a secure intercom system. However, there is a side entrance to a communal garden to the rear of the block with access to a metal staircase, leading from each apartment to ground level. The back door has no lock. It is important to understand the layout of the land, just in case I have to make a hasty departure. I may end up murdering him in that flat. What way, I am not sure. *I need to think over his demise in more detail.* I am wary about deviating from my method of killing. My blade is my security, safe in the knowledge it will never let me down. This scenario is like my experience with Raymond Cartwright and Jake Driscoe. You can never predict the outcome. Regardless of the unpredictability of the situation, I need to put my plan into action as soon as possible.

On the fourth day, I wake up and prepare myself for the chance encounter with Stewart Bailey. I have to cancel my martial art class after work but hope it will be worth the compromise. I reach over, pull open the drawer and slide my hand to the back of the bedside cabinet. My fingers rest on the box and take it out of the hiding place. I open the lid and scan the contents inside, focusing on the different styles of jewellery. I gaze at Annabel Taylor's keepsake. The solitary diamond rests on top of the delicate gold band. *It breaks my heart to depart with another token of death. However, it is unavoidable. The ring is the only piece of evidence that can link Stewart Bailey to her murder.*

Once ready, I put on a pair of gloves, polish the metal with a clean handkerchief and put the ring in a small plastic bag, pressing the top with my fingers to close the seal. I head towards the kitchen and rummage in the drawer. *Where are they? I've used them before to get a good night's rest.* I find the packet of sleeping pills between some old mail. *Two, four, six, eight, ten, twelve. That's more than enough.* I take out the pestle and mortar and grind four of the tablets down to a fine powder, scoop out the contents with a teaspoon, place in another bag and seal the top. I put the two bags and the remaining pills into the inside pocket of my suit and leave for work.

In less than half an hour, I arrive at the agency. As I walk out of the lift, I see Stewart Bailey working with the team in one of the rooms and avoid all contact with him. I need our meeting, later on tonight, to appear like a chance encounter away from any kind of public scrutiny. Once the police investigate his death, I do not want to be at the forefront of the inquiry. I keep busy for the rest of the day. I check my phone. There is still no response from Kristina. *I wonder how the criminal profile is progressing? What will she conclude? Her mind must be in turmoil.* In contrast, my mind is clear. I have had time to ponder over my plan. *Let's hope it works out, but I will need to compromise, that's for sure.*

I settle down and reply to my backlog of emails.

Jessica enters my office at six thirty. "I'm finished. Everyone else has left. Are you not going to your martial arts class?"

"Not tonight. I plan to work late and want to check the progress on the bank brief."

"Are you okay to lock up and set the alarm?"

"Sure. No problem."

"See you tomorrow, Mr Scott."

"Goodnight."

As soon as she leaves the building, my head turns to the side, listening, for any kind of noise. *There's no one here you bloody idiot.* I push back the chair, rush towards the cabinet and grasp hold of the rucksack. With a sense of purpose, I take off my suit, shirt, tie, socks and shoes, and drape the clothes over the seat. I stand in the middle of the office in my underwear. A nervous laugh escapes my mouth. *This is just insane.* I put on into my usual attire, ready for my plan of action and let out a huge sigh of relief. I leave the agency by the rear entrance. *I'll come back later and set the alarm. Proof that I was here until then.* I point the key at the Noble, unlocking the door. *It's better to take my car so I can make a hasty retreat, if necessary.* I drive through the most obscure roads leading to Tollcross and park the Noble at the far end of the street, facing the way I need to drive away from the scene of the crime.

I wait.

And wait.

And still, wait.

And continue to wait.

I check the time. It is eight thirty. *You're late Stewart Bailey. I suppose it is the start of the weekend. He's not at home as there are no lights on in the flat. He may well be out for the whole night. Fuck!* I decide to stay another hour before ending the mission. To pass the time, I listen to some music and light a cigarette. I roll down the window, blowing the smoke out into the cold air, and use my ashtray to stub out the cigarette. Now that would be a disaster. *My own DNA found on the end of a butt!* I am about to give up when I see him at the top of the street. He is alone and seems unsteady on his feet. Not much but noticeable. A wry smirk passes across my face. *Perfect.* I get out of the Noble and pace myself to coincide with a chance encounter outside the front door of his flat.

I smile at him. "Hello, Mr Bailey."

He stares in my direction as we pass each other and stops. He bends down, looks under my baseball cap and announces, "Mr Scott? Jayden Scott?"

"How are you?"

"I'm fine. I never recognised you in your casual clothes."

"I've been at my martial arts training tonight."

"Good to see you again," he says, shaking my hand. "I did some work at the agency today."

"I meant to catch up with you for an important chat about the bank brief. Sorry, I was too busy."

"Are you free now? We can go to the pub and discuss the campaign."

"I'm not appropriately dressed."

"I suppose not. Do you want a drink?" He points at the building. "I live up there."

"Are you sure it's not too much trouble?"

"Not at all. We're business partners."

He unlocks the front entrance.

I follow him to the top floor.

"Come in," he says, opening the door.

Despite the dull nature of the apartment block, the flat is warm, minimal, stylish, and tidy. He takes off his overcoat and strides towards the living room. "Take a seat. What would you like to drink?"

I sit on the couch. "Whisky. If you have any?"

He nods. "Ice?"

"Neat, please."

He pours the measure and one for himself.

"Cheers," he says, as the glasses clink together. "I'll show you our efforts so far on the campaigns. Have you seen them yet?"

"No."

"It's impressive."

Stewart Bailey opens the files on his laptop, downloading two advertisements related to the bank brief. I watch with interest at the effort my team has made on the campaign, showing a more caring, community-based approach to the interpretation of the message. *Bloody idiot bankers. They've ruined our economy and now seek absolution.*

"What do you think?"

"To be honest, the work is fantastic. My only concern is the association with Bailey Communications because of your past."

His eyes widen. "We agreed it wasn't an issue, Mr Scott?"

"You know what the media are like if they find out about a scandal. I'm not sure whether to take the risk?"

"My company has an excellent track record with prestigious clients. It has never been a problem before." He takes a large gulp of whisky and refills the glass. "NEVER," he repeats.

"I understand. There's also a personal matter to consider."

"What?"

"The murder of Annabel Taylor."

He shifts in his seat. "Why?"

"She had an affair with my father."

His hand brushes across his forehead. "You're Edward Scott's son?"

"Yes."

There is an awkward silence.

After several moments, he declares, "I'm not sure what to say. All I can do is reassure you I had nothing to do with her murder or your father's disappearance."

"I believe you."

"What a small world," he says in disbelief. "Refill?"

I nod. "Thank you. It's a relief having someone to talk to about the situation. A person who understands. Annabel Taylor betrayed you and my father betrayed my mother and now they're both dead."

He takes a mouthful of whisky and appears to relax, ignoring my last comment. "I loved my ex-partner very much. I couldn't deal with her seeing another man. I became quite obsessed, to the point I kept a scrapbook of her life and death including your father. The journal was in police custody. They gave it back once the trial collapsed."

"Do you have the book? Can I see the content?"

"I'm not sure. I keep it locked away. It's too personal."

"It would mean a lot, Mr Bailey."

He gets up, unsteady on his feet. "I'll be back in a minute."

I stare at his glass and ponder over whether to spike the whisky with the sleeping powder and decide against it for various reasons. *I won't need to drug him. He seems to be doing a good job himself. I like him. Pity he has to die. Silly bastard is too drunk to think straight. He's playing right into my hands.* I fill up the tumbler with another drink and check the time. It is ten o'clock. *I must act soon. This is dragging on way too long. However, I'm interested in the scrapbook. I want to see the content out of curiosity.*

He returns holding an A4 book with a red cover. "Here you go. Take off your gloves."

"It's not necessary. I have to leave shortly."

He drinks more whisky while I flip through the collection. Stewart and Annabel appear happy together. And then, I see Annabel Taylor with my father walking along the street. *Stewart Bailey is a stalker. Perfect plot.* There are many newspaper headlines about her death and his case that never made it to court due to technical errors by the police. On the last page, there is information on the disappearance of Edward Scott.

"That must have been a nightmare, Stewart."

"Such a living hell, Jayden."

"I understand. It's not been an easy situation for both of us."

He slurs. "We've both lost someone special."

I put the book on the table. "Thank you for sharing your scrapbook. Let's start afresh. Why don't you come to the agency next week? We can go for lunch and have a proper chat about the campaign?"

"That would be great, Mr Scott. You're a good man."

I take out my packet of cigarettes. "Do you mind if I smoke?"

"No, but you must go outside." He gets up. "I have a veranda. Sorry, it's a bit cold."

"No problem."

I open the door and admire the Edinburgh skyline. "What a fantastic sight."

He walks out onto the balcony. "I'm so lucky to have this view."

We both drink in the atmosphere.

"It's beautiful. I'll get your whisky," I tell him.

I return to the living area. Before I pick up his glass, I remove the ring from the plastic bag, concealing the keepsake in the palm of my hand. My heart breaks to have to part with this token of death. As I approach him on the veranda, he leans against the railings and reaches out for the glass. My killer instinct takes over. It all happens so fast. *Do it now!* As he turns to view the city, I slip the diamond ring into his suit pocket, grab hold of him from behind and with one almighty PUSH, he disappears over the edge of the balcony. I move closer and dare to peer over the railing. Our eyes lock together. There is a look of terror on his face. I watch his last moments of life. Time seems to stand still. It almost appears in slow motion; his arms and legs splay out to the side, desperately trying to cling on to life, the remnants of whisky spilling into the air as he clutches hold of the glass. Just then, time shifts, his body falls to the ground like a dead weight, crashing on top of a car roof.

THUD!

I check my watch. It is twenty past ten.

I rush back into the flat, open the scrapbook, grab the drink, gulp down the contents and place it in my rucksack. As a last-minute gesture, I stare at his laptop sitting on the table. I close the files, click on the word document and type the following message:

This is too much of a burden.

I need to go! Get out before it's too late. Fire escape or front door? Front door or fire escape? I make my way towards the front door and peer through the spyhole only to get the shock of my life. I see the distorted image of a woman's face. There is a knock. She waits and presses the bell over and over again with a sense of urgency.

"Stewart, it's Sally from downstairs. Something's happened outside. Are you there? Answer the door."

I notice another voice. "What the hell is going on?"

She says to the man, "I'm not sure, Brian. There's been an accident. I heard a commotion in the street and looked out of my window. There's a body on top of a car. I came to get Stewart. He's not answering. I'm positive our neighbour is home. I heard him earlier and the lights are on but there's no answer." Her voice trails off. "You don't suppose…"

The man bangs on the door.

Get out of here now!

I rush towards the rear of the flat and try to open the fire exit. I notice the lock. *Shit!* The pounding continues in the background adding to an already intense situation. *Where the fuck is the key?* I am like an animal trapped in a cage with no means of escape. *Where would he keep it? Think! Think!* I run through to the kitchen, my eyes dart from left to right looking for a holder. There, on the side wall, hanging on the hooks are different keys. I grab the smallest one attached to a silver skull and crossbones keyring.

"Is anyone there?" shouts the man before he kicks the front door.

Please work. I catch my breath and exhale. *Stay calm.* I put the small key into the lock, turn the handle and push. A gush of cold air smacks into my face. At that moment, there is the sound of splintering wood, and voices in the hallway. I close the exit and lock it from the outside, slipping the key in my pocket. *Go, go, go!* With a notable increase in strength, I grab hold of the metal railing at the same time as I lunge forward, allowing my legs to cover three or four steps at a time. Once at the bottom, I go to the side of the building, veer left and only dare to watch the scene of the crime from a safe distance. As I drive away, I focus on the rear-view mirror; onlookers point up at the two neighbours peering over the balcony, other people are on their mobile phones and the rest stare at the dead body on top of the car.

I hear the distant sound of sirens speeding towards Tollcross.

Now, it is just a waiting game.

4

SUSPICIOUS MINDS

"We've all got the power in our hands to kill, but most people are afraid to use it. The ones who aren't afraid control life itself."
(Richard Ramirez)

Exhilaration.

It is the nature of the kill. I have no control over the adrenaline rush surging through my body. It is like an electrical current shooting through my veins, the voltage finding no way to escape, trapped in a closed circuit. My breathing locks in a battle to reduce the thumping inside my chest. Beads of sweat gather on my forehead and upper lip, trying to combat the sudden increase in temperature. It is euphoric. I grip the steering wheel, want to push my foot down on the accelerator, but find myself in a 20mph zone. With senses on high alert, my body responds. I require an outlet to unleash the build-up of sexual tension. I want to double back towards the city centre to the strip club Undressed To Kill. *No! Return to the office. I need to forget about my carnal desires. Calm down. Lock up the agency and go home.* No matter how much I try to control these out-of-control emotions, the nervous energy has no means of escape.

Enough!

I slam my foot on the break and can only describe my state of mind as completely insane. With tense fingers, I grip onto the steering wheel and feel the beast inside, welling up from the pit of my stomach as it escapes between each breath from my throat as a hoarse growl. The noise loses momentum with each release.

It is such a relief.

I compose myself.

For now.

I drive through the quiet streets of Edinburgh, light a cigarette, breathe the smoke, deep, deeper into my lungs, deliberating over my close encounter. *My world is insane at the moment.* I wonder how long it will take for the police to identify Annabel Taylor's ring and make the connection. *One to two weeks?* The sooner the better. I need Kristina Cooper back in my life. I think over the events, hoping that I have left no trace elements in the flat. There is also the message I typed on the computer and the open scrapbook which should speed up the investigation.

My senses are still on high alert. There is only one way to get back to normal. Once I close the agency, I need to return to the city and visit Koko Kanu at the strip club. *It will be the last visit. I have to commit my life and love towards Kristina. Just one more time.* I park the car at the rear of the building and rush up the stairs. Once inside my office, I slump down on the chair and let out a deep breath. I put my hand into the trouser pocket, my fingers caressing the metal object, take it out, and scrutinise the silver skull and crossbones keyring. It is not my usual keepsake but an appropriate substitute. *I'll add this to my collection later.* I change into my suit and decide to text Kristina. After all, she is the reason I killed Stewart Bailey.

I miss you. Please get in touch.

I pour a large whisky and wait for her reply. I click down the content on my computer and turn off the equipment. To my surprise, she video calls instead of sending a message. I slide the bar over to connect and look at her beautiful face on the screen. She appears irritable.

"Good to see you."

"You too, Jayden."

"How are you, my darling?"

"Not so bad." Before I can answer she asks, "Where are you?"

"Still at work."

"It's late."

"I know. I've just finished. I had a few campaigns to check."

"At least you're keeping busy."

"How are you getting on with your profile?"

"The analysis is going well. I'm looking at the evidence."

"And...?"

"I can't talk about the investigation, Jayden. I don't want to discuss the case."

"Okay, okay."

She sighs.

"Have you gone back to work?"

"Yes, everything seems to have settled down. I still get a few flashbacks of the crash. I keep in touch with Clarissa Evans. We both help each other come to terms with our ordeal."

I lose my temper. "I should be the one to provide support. Why don't you want to meet?"

"Calm down, Jayden."

"I won't calm down. This is insane. I'll come to Lincoln and see you within the next few weeks."

"No!"

"Yes!"

"Let's leave it for a while. I have to be sure…"

I interrupt. "Sure of what?"

"I need to know you're not involved in her murder."

"For fuck sake!"

I close the call.

Stupid bitch. I'm innocent. You'll soon find out.

Kristina calls back.

I hesitate but answer.

"Why did you disconnect?"

"This is all too much. I can't keep justifying my innocence on this matter and never even knew Annabel Taylor. I don't want to discuss that woman anymore. We need to talk about us. I miss you."

She sighs and drops her shoulders. "I miss you, too."

"Let's aim to meet in a few weeks time, once this settles down."

Kristina nods in agreement.

"I have a potential business meeting in Nottingham. I can visit you for a few days."

She nods again.

My hand reaches out to touch her face on the screen.

"I hope you're not lying, Jayden."

"I would never lie to you. EVER!"

"Thank you."

"For what?"

"I needed you to say those words."

I stare at her beautiful features. My groin stirs. I unzip my trousers, lose myself in the moment, stroking the shaft of my penis. The after-kill-tension is unbearable, unbelievably torturous.

"Are you okay?" she declares.

I roll my eyes. "I'm thinking about your body. It's very distracting."

For the first time in ages, she laughs. "I see nothing changes."

"I miss you, not just your body, Kristina."

"We'll see each other soon."

"Sooner rather than later."

"I need to go, Jayden. It's getting late."

I continue to secretly masturbate until we say our goodbyes. I am glad she called back. We seem to have worked out a compromise. My plan is that she will find out about Stewart Bailey's guilt with the forensic evidence of Annabel's Taylor ring hidden in his pocket, the scrapbook, his confession on the laptop and our lives can return to some kind of normality. Right now, the intensity of my sexual frustration is evident. I zip up my trousers and pour another measure of whisky, turn on the new phone and call a taxi to go to the city centre. I raid the safe and take much more than I need, several thousand to be precise. While I wait for the cab to arrive, I check my inbox for any contact from SocialMisfit. There are two unopened messages:

We accept your financial offer.

Please get in touch with the details. We'll clear up this matter within the next two to three weeks as requested.

I reply.

I'll be in Nottingham over the next few weeks and require a face-to-face meeting to fine-tune the plan and exchange money. I prefer to pay by cash rather than bitcoin transaction over the internet.

He responds.

Are you sure? I like to do my financial transactions online?

The conversation continues.

Positive. I want to meet in person.

We'll organise this over the next few days. I will be your only contact. Remember, I'm the middleman between you and Shoot To Kill.

That's fine. I'll be in touch soon, SocialMisfit.

I look forward to meeting you, Edward Cooper.

Satisfied with the outcome, I set the agency alarm. I note the time, twenty past eleven, and wait at the back door for the taxi to arrive. Ten minutes later, I get in the cab and give him directions to the strip club. The traffic is busy and comes to a complete standstill just before the city centre.

"I'll give you a flat rate," he says.

"Thanks. What's the problem?"

"Not sure. I'll check with the control room."

He picks up the radio. "This is Black Cab 13. I'm on my way to Tollcross. What's the problem at the West End? Over."

I listen to the static on the radio.

"Is there anyone there?" he says. "What's the problem HQ?"

"There's an accident. The traffic is horrendous."

He turns the control to mute.

I am unable to hear the response.

"Really?"

"In Tollcross?"

"That will fuck up our whole night."

"Speak later."

"What's the problem?" I ask.

"There's an accident at Tollcross. This may take a while."

"What's happened, do you know?"

"Suicide, apparently. Very nasty. The cops are crawling all over the place."

"I've changed my mind. Can we go back to Leith? Firth of Forth Apartments."

"No problem, mate."

I pay the driver, stand in the car park and must decide what to do. Still as intense as the point of kill, the need to release this build-up of sexual tension is at the forefront of my mind, consuming my every thought, powerful, waiting, wanting a release, ready to explode in a violent eruption. With extreme excitement, I walk the short distance to the bustling area of Leith and enter the hotel which is well-known for high-end escorts. I book a room and order a double whisky, relish the burning sensation in my throat, increasing my sexual desire even more and wait. It is busy just after midnight, full of businessmen and escorts, mingling to prepare for the inevitable.

A woman catches my eye.

I stare back.

The demure style is exquisite: black dress, stilettos, red lips and black stockings on those elegantly crossed legs. My groin stirs. She looks like Kristina Cooper but much more sophisticated. I raise my glass in her direction. She acknowledges with a smile.

I turn my back, order another whisky and wait.

My beautiful escort will come.

I smell her scent and shift round.

Our eyes lock.

"Can I get you a drink?"

"Si, vino rosso, per favore."

I order a bottle of the finest Italian red.

She watches as I pour the wine.

"Do you speak English?"

"Si."

I laugh.

"Yes, I do," she declares in a distinct accent.

"Italiano. Bellissimo."

She smiles.

"You're gorgeous."

"Grazie."

"What's your name?"

"Caterina. You?"

"Jayden Scott."

"Piacere di conoscerti."

"Nice to meet you, too."

She sighs, her eyes divert upwards, thinking, as she translates from Italian to English. "We don't need to socialise. My fee is £200 per hour."

"I want to spend a lot of time with you. What a hectic day. I need to wind down. Two thousand up front. Can you stay the whole night?"

"Up front?"

"In advance. I'll pay the money when we go to my room."

She takes a sip of wine and nods.

I find out she is twenty-six years old from Florence in the Tuscany region of Italy. Caterina is in Edinburgh to continue her studies in the field of forensic science: biological and toxicological. She works as an escort to fund part of her education and living costs. This Italian woman is not only beautiful but clever.

She relaxes. "And what do you do, Jayden?"

"I'm a serial killer. The police require your skills to catch an elusive murderer."

She thinks for a moment and laughs.

I stare at her for several moments, watching her nervous smile. "It's a joke. I run an advertising agency, invest in a few deals here and there, work hard and play even harder."

"Where do you live?"

I lie. "London. I'm here on business."

"Nice to meet you. You seem like a lovely gentleman."

I reach over and touch her hand.

Caterina moves it away.

"I'm all about intensity and intimacy. If you don't want that level of interaction, you need to go."

She thinks about my proposition. "That's fine."

"Good. We understand each other."

I order another bottle of wine and leave the bar.

I am ready, more than ready to consume this image of beauty. The burning lust is evident but I prefer to treat this woman to my passionate side unlike the whore at the motorway petrol station or my wild, drug-induced side with Koko Kanu. I place the bottle on the dresser. She stands by my side as I pour the wine. I turn and brush my lips against her cheek and offer the glass. It is these intimate gestures that stir my groin. My breathing becomes heavier in anticipation of the sexual act, just like my after-kill state of mind.

"To our night with each other," I declare.

"Sei uno gentiluomo, Jayden Scott."

Our glasses clink together.

Caterina's accent is all too much. I take the glass out of her hand and kiss those luscious lips, my fingers wandering over the curves, up her dress to the stocking tops, touching between her thighs. I want to fucking rip off my escort's clothes but refrain, teasing to the point of orgasm. She kisses my mouth, wanting more. I stop, pick up the glass of wine, take a large mouthful and observe her reaction. I see her chest rise and fall, eyes wide in anticipation, lips plump with desire, body ripe and ready.

I sit down on the edge of the bed.

"Undress, slowly. I want to watch you." I pull down my trousers and masturbate, staring at her every move. She gasps, removes the black dress and wants to take off the matching set of lacy underwear. "Don't, not yet. Touch yourself."

Caterina's hand moves to the top of her underwear, sliding down to caress the mound of flesh. She loses herself to the pleasure of touch as her fingertips wander across her flat stomach up towards the straps, releasing those full breasts as she tucks the cups of the bra under her cleavage. I continue to masturbate. She continues to tease her body. Unable to stand it anymore, I remove the rest of my clothes, put on a condom and caress her olive skin. I pull down her panties and leave on the stockings, shoes and bra. I lift her up as she wraps her legs around my torso. We fall onto the bed. She goes on top, moving back and forth, up and down, writhing, grinding in a sexual frenzy. I grab hold of Caterina's body and flip her over and take off all her clothes. We fuck for hours in every position possible, delaying the inevitable until a climactic conclusion. The remainder of the night consists of short naps, wild passion, tender lovemaking and multiple orgasms until we can no longer function, no longer continue, no longer stay awake.

Sometime later, her hand caresses the side of my face. "Buongiorno, Jayden Scott. Come ti senti?"

I groan. "What time is it? Go to sleep."

"Eleven o'clock."

"Shit!" I open my eyes. "Why is it so late?"

"Because we had an excellent night."

"We did indeed."

Before I know it, she is back on top, wanting more.

My body responds.

It is quick, functional and to the point for us both.

"I'm taking the day off. I deserve a break."

I deal with business first, text Kristina to say I will call tomorrow, book into the hotel for another night, eat breakfast, indulge in some serious debauchery for the next twenty-four hours, swap numbers, hand over two thousand pounds and return home a stress-free killer, ready to face Inspector Canmore, if necessary.

****

As soon as I get home, I turn on the lunchtime news and wait for the local bulletin. The reporter is outside Stewart Bailey's apartment block, the area sealed off with crime scene tape. Previous interviews with witnesses testify about the fall to his death, watching, as he landed on top of the car. The report highlights his sordid obsession and link to Annabel Taylor as well as her inexplicable murder. There is no mention of my father. *So far, so good.* In the background, I see the forensic team come out of the flat. The evidence about his 'suicide note' on his computer and the ring will emerge and there is also his scrapbook. *It is a waiting game.* I have to stay calm and decide to go to the office. I have not heard from Jessica Logan. We need to catch up on several projects, especially the bank campaign. I cannot have anymore links to Stewart Bailey or the bank's owner, Mr Guthrie. It is time to cut all ties with that contract. I must distance the agency as much as possible from this situation. Deep down, I know Inspector Canmore will pay a visit and knock on my door.

I leave the flat and drive towards Leith.

Feeling refreshed after the sex feast with my escort, I stride through the doors of the agency, ready to face the day.

"Good afternoon," I say to the receptionist.

She smiles.

I head straight to my office. I recall the events of the other evening after my return from Tollcross and scan the room. Everything seems fine. I switch on the computer and wait. I think about Stewart Bailey's last moments, falling to his death and experience a deep sense of sadness that I had to relinquish Annabel Taylor's ring in order to set him up. *Somehow, I will get that keepsake back and my father's gold band.* My legitimate phone rings, interrupting my thoughts.

"How are you, my boy?"

"Charles, I'm glad you called. Is everything okay?"

"Yes. I wrote a letter of complaint to DCI Grace McFarlane about Inspector Canmore's behaviour. This may stall the reopening of the case, perhaps."

"Thanks. You're a good man."

"I do this because I love your mother and feel responsible for the situation. It goes against my faith, but I have faith in you, Jayden."

"You've no idea how much I need your support right now."

"I do. That's why I want to help. Whatever the outcome, we require closure to move on. Let's hope and pray Inspector Canmore never uncovers your father's body."

"He won't. It's concealed to a depth which is hard to find."

"Please, I don't want to hear the details."

"Sorry. I'm certain we'll be able to move on. In the meantime, we need to wait."

"I hope fate is on our side."

"For sure. Fate is about choices. We've made the right decisions."

"Hallelujah. Take care."

"Goodbye, Charles."

The Reverend's complaint might delay the search. I have my doubts. It is irrelevant anyway because Inspector Canmore is a dead man. The timing of my trip to Nottingham to meet SocialMisfit needs to coincide with my visit to London. I can see Kristina on my way there and also when I return to Scotland. I check my diary. Three weeks from now, my nemesis will die by the beginning of March. That should be enough time for the investigation into Stewart Bailey's death to emerge and the clear links to Annabel Taylor's murder. Superintendent Hunter can inform Kristina about the case. She will find out I am an innocent victim of the justice system.

I go through my emails. There is one from Jessica Logan with high importance. It is about the bank brief. I must go and see her today. First, I check my unofficial phone and send a message to SocialMisfit.

I'll meet you in the park at the back of the National Justice Museum in Nottingham on Wednesday, 14th February at 11.00. The name of the target is Inspector Nicholas Canmore who works for Police Scotland in Edinburgh. Speak to you later.

I chuckle to myself. I like the idea of meeting him there. The historic building contains two courtrooms, underground jail and a site for executions. I think about Canmore's execution and want a bullet straight through his fucking head. I make a gesture with my fingers in the shape of a gun and click down my thumb and say, "BANG, you're DEAD!"

With a sense of triumph, I go and meet Miss Logan. She sits alone in one of the meeting rooms, lost in thought, reading content on the computer. I knock on the glass window. She gestures with her hand to enter the room.

"Thank God you're back, Mr Scott. I've just read about the situation. This is a nightmare. Have you seen the news report about Stewart Bailey and his links to that awful murder over seven years ago?"

"Yes, I saw it online. Tragic."

"What shall we do? The bank brief is a massive amount of money for the business."

"Don't worry. I knew about his link to Annabel Taylor's crime, but the case never made it to court and gave him the benefit of the doubt."

"Why did you not say anything? I hope we're not associated with his dastardly deeds in the media."

"Let me talk to Mr Guthrie about the predicament. I'll tell him to keep the agency out of this dilemma. We can also cancel our contract."

"Really?" Jessica's face is full of tension but eases at my reassurance. "Thanks, Mr Scott. It's better if you deal with Mr Guthrie."

I nod.

"I wonder if Stewart Bailey killed that woman?" she says. "Perhaps the burden was too much? I've just read the news which indicates there may be evidence to implicate his guilt."

Perfect.

"Mr Scott..."

"What evidence?"

"Something about a suicide note and item of jewellery found at the scene of his death."

The ring! This is going better than expected.

"Let's not speculate," I declare. "We need to wait. Remember, innocent until proven guilty."

"You're right. He seemed like a genuine person. It makes little sense?"

"We all have our secrets, Miss Logan."

"This is true."

"Put it to the back of your mind. Would you call Richard McKenzie and see how the perfume brand is progressing? Tell him I will come to London in a few weeks' time. We can focus our efforts on that brief as well as the government contracts on knife crime and mental health. I'll negotiate extra income on these campaigns. We'll be fine."

"Thanks for your support."

I turn to leave. "My pleasure. Speak to you later."

The day gets better. I watch the updates of my case on the online news. Reports reveal that it is a suspected suicide and that "further sources of evidence are under investigation which should take a few days to establish." *Yes! Yes! Yes! This evidence will filter through to my darling criminologist. Whatever profile she redeems from her box file of information, there is only one guilty man in this sordid affair—Stewart Bailey. And, she needs to apologise for her behaviour over the last few weeks.*

With a sigh of relief, my attention turns to Mr Guthrie. I decide to call him and end our contract. We don't need him anymore.

I dial the number.

Someone picks up the phone.

I say, "It's Jayden Scott."

Silence.

"Hello, Mr Guthrie?"

"Sorry, my mind is deep in thought at the moment, young man."

"I saw the news about Stewart Bailey."

"The situation is hard to believe. I'm in a state of shock. I supported and believed in his innocence for the last seven years."

"He may well have nothing to do with her death, but it's doubtful."

"It appears that way. I'm devastated."

"I need to terminate our contract. I have to think about the agency's reputation."

He sighs.

"Nothing personal."

"I understand."

There is an awkward silence.

"You might get a visit from a police officer, Inspector Canmore. He came this morning. I had to mention that Stewart Bailey was working on a campaign for your agency on our behalf."

"Don't worry. I'll deal with the situation."

"Thanks, Jayden. Sorry to bring so much trouble to your door. I had no idea of his secret life."

"No problem. Please, take good care."

He hangs up the phone.

I look forward to our meeting, Inspector Canmore.

I check the clock. It is just after six. Time to go home. There are still several employees working on briefs, ready to pitch for potential new clients. No doubt, they will stay until the early hours of the morning. I leave the agency with the intention to return to the flat and relax. As I drive towards Leith, I connect the second phone to the bluetooth in my car and switch on the speaker. I need to call Kristina and find out if she knows anything. However, it is only two days into the Stewart Bailey investigation.

I press on her name.

She answers. "Hi, Jayden. How are you?"

"I'm fine."

"You busy?"

I think about the Italian escort from the previous night, stirring my groin. "Very busy."

"Me too. I have a lot of work to do…and…well….it doesn't matter."

I suspect she wants to speak about the profile but wait for her to decide whether she will mention anything about Annabel Taylor or Stewart Bailey.

"Is everything okay, Kristina?"

"Yes, fine."

That's a good sign.

"I still want to come to Lincoln next weekend. Would you like to meet?"

"Yes, we need to talk face to face."

"I'll stay with you for a few days and head off to London. On my return, I have a meeting in Nottingham. After that, I can travel back to Lincoln before heading home to Edinburgh."

"That's a good plan."

"I miss you."

"Me too, Jayden."

I end the call.

Kristina sounds different. Submissive, not as feisty and defiant. She knows something from the news reports. It shows in the tone of her voice. This is going much better than expected. I am back in charge of the situation and the master of my own destiny. My deceit is no longer spinning out of control. I am now one step ahead of everyone and everything. The threads binding together my web of lies are stronger than before, the more the narrative unfolds. I have the loyal support of the Reverend, the Annabel Taylor murder is not an issue anymore and Kristina Cooper can apologise, SocialMisfit is the dark to her light, Shoot To Kill will eradicate my nemesis, Inspector Canmore dies and nobody must ever find my father's skeletal remains. I breathe a sigh of relief. The pressure over the last few weeks, days, hours and minutes, fuels the desire for more sex. It is almost unbearable. I get ready to call the Italian escort but realise I have to focus my efforts and loyalty on my beautiful criminologist.

A battle ensues in my mind, arguing with an imaginary voice in my head. *Phone Caterina or visit Koko Kanu. Just one more time. No, I need to be faithful. You'll never be true to anybody. You're a delusional liar, killer, cheat and grandmaster manipulator. DO IT! Have a great night. Forget about your life with Kristina Cooper. She is too good for your pitiful existence, anyway.*

"STOP!" I shout.

The negative voice ceases to exist.

"Where the fuck did that come from?"

I park the Noble in a side street and try to regain some kind of control, light a cigarette and calm down. "There's no room in my life for negativity and imaginary voices. Get a bloody grip," I tell myself.

I restart the car, continue on my journey and prepare to relax on my own for the rest of the evening. I put all these negative thoughts down to the stress of my situation, or perhaps, I am going insane due to the continual fight to establish my innocence through elaborate scheming, debauchery, and having to dig my way out of this dark web of lies. As I turn the corner to park the vehicle in my private space, I see him there, lurking like a stalker to harass and intimidate his prime suspect.

My fighting spirit returns. I push all negative thoughts aside and mutter, "I'm ready, you bastard."

I get out of the Noble.

He winds down the window.

"Nice to meet you again, Inspector Canmore."

"You got a minute, Mr Scott?"

I turn and look him straight in the eye. "For you. Always."

He smirks.

I invite him to the apartment.

There is an awkward, stony silence in the lift. I open the door to the flat and hang up my coat. I head to the living area. He follows. We stand and stare at each other, both assessing the other, until I break the silence.

"Coffee, tea, wine, whisky, anything else?"

"Brandy."

"You're driving."

"I'm the law. I'll do what I want."

"Fair enough."

I pour us both a large measure. "How can I help?"

He takes out a notebook and pen from his pocket. "I need to ask a few questions."

"What?"

"Your whereabouts on Friday night."

"Why?"

"Answer the question."

I comply. "I was in my office until I locked up the agency just after eleven."

"Why so late?"

"We work all hours in this industry, Inspector Canmore. I had a few campaigns to assess, spoke to my partner on video chat and left."

"What time?"

"I can check my data." I take the phone out of my pocket and click on the log. "She called at 10.50."

"Dr Cooper?"

"Yes."

"You do realise she's a profiler on the Annabel Taylor murder?"

"I know about the case. We tell each other everything but not confidential intelligence."

He smiles. "I hope not. Too much insider information considering you're a prime suspect."

"No, I'm not."

"Yes, you are, Mr Scott."

I sigh.

"Back to the night in question. You stayed here until after eleven?"

"Yes."

"I thought you had a martial arts class on a Friday evening or a date with your woman at the strip club?"

I grin. "Not this week. Too busy with work."

"Does Dr Cooper know about your shady past?"

"That's none of your business, Inspector Canmore."

He continues. "Was there anyone in the agency?"

"Miss Logan was there until six thirty but everyone else had gone."

"So, you don't have an alibi?"

"Alibi for what?"

"The death of Stewart Bailey. He worked for you, Mr Scott. The man found on top of the car. Apparent suicide. The other half of Annabel Taylor. A convenient scapegoat for her murder."

"I saw the news footage. How tragic."

He smirks. "Did you have anything to do with his death?"

"No."

His phone rings.

"I need to take this call."

He heads out to the hall. I gulp down the brandy and refill the glass. I hear his tone but not the words. Several minutes pass. Inspector Canmore re-enters the living area, his face, pale. He picks up the tumbler and does the same, polishing off the measure.

"Pour another one, Jayden."

"What's up?"

He gulps it down and rubs his temples with his fingertips. "I don't have to ask any more questions at the moment."

I can tell his mind is in turmoil.

"There is new evidence to implicate Stewart Bailey with Annabel Taylor's murder. A key piece of forensics. We found her missing ring... after all this time."

"What ring?"

"Nothing. I need to end this informal interview and get back to the station. I'll be in touch once I check out your information. I take it there are records of when you locked up the agency."

I nod a triumphant gesture.

He turns to leave.

"Wait! What about my father's case?"

"The search takes place at the start of next month. This may be over for one victim but another one still remains unsolved."

Inspector Canmore marches towards the door, and stops, dead in his tracks. He turns around, almost in slow motion, looking up from below his inquisitive brow. His head moves to the side contemplating the situation. He points an accusatory finger in my direction. "I have your father's ring, Mr Scott, and now another one materialises at the death scene of Stewart Bailey who works for your agency. What a coincidence."

"You're crazy, Inspector Canmore. Give up your obsession with my involvement on these issues. I had nothing to do with either."

"I'm not giving up. No matter what evidence proves your innocence. I'll bring you down."

On that note, he leaves the flat.

****

Inspector Canmore is clever. I acknowledge and admire that side of his personality. However, the evidence is overwhelming against Stewart Bailey. I left no trace elements in his flat. The week passes by with no more intervention or contact from my nemesis. The news feed on Stewart Bailey's suicide, confession, scrapbook pictures and involvement in the death of his ex-partner fades into the background. I switch off and continue to plan my next move. It is the night before my trip to Lincoln. I message SocialMisfit to complete the plans for his murder. I gave him the information on Inspector Canmore. It is now up to Shoot To Kill to end his life. My partner in crime has someone following Canmore's every move to establish his routine. I insist on a gunshot wound to the head and wait in anticipation to meet up with SocialMisfit in Nottingham, but first, I need to visit Kristina Cooper to reconcile our differences and get back on track.

I decide to video call.

She answers.

"Hey, sweetheart. How are you?"

"I'm fine, Jayden. I decided to work late tonight. I can enjoy our long weekend together without having to worry about my workload."

"Great. I've planned the visit to coincide with my meetings in London and Nottingham. See you tomorrow afternoon."

"I can't wait to meet you."

"The feeling is mutual. I need your body, so, SO, SO, SO MUCH!"

She laughs.

"It's great to see you smile, Kristina."

"I'm happy at the moment. I'll tell you everything when we meet each other. This is not a conversation to discuss over the phone."

"Sounds intriguing. You get on with your work. See you soon."

"Good night, Jayden."

I pack my case, including my killer outfit to meet SocialMisfit, check the money in the briefcase, make a bowl of pasta and settle down for the evening. The ten o'clock news comes on the television. Just then, the doorbell rings. *Who on earth is that?* I peer through the spyhole. *For fuck sake, what does she want?* The noise is persistent. I open the door. She wears a short trench coat and high heels, her lips a deep shade of red.

"Buonasera, Jayden Scott."

"What the hell are you doing here?"

"I thought you might like some company. Are you alone?"

"Yes, but that's irrelevant. How did you find my address? More to the point, how did you get into the building?"

"You were not hard to locate online. I noted you lived in Edinburgh and London. The concierge said to come up."

"Did he now?"

My neighbour comes out of the apartment across the landing and raises an eyebrow. "Hello, Jayden. How are you?"

"I'm fine," I say, grabbing hold of Caterina's arm and pull her into the flat.

He smirks. "Have a good night."

"You too."

We stand in the hallway. Now I am over the initial shock, my groin stirs. My Italian lady is a vision of sexual beauty. She steps forward, kissing my lips, lingering, long, slow, and passionate. I am tempted but must refuse. I think of Kristina Cooper. She is the important one at the moment, not this escort, despite my undeniable arousal.

"You need to go. I don't want to do this tonight. I have a busy day tomorrow. Another time, perhaps."

Disappointment passes across her face.

I shrug my shoulders.

She moves forward.

I push her away. "Stop it!"

Caterina turns to leave the flat.

I feel a sense of relief.

"Call when you're ready."

"Wait!"

I grab hold of her wrist, undo the belt on her coat to reveal her naked body underneath and gasp. Right there in the hallway, I perform the ultimate act of intimate betrayal as my tongue finds the point of pleasure. She orgasms on my face. I sit on the floor with my head in my hands. *I'm sorry, Kristina. It's the last time. I promise.*

"Gesu Cristo. Are you okay, Jayden?"

"Yes. Please go."

She leaves the flat without another word.

My remorse is short and sweet.

I receive a text from Kristina.

"Thinking of you. Can't wait to see you tomorrow. Let's start again. I adore and trust you more than ever."

I get up off the floor and go for a shower. There is no doubt that my criminologist knows the details of the Bailey investigation. She is right. It is time to start afresh. I think about her body. My sexual appetite is out of control at the moment. One that only she can truly satisfy. This is her fault. I have not seen my beautiful criminologist for weeks. That denial has sent my sex drive into overdrive despite the encounter with Caterina at the hotel on the night of Stewart Bailey's murder. I head off to the bedroom and try to sleep. However, I am more than aware of my state of arousal.

I wake up late in the morning. I stretch out in bed and take a deep breath. The day has come to face the most important woman in my life. I get up, have a shower, dress and leave to drive to Lincoln. The treacherous A1 motorway is busy. Several hours later, I stop at the same service station to grab a coffee. There is no sign of the hooker I met on the way back from Lincoln. I am keen to reunite with Kristina, but moreso, my trip to Nottingham to meet SocialMisfit. The man is intriguing with a devious mind. Not unlike myself. We can exchange money and arrange a date and place to kill Inspector Canmore. I hope it all goes well. I am back in control for the first time in a while. Not since my confessional encounter with Charles in the church at New Year. A lot has happened over the last few months, but now, life is good.

I ponder over the events in my mind. *My confession, the Reverend's wrath then support, our trip to the cottage, the plane crash, Kristina's stony silence, Stewart Bailey's murder, the service station whore and Italian escort, Inspector Canmore, and finally, the darker side of the internet and SocialMisfit.*

Jesus Christ! No wonder I'm going insane. There is only so much that one individual can handle. My negative voice is right, I am not only a psychopathic serial killer but a master of manipulation. I chuckle to myself, relishing my new title. Nevertheless, despite my manipulative behaviour, it is necessary to spend time with Kristina and live a normal life.

Five hours later, I park the Noble outside her flat just after three o'clock. *I wonder what news she has about the Annabel Taylor murder? This is too exciting for words.* I lift my bag out of the car, leave the case full of money, and bound up the stairs. I inhale a deep breath and ring the bell. It seems to take ages for her to answer the door. Much to my surprise, an old lady stands in the doorway. She is small, petite, peering over the rim of her glasses.

"Hello, you must be Jayden Scott?"

"Yes. Who are you?"

"Clarissa Evans."

I stare at her for a moment, and then, her name registers in my mind. The person from the plane crash. The interfering old bitch who supports my woman in her recovery. She is the reason that Kristina never spoke much about the accident. I stretch out my hand. "Nice to meet you."

Clarissa places her palm on mine, makes contact and flinches, pulling it away. "And you..."

We stare at each other. The battleaxe cocks her head to the side, looks up, and contemplates. The muscles in her face slacken as she puts a forefinger and thumb on her chin, rubbing it while she thinks.

"Are you okay?"

The old woman refocuses. "I'm not sure."

I roll my eyes. "Is Kristina here?"

"Yes, she's in the kitchen making a light snack."

Clarissa continues to stand at the door and blocks my entry.

"Can you move out of the way?"

She steps aside. "Please, come in."

What a fucking silly woman.

I leave my bag and her in the hallway. As I march towards the kitchen, I smell the distinct aroma of fresh baking. Kristina runs in my direction and wraps her arms around my neck. My fingers brush against her face before my mouth connects with her soft lips. She responds. Nothing else exists at that moment. This is my destiny, she is my destiny, we are our destiny. Still clinging on, she says, "I've missed you."

"I know. I've missed you too," I reply, cupping her face in my hands. I place a small kiss on her cheek. "Very much."

We compose ourselves. I turn around and Clarissa stands in the doorway, watching our every move, knitting her brow together. "How sweet," she declares.

Kristina laughs. "Both of you go to the living room. I'll bring the tea and cake."

There is an awkward silence.

The old woman avoids my gaze.

"Is there something wrong, Clarissa?"

"No. Yes. This is not right…"

"What?"

"I'm not sure."

She appears lost in thought.

There is another awkward silence.

"It's nice to meet you at last," I say. "Kristina never stops talking about you."

"That's good to know."

"How are you coping with the horrific ordeal?"

"Much better. We've supported each other through this crisis."

"I also worry about *my* girlfriend."

"She's fine. I love her like my own daughter. We were meant to meet. Kristina needs my support because of the fractious relationship with her own mother."

Interfering bitch. "That's very kind of you."

Kristina interrupts the conversation. "Here you go. Afternoon tea is ready."

I take the heavy tray out of her hands and place it on the table. "You're full of surprises, Miss Cooper."

"I wanted to do something special for us."

"Thank you," says Clarissa.

I pour the drink and serve the cake.

We talk about the plane crash and how they support each other. Kristina also declares that this woman has some kind of sixth sense. *She is uneasy in my presence, that's for sure. What's going through her mind? Clarissa better not create any trouble with her mumbo jumbo nonsense. I need Kristina on my side. My plan is flawless so far. I don't need another distraction on top of everything else.* I endure the conversation for the rest of the afternoon. It is torture. I want to be on my own with my woman. At last, the old bag decides to depart.

"Thank you so much for a wonderful day, Kristina."

"My pleasure."

I look her straight in the eye. "I'll be here for the next few days."

With a wry smile, she says, "I better leave you two alone. I can catch up with you mid-week, my dear."

We walk her to the door.

"Take good care," declares Clarissa. She turns towards Kristina with a serious look on her face, avoids my gaze and takes hold of her hand. "We need to talk in private."

Kristina falters. "Of course... soon."

She lets go of her hand and says, "Goodbye."

"Goodbye," we both say together.

At fucking last. I close the door.

"Sorry, Jayden. Clarissa insisted on meeting you. I wonder what she wants to talk about?"

"Who knows? She's gone now," I reply, licking my lips. "Your cake was delicious."

Kristina laughs. "Bring your bag through to the bedroom."

We lie on top of the bed: touch, kiss, talk, but the sexual act is never far from my mind. I want to wait until after we discuss the Taylor murder. It is an intimate moment. We re-establish our special bond. This time, our link must be unbreakable. My beautiful criminologist does not mention the case. I do not encourage the conversation, for now.

"What shall we do tonight, Kristina?"

"Not sure?"

I laugh. "An early night?"

She chuckles. "You're so predictable."

"Why don't we order food, relax and enjoy our time together."

"Sounds like a great idea."

"What do you fancy?"

"You," she says in a playful voice.

"It's good to see you smile."

"I'm happy, that's why. What a stressful month."

"Let's put it behind us. However, we need to talk about the Annabel Taylor case. The details are all over the news."

"I've seen the footage. Later?"

"Sooner rather than later," I insist.

Kristina ignores my words. "Can you order the food? I want to go for a bath."

"Of course."

I scan the restaurants on my phone, deciding on some fish and sushi dishes. It is an hour for delivery. I hear Kristina run the water, change into some comfortable clothes, give her time to settle, go to the kitchen and pour two glasses of wine. *I need to find out what my criminologist knows about the Taylor case. How far did Kristina get with the profile? What does she think about Stewart Bailey's involvement?* I gulp down the contents of my glass and refill. I make my way towards the bathroom holding them by the thin stem and push the door open with my foot. Kristina flinches, placing both hands on her breasts as she crosses one leg over the other, wary, hiding.

"Why are you covering up your body?"

"I was lost in thought and got a fright."

"Don't be scared, Kristina."

"I'm not. It was just unexpected. Why so serious, Jayden?"

I sigh, handing her the glass of wine. She relaxes. I pull over the chair, sit down, bend over and whisper, "We need to talk."

"Did you order dinner?"

"Fish and sushi."

"Lovely."

I wait.

She pauses.

I stare into those beautiful eyes.

Kristina looks in my direction.

I take a drink.

Her hand reaches out to turn on the hot water tap.

I continue to wait.

"I'm sorry for the accusations," she blurts out. "Really sorry. This is awkward. I'm not sure what to say."

"Do you want to talk about it over dinner?"

She nods.

"We need to get it out of the way. I can't relax and enjoy your company with this issue in the background."

"You're right."

"I'll leave you to have your bath."

I go to the living area and notice the box file sitting on the table in the corner of the room. I take out the A4 notebook and open the first page. As I sift through the content, there is a lot of written description of Annabel Taylor's life. As I turn the pages, the writing style changes to a more formal approach. There are three columns of notes:

Category	Stewart Bailey	Jayden Scott
Age	48	30
Murder age	41	23
Gender	Male	Male
Status	Entrepreneur/Owner	Entrepreneur/Owner
Occupation	PR Consultant	Advertising Agency
Address	Edinburgh (Tollcross)	Edinburgh (Dean Village)
Murder location	Tollcross	Tollcross
Relationship	Ex-lover	Father's mistress
Murder weapon	Knife	Knife
Leisure	Meet friends	Martial Art
Motive	**JEALOUSY**	**REVENGE**
Stolen items	Mobile phone, purse and ring	Mobile phone, purse and ring
Type of killer	Missionary	Missionary
Expert (knife)	No evidence	Perhaps?
Type of killing	Personal	Personal
Modus operandi	Single operator	Single operator
Circumstantial evidence	Ring, scrapbook, suicide note	Martial Art Specialist

So far, it is a mesmerising read. I listen to her come out of the bathroom, throw the notebook back in the box, rush towards the sofa and drink my wine. *She's clever linking my martial arts training to this type of kill. But the ring will seal his fate, that's for sure. All I have to do now is deal with SocialMisfit and Inspector Canmore and this comes to an end. Stewart Bailey's murder or suicide will remain unsolved, just like my father, with no evidence to link his death to myself. I can't wait to meet my new partner in crime. No matter how much SocialMisfit searches, he'll never find the real Edward Cooper because that person doesn't exist, only in my deranged mind.* I place the glass on the table and go to find my criminologist. Kristina sits on the edge of the bed and wears a black robe, gazing into the mirror as she moisturises her face.

I watch her for a while.

"Where do you want to eat?" I ask. "Small table in front of the fire or large one in the corner?"

"Small table. It's more intimate."

"I'll get everything ready for dinner."

"Thank you."

I set the table, light a few candles, turn on the music player, sit down and wait for the food as well as our talk. *I've not felt this relaxed in ages.* With a carefree attitude, I check my illegitimate phone. There is a message from SocialMisfit.

I'll meet you on Wednesday at 11.00 behind the National Justice Museum. Don't be late, Edward Cooper.

I chuckle and type a response. I love my new name.

Likewise, SocialMisfit. I am in Lincoln at the moment. I have several meetings in London for a few days and will stop off in Nottingham on my way back. See you soon.

Just then, I jump out of my seat as the doorbell rings.

"I'll get the food, Jayden."

"Thanks." I pour us both another glass of wine, ready for our conversation. "The plates and cutlery are through here."

Kristina enters the living room. "This is nice. Thank you for making such an effort." She puts the bag on the table and picks up the glass. "You can serve."

I split up the meal.

We sit down to eat.

"So…" I declare.

"Well…" she replies.

"I take it you have come to some kind of conclusion on the Annabel Taylor murder?"

Kristina nods, chewing a mouthful of food. She takes a small sip of wine. "I have but not from my profile. That's not finished yet."

I raise an eyebrow.

"I've put together information on you and Stewart Bailey."

"Have you now?"

"Sorry, I had to be sure."

"No need to apologise."

"I saw the news report about his apparent suicide."

"Did you?"

She nods. "I also received a phone call from Superintendent Hunter last night before you called. He confirmed that Miss Taylor's missing ring turned up in Stewart Bailey's pocket. There's no mistake. Forensic tests reveal it is Annabel Taylor's DNA. And just before Stewart Bailey took his own life, he left his scrapbook of him and his ex-partner on the table. He also wrote a suicide message on his computer."

"What a relief. This has driven a wedge between us."

"Perhaps it's a relief for Stewart Bailey. What a burden to bear over such a long period of time."

"I'm not sure what to say?"

"There's no need to say anything. Marcus has closed the case on Annabel Taylor."

THANK FUCK! "Good. We don't need all this doubt between us both. But remember, we still have to deal with the search in Argyll. Inspector Canmore is a lunatic, Kristina."

"I have come to that conclusion. Superintendent Hunter also doubts his sanity."

"Why? What did he say? Does he know about us?"

"I never mentioned our involvement with each other. He said Inspector Canmore was wrong seven years ago and is wrong now, about everything, including your father."

I smirk.

"I got a verbal invitation from Superintendent Hunter to go to The Charity Ball on the 3rd of March. I checked. It's on Saturday evening. I will return the box files in the next few days."

I feel a pang of jealousy about Hunter asking her to the event. I am just about to explode but let her continue.

"Do you mind? It might be the ideal place to speak to Inspector Canmore about the search in Argyll. I'll try and get him to call it off."

This could be the perfect opportunity for Shoot To Kill to end his life.

"What do you think, Jayden?"

"Sounds like a plan, Dr Cooper. Make it clear to Superintendent Hunter that you're not available."

She wraps her arms around my neck. "Are you jealous?"

"Not one bit!"

"It's all going to work out."

"I never had any doubt."

The food is fantastic and we share another bottle of wine. I am calm, in control, and happy with Kristina. At end of the evening, I take hold of her hand, lead her towards the bedroom, close the door and indulge in some of the most intimate lovemaking of my whole life.

I am back: back where I belong.

5

THE HUNT

"I love to hunt."
(David Berkowitz)

In the life of a policeman, I hate the start of the week, especially on a cold, dreary Monday morning in Scotland. I stride through the doors of the station and acknowledge the young officer at the reception.

"Good morning, Peters."

"How are you today, Inspector Canmore?"

"Not good. The day can only get better."

"I'm not so sure. Have you heard the news?"

"What?"

"Superintendent Marcus Hunter closed the file on the Annabel Taylor murder."

"He did what!?"

"There is too much evidence to implicate Stewart Bailey."

"Like hell, there's not. That man is insane."

I march off without another word, storm up the stairs and slam the door. As soon as I sit down on my chair, I get up, run out of the office and head towards Hunter's room, my face flush, the more I think about his decision. I barge through the door without knocking. The place is empty. I scan his office. Everything is neat and tidy like his stupid mind. There is a piece of paper on his desk with a name and mobile number. I take out my notebook and write it down before heading back to my floor. It is necessary to make several important phone calls. But first, I consider the timeline of events leading up to Stewart Bailey's death.

Stewart Bailey died nine days ago on the Friday night in Tollcross.
Partner on a bank brief for Mr Scott's advertising agency.
Possible scapegoat to cover Jayden Scott's involvement in Annabel Taylor's murder?

Jayden at work on the night of Stewart Bailey's 'suicide'.
On his own from 18.30 until after 23.00.
Over a four hour window of opportunity.
Did Jayden Scott meet Stewart Bailey?
Was he in the victim's flat or at the agency?
Time of Stewart Bailey's death, 22.20.
Spoke to Kristina Cooper at 22.50 from his office.
Tollcross to Leith in half an hour?
Sets the alarm and leaves the office at 23.20.
Stewart Bailey's crime scene results? Contact Sarah McLeod?
She owes a favour for her conduct on the Edward Scott files she sent to Marcus
Hunter seven years ago.

I ponder over the information, staring at the timeline of events.
The key question is whether Jayden Scott could drive from Tollcross
to Leith in half an hour? I will do this trip later on tonight and
monitor the time of the journey. Even if Mr Scott had something to
do with Stewart Bailey's demise, how could he communicate with
Kristina Cooper so soon after his involvement? Anyone in their right
mind would appear nervous and out of control. However, he is a
devious bastard. And the ring? Another one turns up in Stewart
Bailey's pocket. A thought enters my mind about the last
conversation I had with Jayden Scott when I left his flat. *First, there is
the disappearance of Edward Scott. Cause unknown but I found his ring in the
hallway of the family home. Did Jayden Scott lose it on the night of his
nosebleed? Was all the pressure too much? And then, Annabel Taylor's ring
turns up after seven years just as Dr Cooper tries to establish a profile of the
murderer. Are the rings a keepsake? Are these trophies of a more sinister mind?
Did he kill Stewart Bailey and leave the ring as evidence to condemn him and
admonish himself? Am I dealing with the same killer for both crimes?* I need
to talk to someone in confidence. I email Sergeant Jack Murray to
come to my office later in the day. He is my voice of reason and
knows the suspect. Besides, Jack's role is important in the new
search to take place at the cottage in Argyll. In the meantime, I
phone Sarah McLeod to discuss the Bailey case.

She answers. "Good morning, Inspector Canmore."

"Hello, Sarah. How are you?"

"I'm fine."

"I'll get straight to the point."

"Yes."

"I suspect the information is not in the archives? I need you to send the forensic results for the Stewart Bailey suicide."

"No, the documents are not online yet. It's not your case."

"Can you send the report? You owe me a favour after your conduct on the Edward Scott files."

She pauses.

"I want to review the results. Hunter has closed the case. It doesn't make any difference whether you send them or not."

"Okay, don't mention my involvement if this goes wrong."

"It won't. I'm determined to wrap this up once and for all. Jayden Scott is the key to Edward Scott, Annabel Taylor and Stewart Bailey."

"Are you sure?"

"Absolutely. I'm not messing about anymore."

"Good luck. There's no evidence to incriminate your suspect."

"That's the problem. It's all too perfect."

"I know what you mean."

"Watch and wait. Please forward the files to my fax machine, not the central number. Can you send the report as soon as possible?"

"I'll do that now."

"Thanks."

I sit down, glare at the machine, tapping my fingers on the table, waiting for the results. In the meantime, I take out my notebook and stare at the number I stole from Superintendent Hunter's office. I wonder if this person has doubts over Jayden Scott's involvement? There is only one way to find out. My hand hovers over the phone. *This will be awkward but I have to make the call. Pick it up and dial the number.* As I am about to take the plunge, there is a knock on the door. *Bloody hell! Bad timing.*

"Who's there?"

He enters.

I smile. "Come and sit down, Jack."

"Cheers."

"That was quick!"

"I got your message. I was already here on another case."

"What a stroke of luck."

"How are you, Skipper?"

My brow pinches together. "I need your advice."

He laughs. "That's nothing new."

"I value your opinion."

He winks. "How can I help?"

"Do you remember the disappearance of Edward Scott?"

"It's hard to forget."

"We're reopening the case. Can you conduct another search at the cottage in Argyll? This time you're not leaving until we find evidence."

"When? I have a tight schedule over the next month."

"As soon as possible."

He scratches his head. "Resources are scarce at the moment."

"I know but this is important."

"I can reschedule my appointments. I'll try and do the job within the next three weeks."

"Thanks, Jack. Much appreciated."

He stares in my direction. "Anything else? You could have emailed about the search. What's going on?"

"Jayden Scott. He might have something to do with another murder although it's an apparent suicide."

"Who?"

"Stewart Bailey. Over a week ago. Found on top of a car at Tollcross. Jumped to his death."

"I heard about it on the news."

"He's Annabel Taylor's ex-partner. Mistress of Edward Scott. Business associate to Jayden Scott."

"Really?"

"Our suspect is the deadly connection to this trio."

"What proof do you have, Skipper?"

"My gut instinct."

"You need to find evidence."

"That's the problem. The crime scenes are immaculate. He's a clever killer, that much is true."

"I'll conduct the search. You have to go back over the evidence on Edward Scott and get access to Stewart Bailey's suicide report. Be thorough, Skipper."

"I already requested the Bailey files from Sarah McLeod. They arrive today."

"Good. Let's proceed with caution and find proof, that's if your gut instinct is correct."

"My gut instinct is never wrong, Jack."

He nods in agreement. "I've got your back this time."

"Thanks. I also have the support of DCI Grace McFarlane in terms of resources and funding unlike Superintendent Hunter when he was my superior officer."

He laughs. "I remember the conversation with him to call off the last search and thought it was you on the phone. Too funny."

"That man is a nightmare."

"Just a bit! I'll be in touch about the investigation. In the meantime, find evidence, something, anything."

"I must revisit Edward Scott's files and have an important call to make."

"Who?"

"I'll update you in due course."

He gets up to leave. "Sounds interesting. I better go. Busy as usual."

"Thanks for the advice."

He slaps my back. "Good luck, Skipper."

I look at the fax machine, willing it into action. *Come on, send the Bailey files, Sarah.* I contact the archives department in the basement of the police station and arrange to pick up the Edward Scott files in the afternoon. I could download the material online but there is too much information to print out. I can only stare at a screen for so long. The originals are better. In the meantime, I lift the phone and dial the number from my notebook.

"Hello."

"Dr Cooper?"

"Yes…"

"Inspector Nicholas Canmore from Police Scotland."

There is no reply.

"Hello, Kristina."

"How can I help you?"

"I'm not sure where to start."

"Start at the beginning."

"This is awkward because of your involvement with Jayden Scott. I'll get straight to the point. I am positive he killed his father, Annabel Taylor and Stewart Bailey."

She gasps. "Why?"

I blurt out, "It's the rings."

"What?"

"I found his father's wedding band in the hallway of his family home seven years ago. And now, Annabel Taylor's ring turns up in Stewart Bailey's pocket."

"Superintendent Hunter confirmed that the DNA evidence on the ring belongs to Annabel Taylor. Therefore, one plus one equals two. Stewart Bailey murdered his ex-partner. How did you come to the conclusion that Jayden killed all three?"

"You don't have a clue, do you?"

"What?"

"Stewart Bailey was a public relations consultant on a brief with Mr Scott's advertising agency."

"Are you sure?"

"Yes, secrets and lies, Dr Cooper."

"Wait a minute. We don't discuss his business clients."

"This is an exception. Bailey is the main suspect in the Taylor murder and she was his father's mistress. Why did he not tell you they worked together?"

"I have no idea."

She changes the subject. "And does Jayden know you have his father's ring?"

"Yes. He said his father must have dropped his wedding band. I don't believe him. These rings are tokenistic gestures of a serial murderer. I'm just away to scrutinise Edward Scott's file to see if I missed anything. Mr Scott was also on his own in the office, with no witnesses, on the night of Stewart Bailey's apparent suicide. He could have been at his flat, he may have pushed him over that balcony, went back to the agency and answered your call before he left."

"I doubt that very much. When I spoke to him, he appeared normal, but then again, people who commit multiple murders have no remorse or guilt." She falters for a few seconds, contemplating the situation. "Who, how, why are you so sure of his involvement?"

"Gut instinct. I will prove it this time."

"You're delusional, Inspector Canmore. There's no evidence. None."

"Don't you think that's strange. The crime scenes are too clean. It's premeditated. Planned to perfection from the mind of a clever killer. I'll find the connection to all three murders," I shout. "I'm bringing that psychopath down."

"You have no evidence to back up your claim. This is harassment. Now I understand your level of obsession."

"I must warn you, Dr Cooper. You're involved with the wrong man and could be in mortal danger because of your link to the Taylor profile. Be careful."

"I can take care of myself. I have yet to finish my analysis of the Annabel Taylor murder. Just because the case is closed, I'll complete it based on the evidence. I'm a professional, Inspector Canmore, despite my relationship with Jayden Scott."

"Good."

"We can talk again at The Charity Ball. Are you going?"

"Yes, I'll be there."

"Please consider all the facts. I'm here if you require anymore information."

"I have your number if I need advice. Thank you for your call."

"No, thank you for speaking in such a calm manner despite my revelations. I will unravel his web of lies. The net is closing in on your partner, Dr Cooper."

She falters, again. "… Goodbye, Inspector Canmore."

I contemplate the conversation. *That went well. I wonder what she truly thinks? Too controlled? She'll come to the same conclusion. I'll put a tail on that bastard and spy on his every move.* I call his work to discover that Jayden Scott has left Lincoln and is away on business at the London agency. I find the contact details of one of my old mates, Larry Parker, to ask him to follow my suspect for the next few days. He is a retired officer from the Metropolitan Police. I pick up the phone and dial the number.

"Hello. Who's calling?" he grumbles. "I'm having my afternoon nap."

"Larry, good to hear your grumpy voice. I see nothing changes. Inspector Nicholas Canmore of Police Scotland."

He perks up. "Hey, Skipper. How can I help?"

"I'll get straight to the point. Can you do surveillance work on a prime suspect in a murder case? Are you interested?"

"Oh yes! My life is boring since I retired and need a new challenge. When do I start?"

"Now."

"Where about?" he says with excitement.

"London. Westminster area."

"For how long?"

"I'm not sure. Follow him for a couple of days."

"Okay doke."

"I'll make certain you're compensated for your efforts."

He laughs. "I'm not bloody doing it for nothing!"

I chuckle, having no idea how to fund this venture. I will need to claim the expenses against the budget for the search in Argyll which should take place at the beginning of March. I give him Jayden Scott's address to his flat and the London agency, my mobile number and email a photograph of the target.

"I'll transfer part of the payment into your business account. Keep a note of all your expenses."

"I know the drill, Inspector Canmore."

"Contact me on a daily basis. I need you to track his every move."

"Do you want to give any additional details about the suspect?"

"Not at the moment, Larry."

"Fair enough."

"Stay in touch."

I hang up the phone.

Just then, I see the fax machine light blinking on and off. Several moments later, page after page of evidence arrives from Sarah McLeod. I gather up the documents and place them in a folder. With a sense of purpose, I read over the information for the rest of the afternoon. The crime scene is clean. Too sterile. All clues in the Stewart Bailey files lead to only one scenario. Suicide. However, there were two neighbours, Sally Walker and Brian Wallace, who gained access to his apartment after he fell to his death. *Although the interviews reveal nothing of significance, I'll make a point of speaking to both of them when I go there later on.* As day turns into night, I place three fingers on my forehead, trying to relieve the pressure accumulating behind my eyes. I must find some new leads. I gaze up at the clock. It is after seven. I gather the evidence and lock the file in my cabinet. It is time to head to Tollcross to assess the area and make the journey from Stewart Bailey's flat to the agency in half an hour. I put on my heavy overcoat, ready to embrace the winter weather outside. As I walk past the reception, I say goodbye to Constable Peters.

"Wait, Inspector Canmore!"

I turn around.

She holds a small package.

"This arrived for you a few hours ago from Sarah McLeod. She called and insisted that I give it you in person."

I scan the area.

We are alone.

In a low tone of voice, she says, "What's inside?"

"I'm not sure?"

I open the brown envelope and peer at the contents.

"Well…?"

I take out the two pieces of evidence with tags on each item.

Constable Peters gasps.

We both stare at Annabel Taylor's ring and a set of keys which can only be the gateway to Stewart Bailey's flat.

"Not a word to anyone, Peters."

She nods.

The hunt begins.

****

I drive towards Tollcross, the anticipation unbearable, knowing these keys allow access to his apartment. Tapping my fingers on the steering wheel, I wait at each red light, the traffic head to tail as endless lines of cars crawl through the city centre. I take a left turn and head through the backstreets to my destination, park the car at the end of the road and walk the short distance to his flat. I strain my neck to peer up at his top-floor residence from the main road. My eyes focus on the balcony, following the drop to street level. I get the bunch of keys out of my coat pocket and open the front door. A gust of wind hits my face from the passageway. It leads to the back of the residence. The door is ajar, creating a vacuum of swirling air as soon as someone enters the front of the building. I go to the garden and stare up at the block of flats. The fire escape zigzags from the exit point of each apartment with sharp turns down to the ground floor. I proceed up the stairs to his apartment. *I'll speak to the witnesses Sally Walker or Brian Wallace on my way out. I need to get in that flat, right now.*

I put the key in the lock, turn the handle, push and enter the residence. It is quiet, dark, an eerie silence clings to the chill in the air. I find the switch in the entrance. There is no power. My mobile phone has a light. I take it out of my pocket and press on the flashlight. As I exhale, the air from my breath is visible creating a plume of icy cold condensation. I watch it float and disperse through the thin beam of light. *Damn! I should have brought a torch.* I check out the hallway. There are several doors which lead to the bedrooms and bathroom and one in the corner of the hall which looks like a fire escape. I walk towards the sitting room at the front of the flat. My eyes strain to make out the shapes of furniture. Once my senses adjust, I am more coherent, find the doors to the balcony, open them up and step outside.

The silhouette of the rooftops stretches for miles across the city skyline. I look down to the street below. *What an awful way to die. Did Stewart Bailey jump or was he pushed? If Jayden Scott came here, he left no trace. Then again, there is no evidence at any of the crime scenes, especially Edward Scott. Where on earth did the sordid act take place? Somewhere between Annabel Taylor's flat and his family home. You're a devious bastard, Jayden Scott. I'm watching your every move.* Lost in thought, I jump out of my skin when I hear a voice.

"Who the hell are you?"

I spin around and stare at the figure.

She takes a deep breath. "Well...?"

"What a fright!" I reach for my badge. "Inspector Nicholas Canmore of Police Scotland."

The woman says, "You left the front door ajar. My name is Sally Walker. I live downstairs."

"Miss Walker. I was about to pay you a visit."

"Why?"

"I need to ask a few questions."

"I've already spoken to the police."

"I read your statement and want to see if we missed anything."

"What do you mean?"

I rub my hands together. "Can we go to your apartment? It's too cold here."

Sally hesitates. "Alright."

Once outside, she asks to look at my identification, again. "Just checking. One needs to be careful these days." I follow her to the flat below. "Tea or coffee?"

"Coffee, please. Black. Two sugars."

She points. "Go through there. I'll make us a hot drink."

It is warm and inviting with an open-flame fire. There is a cello in the corner of the room and a violin case on the table. *Professional musician, perhaps?* This apartment is the same layout as my suicide victim. I gaze up at the ceiling, then over at the balcony, and think about Stewart Bailey's last moments. *I don't believe he took his own life because he never killed Annabel Taylor. That theory is a load of bullshit.* I take her ring out of my pocket and stare at the solitary diamond. *Three victims, three lifes and two rings. Edward, Annabel and Stewart, all linked together in a deadly tale of murder, death, sex, love and intrigue.*

Sally enters the room.

"Here you go. This will heat you up."

"Thank you."

"How can I help, Inspector Canmore?"

"I've seen your statement but need you to go over it again, just to be sure."

"Sure of what?"

"That we've not missed anything."

She pauses. "If you insist."

Sally describes the events of that evening with clarity and consistency. The same story as her initial report. However, now I am here, I have the opportunity to tease out the finer details deep within her subconscious mind. I think about my training and must not make any leading remarks.

"Thank you for such a detailed description."

She beams. "You're welcome."

"Let's take you back to that night. You said you heard him going into his flat."

"Yes, that was just after nine."

"I see that your apartment is the same layout. Do you notice the noise upstairs?"

"Not much. This is an old stone building. I hear his front door bang shut. That's why I know it was after nine when he came home."

"Perfect."

"I go up for a coffee and a chat sometimes."

"What's he like? His character?"

"Kind, caring and considerate. We've been friends a long time." She stares for a moment. "Just friends though, nothing more. I supported him through the murder accusations of his ex-partner and vice versa with my relationship break-up."

"You knew Annabel Taylor?"

"Yes."

"Is he capable of murder?"

Sally stands up. "Absolutely NOT!"

"Stay calm. Your opinion is of great value."

She sits down. "Thank you."

"Back to the night in question. When you noticed the commotion in the street, you went to his flat?"

"For moral support. The scene outside was horrific."

"Stewart never answered, however, you knew he was at home."

"Correct. It did cross my mind it might be him lying on top of the car. Brian, the guy below my apartment, kicked in the door." She laughs. "Bit of a rough brute but I like him."

"What did you do when you entered the flat?"

"Called out his name. There was no reply."

"Did you notice anything out of place?"

"Just the silence. And there was a momentary chill in the air."

"Continue."

"We went to the living area and opened the doors to the balcony."

"So, they were closed?"

"Yes."

"Warm?"

"Yes."

"Go back to when you went into the apartment. Where did the cold air come from?"

"I'm not sure?"

"Straight ahead?"

"No, it came from the side as we entered the house. I'll show you."

She gets up.

I follow.

Sally turns around. "From this direction," she says, stretching out her right arm. We both turn our head at the same time and stare at the fire escape door. Miss Walker gasps. "Do you think someone else was in his home, Inspector Canmore?"

"It's possible."

"Is this now a murder investigation?"

"Let's not speculate."

"You're right. It's necessary to find solid evidence first."

"You sound more and more like a detective with each new clue." She laughs.

"How do you open the fire escape?"

Sally goes into the living area and searches her bag. She produces a bunch of keys and finds the smallest on the keyring. "This opens the door," exclaims Miss Walker.

"Stewart must have the same one." I check the bunch in my pocket. "No, it's not here."

"He keeps extra keys in the kitchen hanging on a hook."

"Do you have a powerful torch? I want to go back to his flat."

"Hang on a minute." She enters a cupboard in the hallway and returns with the light. "Here you go. I will come with you."

I hesitate then nod my head.

We enter the residence.

I take the lead to the kitchen.

"Sally, you hold the torch. I'll search for the key."

She grasps hold of the light.

I check and double check. "It's not there."

"Do you really think someone left by the fire escape?"

"Maybe?"

"Did that person push him over the balcony?"

"Perhaps?"

"How awful."

"Not a word, Miss Walker. This is confidential information."

"I won't say anything," she says, making a gesture with her fingers across her mouth. "This is unbelievable."

I take Sally back to her flat.

"Do you have a business card," she gushes. "I'll call you if I remember any other important facts."

I pass over my details. "Here you go."

She smiles. "Thank you, Inspector Canmore."

I catch her glancing at my left hand.

I am just about to say, "No, I'm not married," but declare, "Goodbye, Miss Walker."

I make my way into the garden and walk up the metal stairs to the back of his flat. As I pass, Sally watches out of the kitchen window and waves in my direction. I return the gesture. When I get to the top, I look at the time. It is ten o'clock. I sit on the step and wait for another twenty minutes pondering over her statement. *This is the only means of escape. If Jayden Scott was in that apartment with Stewart Bailey, he must have got one hell of a shock as his neighbour kicked in the door. The key is gone from the rack but there is a possibility it may be somewhere else in his home. I'll come back during the day and look for the missing key.* I glance at my watch. Quarter past ten. My thoughts turn to Sally Walker. *Mid to late thirties, perhaps. I can check the credentials on her statement. No wedding ring. No sign of a partner. Intriguing. Charming. Delightful.* I hear a window open. She pops her head out and looks up through the space between the stairs.

"Is everything okay, Inspector Canmore?"

"Yes, I'm just leaving."

"Alright. Good night."

"Goodbye, Miss Walker."

Twenty past ten.

I stand up, race down the fire escape and catch sight of Sally out the corner of my eye peering out of the window, but keep on going. *What an idiot! She must think I'm a right lunatic.* I follow the path at the back of the building which leads to the main road, look to my right, stare at the cars under his flat and stride towards my vehicle. I head off through the quieter streets from the city centre to Leith and arrive outside the agency twenty-five minutes later. *It is possible. You were there you scheming bastard. You're clever but not clever enough. I am closing in on your web of lies. However, I must find evidence.* As I ponder over my next move, the phone rings. It is Larry Parker.

"Sorry, it's late. I thought you might like an update."

"I'm still working. It's not a problem. How did you get on?"

"Jayden Scott was at the London agency all day. I followed him home after seven. Our target left the flat at nine, took the tube to Piccadilly Circus and walked the short distance to the Diamond Life Casino. Mr Scott stayed there until the early hours of the morning. He must be a regular because he knows the staff. Pretty good Black Jack player as well."

"So, he's a gambling man."

"Slick operator."

"I agree. Did you find out anything else?"

"I did a background check on the casino. Weird situation. Almost three years ago, the owner Raymond Cartwright and Jake

Driscoe were killed in a showdown at a warehouse near Dover. Both shot and burned to death in an arson attack. They were also part of a child trafficking ring. Possible gangland warfare. However, there are no suspects for this crime."

"That's interesting. Although it's not relevant to my case. Follow him for the next few days."

"I must admit, I'm enjoying this surveillance."

"Keep up the good work, Larry."

"Thanks, Skipper."

Although it is late, I head back to the police station to plan for the following day. As I walk through the doors and pass the reception, Constable Peters is still on duty. She is busy with another officer dealing with a drink driving offence. I take the stairs to the third floor. There are not many people around. What a long day. I close the office door, slump into my chair, reach for the filing cabinet and lift out the Stewart Bailey file. I find the document on Sally Walker. She is a music teacher, thirty-eight years old, single and lives alone in her home in Tollcross. She might have a partner? I stare at the photograph in the corner of the document. Sally is confident, petite, pretty, with sandy brown hair, blue eyes, thin upper lip and beautiful smile. *I'm sure there's a mutual attraction. It's time to move on from my divorce. I've been on my own too long. I'll make a point of visiting her again when I return to Stewart Bailey's flat and ask her out to dinner.* For now, I must find proof to implicate my main suspect.

I open the report on Edward Scott, sifting through the documents. Not exactly following protocol, I put together the names and numbers over the last few years of Jayden Scott's contacts from mobile phone records I got from his contractor. Due to time constraints, I had little chance to check all the information. *I'll get Peters to work on this over the next few weeks.* I am just about to close the file when a detail catches my eye. I lean closer, eyes wide, staring at the evidence. On the list, there is a familiar name from Larry Parker about the Diamond Life Casino: **Raymond Cartwright**. Why do these murder connections come back to one person or has my imagination gone too far this time?

I browse online for information. It is an interesting cold case. The owner is a nasty looking bastard. Again, there is no evidence at the scene of the crime. The footage confirms that it appears to be a showdown between two people, Cartwright and Driscoe, but further forensics suggest that someone doused the hangar with petrol and set it alight, so there was someone else involved. I think this is a red herring but will ask Peters to check this person against Jayden Scott's contacts over the last seven years.

I pick up the phone.

Constable Peters answers.

"Can you get cover for the desk? Come up to my office."

"Right away, Inspector Canmore."

Five minutes later, she knocks on the door.

"Come in, Peters."

"You're working late tonight. I never expected you to return. Did you go to Stewart Bailey's flat?"

"Yes, the electricity is cut off. I left it for now."

"How can I help?"

"I need you to check Jayden Scott's phone contacts over the last seven years. It will take several weeks. This must be a priority. No more reception duty for a while. I hand over the lists. You can take a desk in the incident room. I'll contact your line manager and let him know. You're on my team along with Sarah McLeod and Jack Murray."

She beams. "Thank you."

"Be thorough, Peters. Check every person. Find out where they are now."

"Understood."

"You can return to your reception duties."

"Yes, Sir."

Once she leaves, I pack the documents into my briefcase along with Annabel Taylor's ring and Stewart Bailey's keys and write down the itinerary for the next day in my diary.

Contact Jack to set a date and time for the search in Argyll.
Check ALL the case files, again.
Daily updates from Constable Peters
Go back to Stewart Bailey's flat and look for the fire escape key.
Revisit the adorable Sally Walker.
Keep in touch with Larry Parker.
Find evidence to prove Jayden Scott's guilt.

I turn off the light and leave the office.

****

I have a restless sleep, tossing and turning in my bed and experience intense dreams with a concoction of familiar faces and scenarios. Edward Scott decomposes in a shallow grave in Argyll. He is still alive, scratching through the surface of the muck, desperate to escape. Annabel Taylor tries to help, the blood from the gash on her neck spills over the damp earth as she claws at the mud with her fingernails. Stewart Bailey watches from a distance, moves forward to kill his ex-partner for her betrayal, however, someone else lurks in the background. The stranger walks up behind Bailey and shoots at point-blank range to the head. Annabel Taylor slumps over the grave, clinging onto a mud-stained hand coming out of the earth. The man from the shadows laughs out loud. It is the evil child trafficker, Raymond Cartwright. Just then, a hand appears on his shoulder. Before he turns around, the killer slits his throat from ear-to-ear, the globules of blood dripping in slow motion from the tip of the blade. Cartwright drops to his knees, reaches for the gaping wound and falls to the ground, gasping for air until his last dying breath. The mystery man is Jayden Edward Scott. He kneels over the multitude of dead bodies and pulls off the rings from each of his victims' fingers. Like the flick of a switch, everything turns a deadly shade of black where no light can escape or penetrate the void. Jayden Scott's distinct voice sounds like an echo from within the dark abyss. "You're next, Inspector Canmore."

I jolt upright.

"Holy shit!"

A nervous sweat covers my entire body. I wipe my forehead with the back of my hand and keep telling myself it is only a dream. My head feels heavy, eyes stinging from lack of sleep. I gaze out of the bedroom window at the night sky and slump back down on the bed. I switch off the alarm. After some time, I drift off and do not wake up until I hear the sound of the letterbox. My eyes open, straining at the sight of daylight flooding through the open blinds. I reach over and pick up my mobile from the bedside cabinet. I check the time. It is five minutes before eleven. There is a text from an unrecognisable number.

I enjoyed our encounter together yesterday albeit on formal business. I hope we can see each other again on a more informal basis, Inspector Canmore.

I text back.

That would be wonderful, Miss Walker.

I am not good at phone messages. Much better face to face. I will visit her when I search Stewart Bailey's flat for the missing key. In the meantime, I need to plan my day. For a change, I want to work from home and ring reception to redirect my calls to my residential number. After the onslaught of the previous day, I intend to take it easy but focus on my itinerary. First, I potter about the flat, eat breakfast and have a shower. As I get out, my thoughts turn to Sally Walker. *It's been a while since I thought about another woman. I'm six years older than Sally. However, I'm still in great shape. I hope this is the start of something special. She's adorable. My kind of lady.* I notice the faint ringtone of my mobile phone. I pull on my boxer shorts and run through to the living room.

"Hello, Jack."

"Hey, Skipper. I dropped by the office. You're not there."

"That's because I'm here."

"Where?"

"At my house."

He pauses. "Are you okay? You never work from home."

"Today is an exception."

"You sound different."

"In what way?"

"Chipper."

I laugh. "I had a productive day yesterday."

"Anything interesting?"

"Lots of things. I will update you when we next see each other. The best news is that Sarah McLeod sent Stewart Bailey's file along with Annabel Taylor's ring and the keys to his flat. I went around last night. There may be several issues to consider. I'll let you know, if and when, evidence corroborates my suspicions."

"Sounds intriguing."

"The investigation is heading in the right direction."

"Great. I also have a day and time for the search in Argyll."

"When?"

"A few weeks from now on Saturday, 3rd March. I can dedicate the whole weekend to try and find Edward Scott's remains."

"That's the evening of The Charity Ball. I take it you won't be going?"

He laughs. "Nope. I have a date with destiny. If he's there, I'll find him, Skipper."

"I'm counting on you, Jack."

"Let's try to meet up for a beer. We can talk."

"What about the end of the week? Friday night? Drop by my office."

"It's a date, Skipper."

"Bye for now."

At last, we will be able to do a proper search of the surrounding area near the cottage. It is the perfect place to conceal a body. I know Jayden Scott took him to Argyll, seven years ago, on his twenty-third birthday. If he can hold a party with his friends, bury his father when they leave, then it is possible for him to kill Stewart Bailey, return to the agency and speak to Kristina Cooper five minutes later on the phone. My trip last night from Tollcross to Leith proves it can be done in twenty-five minutes. Dr Cooper is some kind of sick alibi. Once I acquire more evidence, I will talk to her at The Charity Ball. Kristina Cooper is a clever woman. She is in denial at the moment but will soon realise the gravity of the situation.

It is only a matter of time.

I put on some casual clothes and spend the rest of the afternoon in my study looking over the details of the files, again. Out with the Raymond Cartwright lead there is nothing more to find. I lift the small envelope from my case, take out the ring and stare at the fissures in the solitary diamond. I open the drawer at the side of the bureau and place Annabel Taylor's ring in the box with Edward Scott's gold band. "You both belong together."

A thought crosses my mind.

I grab my phone and press the contact details.

He answers. "Hey, Skipper."

"Larry, just a quick call. I'll catch up with you properly later."

"How can I help?"

"Raymond Cartwright's sidekick. What's the guy's name?"

"Jake Driscoe."

"Thanks."

I hang up.

I connect to the database of the Metropolitan Police. The case is old enough for the files to be stored in the archives. First, I search for Raymond Cartwright and recover the information, skimming the pages for specific details. The charred body is badly burned. I stare at the hands of the skeletal remains. Nothing. I pull up the file on Jake Driscoe. Parts of his body are intact. At the bottom of the autopsy report, several words glare out from the page: "There is an indentation on the fourth digit of the right hand. However, there is no ring?" *Bloody hell!* My mind goes into overdrive. *Did he take the rings? More keepsakes? Tokenistic gestures of the kill. What connection do these two people have with Jayden Scott, if any? Do I have a serial killer on my hands? If so, Kristina Cooper may be in mortal danger.* "STOP!" *I need to slow down and take one step at a time, concentrate on my three main victims, not create new ones.*

I put on a pair of running shoes, thick fleece and grab the key to Stewart Bailey's flat. Daylight fades fast. It is only a half-hour run from my house in Colinton to his flat at Tollcross. I should have at least an hour to search his home before nightfall. However, I take a torch. The run is pleasant and the crisp air helps to clear my head. I order a hot drink at the local coffee shop, five minutes from his apartment, and enter the building.

The flat is freezing cold. I wrap my hands around the cup, gaining comfort from the warm surface. I search each room, start in the kitchen and double check the holder hanging on the wall. No key. I also search the bedrooms but nothing. By the time I make my way to the living area, the light is minimal. I switch on the torch and notice a desk in the corner of the room. I rake in the drawers. There is still no key. The best place to keep one is on the rack in the kitchen close to the fire escape. That is the sensible thing to do. It is not there. Another keepsake for Jayden Scott perhaps, albeit a poor substitute compared to a personal trophy such as a ring. I think about Raymond Cartwright and Jake Driscoe. There may be at least five victims in Jayden Scott's repertoire.

I shudder.

My heartbeat increases. A cold sweat appears on my forehead and a sinking feeling develops in the pit of my stomach like a lead weight. I must find more physical evidence to prove his guilt. However, I need to wait for Constable Peters report on Jayden Scott's mobile contacts. In the meantime, I can only continue with the hunt. The loud noise of the doorbell pierces through the empty silence. I switch off the torch, tiptoe up the hallway, peer through the spyhole and stare at her inquisitive face. I open the door. My hand reaches for her arm and usher Sally into the flat.

She laughs. "What are you doing? I saw blocks of light moving from one place to another in the living room from the street."

"Searching for the key. I got here about an hour ago but had to use the torch."

"I thought it might be you. Any luck?"

"It's not here. I looked everywhere."

"I'm certain he kept it on the rack in the kitchen on a skull and crossbones keyring."

"That would be the obvious choice. Thanks for the additional information about the design. Skull and crossbones. Very useful."

She smiles.

"Does your key open his fire escape?"

"I'm not sure?" Sally hands over her set. "Try it out."

I place it in the keyhole, turn and push. A burst of air enters the flat from the side entrance.

She gasps. "It feels the same as when myself and Brian first came into the apartment."

"Someone else was definitely here."

"Who?"

"That's confidential information, Miss Walker."

"A murder case. How exciting. Not that I mean any disrespect."

"The suspect is dangerous. The evidence against him is circumstantial at the moment until I find some further proof."

"I saw the forensics team here a few weeks ago. I suspect they found nothing or you wouldn't need to snoop around, run down the fire escape like a lunatic and talk to one of the main witnesses."

I chuckle. "You're correct. Thanks for your assistance."

"My pleasure."

We leave Stewart Bailey's flat. I decline the coffee offer and make my excuses to return home. However, I secure a dinner date at the end of the week. We decide to go to Bia Bistro on Friday night. It is my favourite restaurant; intimate, full of character, just like my companion. The meeting and catch up with Jack Murray will have to wait. We say goodbye outside the block of flats. I turn and give her a gentle peck on the cheek. She smiles, happy with the outcome. The air is crisp and helps to focus my mind. I think about what I still need to do before the day ends. I must contact Constable Peters and speak to Larry Parker. When I return home, I prepare a meal and proceed to the study to make a few phone calls.

I dial the number.

She answers.

"Hello."

"I want to check on your progress, Constable Peters."

"It's going well. I started this afternoon. I'm going through the list from the beginning."

"There's no need. I checked the first two years in a lot of detail. You do the last five. The documents have piled up. I've not had time to finish the task to the best of my ability."

"Thanks. That makes this job a little easier."

"Keep up the good work."

"Do you think we'll find anything?"

"I'm not sure. We have to try."

"I'll do my best."

"One more thing before I go. Check to see if there's any correspondence between our suspect and two people called Raymond Cartwright and Jake Driscoe."

"Noted."

"Goodnight, Peters."

I pour a double measure of brandy. The last few days have been a challenge but I am making progress. I gulp down a large mouthful. *That tastes good.* And another. As the alcohol takes effect, I make the final call of the day to Larry Parker.

"Hey, Skipper. How are you?"

"Not bad. I can't hear you too well. Are you driving?"

"Hang on a minute!" he shouts. "I'll close the window. Just having a smoke. Is that better?"

"Yes. Where are you?"

"I'm following our suspect. It looks like he's heading towards the M1. Jayden Scott packed his bags into the boot of his Noble and left London about half an hour ago."

"He might be on his way to Lincoln to visit Dr Cooper or coming back to Edinburgh."

"Who?"

"Kristina Cooper. His partner. She lives near the marina in Lincoln."

"I'm not sure?"

I give him the address.

"I'll let you know soon."

"Okay. Keep on his tail."

"Will do."

"When you return to Edinburgh, call into the office. I take it your keeping a written account of everything he does?"

"Yes. I also have my camera. I've already taken a few photos. Nothing out of the ordinary to report so far, Skipper."

"Keep following our suspect. Don't lose him, Larry."

"I won't. Catch you later."

I close the call.

It is after eleven. I have a few more drinks and retire to bed. My mind wanders. *I'm exhausted. It's been a busy few days. At least everything is in place to progress to the next stage. I need to wait to see how it all unfolds. I have a good team. Peters, Sarah, Jack and Larry. I suppose Sally is also part of the group. She provided a vital piece of information regarding the possibility someone else was in Stewart Bailey's flat. And, I know that someone is Jayden Scott.* I refocus, trying to block out any more thoughts on this case, having had enough for the day.

I close my eyes and fall asleep.

Sometime later, I hear my phone.

BEEP BEEP, BEEP BEEP, BEEP BEEP.

My arm reaches across to the bedside cabinet and grasp hold of my mobile. I open one eye and check the time. It is two o'clock in the morning. My finger slides over the screen to answer the call.

"Hello…" I say in a sleepy voice.

"Sorry to wake you, Inspector Canmore."

"No problem, Larry. Is everything okay?"

"Jayden Scott arrived at his destination."

"Where?"

"Nottingham. He checked into a hotel."

"What the hell is he doing there?"

"I'm not sure. We'll soon find out."

"Track his every move."

"Okay doke. Goodnight, Skipper."

Alert, I sit up in bed.

I think back to the information I have on Jayden Scott. None of his records reveals a contact in Nottingham. If my memory is correct, his recent phone pattern is consistent between the agency in Edinburgh and London, his mother, Reverend McIntyre and Kristina Cooper. Perhaps, it is a new business client?

I scratch my head.

"What the hell is he doing in Nottingham?"

6

MISFITS

"I wish I would have known from the beginning how far this would
have gone."
(David Berkowitz)

I arrive at the hotel in Nottingham just after two o'clock in the
morning to avoid any travel complications. Once inside, I take the
mobile out of my pocket. There are no texts or calls from Kristina.
*Why has she not been in touch over the last few days? I'll make a point to call
her before I leave to see my saviour.* I double check the message on my
second phone to SocialMisfit.

I will meet you in the park at the back of the National Justice
Museum in Nottingham on Wednesday, 14th February at
11.00. The name of the target is Inspector Nicholas Canmore
who works for Police Scotland in Edinburgh. Speak soon.

In the meantime, I book into the hotel, order a large measure of
whisky from the bar and head up to my room. I sit on the edge of
the bed and scan my phone, looking at photographs of her beautiful
face. Kristina Cooper is my soulmate. No more Koko Kanu, high-
end escorts or sleazy hookers. I am ready to settle down for the rest
of my life once I sort out all this unfortunate mess.

I send a text.

Miss you. I will call tomorrow at 09.00.

I gulp down the contents and check the money in the case. Eight
hours from now, we can seal the deal. I close it and go for a shower.
As the soothing water cleanses my body, I experience a deep sense of
satisfaction at my progress. *Charles and my mother are happy, and I have
his support. Everything is more than fine with Kristina. I will see her later on
today as I am going back to Lincoln before returning to Edinburgh. The
Annabel Taylor case is closed. Stewart Bailey is dead. Nicholas Canmore will
die. Life will return to normal. Perhaps Kristina might move to Scotland and*

plan our future together. But wait, the search in Argyll. One can only hope that they never find my father's remains. I get out of the shower, dry my body and wrap the towel around my waist. I lie on top of the bed, thinking about SocialMisfit and our meeting. *What is he like?* I answer my own question. *This devious man is an astute businessman that much I know. Common but clever, I suspect.* My eyes shut. I drift off only to wake to the sound of my mobile phone several hours later. I note the time. Seven in the morning. There is a video call from Kristina. *Not now.* I ignore it and fall back to sleep.

Once awake, I sense a nervous flutter in the pit of my stomach, get out of bed and stare in the mirror at the face of a serial killer. The more I look at these evil features, my heart quickens, pupils dilate and retract at the mere thought of meeting SocialMisfit. I find it hard to contain my excitement, order a cooked breakfast with a large pot of coffee and contemplate whether to phone my beautiful criminologist. *I'll call her soon.* My appetite is insatiable. The food is delicious. I change into my usual clothes. I also have a black baseball cap and sunglasses to obscure most of my facial features. Before I leave to meet SocialMisfit, I phone Kristina. Not on the video link as she will question my whereabouts and my attire.

"Good morning, darling," I say in a cheerful voice.

"Hi there."

There is a long silence.

"Sorry, I missed your call. Why so early?"

"I want to talk."

"Is everything okay?"

"I'm not sure?"

"What's on your mind?"

"… Nothing…"

What's the matter now?

"I have to attend a meeting and should be with you about three or four depending on when I leave London."

"I need to work late today. Lot's of deadlines to reach."

"What are you saying? That you don't want me to come?"

"I'm busy."

"What the hell is going on? We left on such good terms."

"Nothing," she repeats.

"I will ask one more time. What's happened?"

She hesitates.

"I'm still working on the Taylor profile. It doesn't seem appropriate to see you when you're part of my investigation."

"You know it was Stewart Bailey. He had Annabel Taylor's ring. He's the only suspect, Kristina."

"I received a call from Inspector Canmore."

"For fuck sake! What now? That man is obsessed."

"He suspects you in all three murders."

"What three murders?"

"Your father, Annabel Taylor and Stewart Bailey."

I take a deep breath. "Pardon?"

"In his own words, he said, I'm bringing that psychopath down."

"He's the bloody psychopath. A neurotic one as well. Surely, you don't believe a word of his bullshit."

"I'm not sure what to think anymore. Why did you not say Stewart Bailey worked with your agency?"

"Why would I mention him? It was a recent appointment. He's a partner of one of my biggest clients. Nothing gets in the way of my business," I shout. "Nothing!"

"Calm down."

"No, I won't calm down. Listen, Canmore will organise the search in Argyll and not find anything. Stewart Bailey killed Annabel Taylor and took his own life because of the guilt. Any bloody idiot can work that out."

She goes quiet.

"What?"

"He said it's the rings."

"I'm not sure what you're talking about?"

"Inspector Canmore has your father's ring."

"I know he does. He found it in the hallway of our house just after my father disappeared. Serial cheat. That's the real Edward Scott and this is why he took it off."

"How did it get there?"

"I have no idea."

"But…"

"ENOUGH!"

I play a game of reverse psychology.

"If this continues, I'm done. I've had enough. Choose your side, Kristina. I'll see you when you return home from work."

I hang up the phone.

Inspector Canmore is a clever bastard.

I check the time. It is ten thirty. There is no point dwelling on the matter. I grab my cap, sunglasses and case as well as my knife and sheath. I leave the hotel and start up the Noble. I light a cigarette, take a deep drag, then another and another. The hotel is only a five-minute drive away from the National Justice Museum near the Lace Market in Nottingham. Such an appropriate location. Courtrooms, jail and executions conducted on the steps of the ancient building. *"In the midst of life, we are in death."* These are the words of the chaplain at the last public execution at the courthouse in the nineteenth century. I ponder over the possibility of my own capture and what punishment awaits my heinous crimes? A lifetime in prison? Never! I finish the short trip and park the car at the back of the old court house.

I light a smoke, put on my cap and sunglasses, scrutinise the people in the vicinity, wondering which one is SocialMisfit. Just in case, I strap the sheath around my waist, get out of the Noble and stub out the cigarette. I leave the case of money on the passenger seat. Once I find out the plan is in place, he can have the cash. With my senses on high alert, I walk to the back of the building, cross over a bridge that leads to the park and wait. I sit down on a wooden bench. There are several dog walkers but nobody else at this moment. It is 10.55. Another five minutes until I meet my contact. *He better show up, the bastard.* And then, there is no mistake. I notice him in the distance, tall with a slight swagger, walking up the path, the recognisable peak of the baseball cap protruding from underneath his hoodie.

I step towards him.

"SocialMisfit?"

He stops. "Edward Cooper?"

I nod.

"Pleased to meet you," he says in a polite tone.

"Likewise," I say, shaking his hand.

"Let's go for a stroll."

My fingers rests on the hilt of my knife. "Sure."

As we walk, we talk.

"I got someone to check out the target. We know Inspector Canmore's workplace and where he lives. My contact in Edinburgh has been following him for the last few days." He reaches into his rucksack. "Here is his file."

I take the folder. "Impressive."

"We'll put a dossier together to track his every move to find consistency in his daily routine and then set up the kill."

"I have a date, time and place."

"Do you? Where?"

"Saturday, 3rd March, no later than ten o'clock outside the Balmoral Hotel in Edinburgh. He's attending The Charity Ball."

SocialMisfit takes out a small notebook from his back pocket and writes down the details. "He'll definitely be there?"

"Yes."

"We can plan around this event and find a suitable place for the marksman to take out the target."

"You're very efficient."

"I'm just the middleman. Shoot To Kill is the best in the UK."

"Inspector Canmore must die with a bullet to the head."

"If that's your preference. My aim is to please our clients. My contacts are the toughest in the business. After today, we have no need for any more correspondence."

"We do. I need updates on Canmore's every move."

"That costs extra."

"How much?"

"How long do you want us to follow him?"

"Until the day of his death."

"That is just over two weeks away."

"Correct."

"An extra ten thousand."

"Deal. It will be worth every penny."

"Do you have the payment with you?"

"Yes, it's in my car. Wait here. I'll add the additional money. I always carry spare cash for emergencies."

I head back to the Noble, perusing the folder on Inspector Canmore. I stop. There are photographs of him going into Stewart Bailey's block of flats at Tollcross. Once Canmore leaves, he kisses a woman on the cheek. *Well, well, well. My nemesis has a lady friend.* Her face seems familiar. *Think!* Realisation. She is one of the witnesses I saw on television. *Never mix business with pleasure, Inspector Canmore. This gets even better. Such a pretty woman. If he can mess with my relationship, I can now interfere in his life. What is her name? I'll check later.*

In the meantime, I open the door and grab the case from the passenger seat. There is a metal box under my chair with extra cash. I add the money to the horde, glimpse out of the rear-view mirror and notice an old guy with a camera, alone, getting into his car. I wait for him to drive off. He lingers and continues to sit in the red Volvo. *Tourist, perhaps?* I lock up the Noble, quicken my pace and meet back up with SocialMisfit.

"It's all there plus the extra money. A total of eighty thousand."

"If not, the transaction is off, Edward."

"A deal is a deal. I hope you keep to your end of the bargain."

"Always. We provide a professional service."

"Good."

He shakes my hand and we part company.

I return to the car, ecstatic, out of my mind with euphoric pleasure at the mere thought of Canmore's demise. I can visualise the bullet going straight through his brain. This thought is almost as intense as the kill itself. When I experience this level of excitement, my body responds. I need a release but must wait until I get to Lincoln. Kristina better apologise for the disrespectful outburst of doubt, and then, I will use her for my own gratification. She needs to comply, choose a side and remain a loyal partner. I start up the Noble, notice the red Volvo has gone, and head back to the hotel.

Several hours later, I am on the road, ready to deal with all this nonsense with my criminologist, again. *I wonder if she'll be home?* It is only a short drive from Nottingham to Lincoln. The journey passes without incident. I stop at a service station for a coffee. I sit in the café, contemplate the meeting with SocialMisfit and stare out of the window. At that moment, I see a red Volvo leave the car park on the route to Lincoln. *Coincidence or am I being followed?* I convince myself that I am paranoid and relax for the next half an hour, gathering my thoughts. Just over two weeks from now, on Saturday 3rd March, Inspector Canmore dies and Shoot To Kill will put an end to his continual interference in my life. I leave the cafe, smoke a few cigarettes, and gear myself up to face Kristina to defend the accusatory call from my nemesis and my triple murder status. *This is tedious having to maintain my innocence.* It is time to confront my antagonistic partner.

I make the short drive to Lincoln, leave the bag in the car and bound up the stairs to her flat, ring the doorbell, wait, but there is no answer. I check under the flower pot for the key. It is not there. Furious, I return to the Noble, lean against the side of the car, light a cigarette and search for the directions to her department at the university. *If I go now, I might miss her and pass each other. If I stay, she may take hours to get home.* I decide on the latter and light another cigarette, watching the plume of smoke disperse through the air. To pass the time, I read over the file on Inspector Canmore. An hour later she drives into the car park. My intense stare never leaves her sight.

She winds down the window.

"What the hell is going on, Kristina?"

"I'm not sure what you mean?"

"Why did you move the spare key to your flat?"

"It should be under the pot."

"No, it's not. I checked."

"The key is always there. I don't understand?"

I scan the parking lot.

There is nothing out of place.

"Stay in the car. Hand over your keys."

Kristina's eyes widen.

She complies.

I make my way to her apartment. I put the key in the lock and open the door. My killer instinct is on high alert, wary of potential danger. I creep around the flat, putting one foot in front of the other, cautious, ready for any sign of abnormal activity. There is none, so far. I scan the living room, see an array of papers, articles and notes. My gaze lingers at the open book on the table. I flip it over and look at the title. *Serial Homicide: Profiling of Victims and Offenders for Policing.* Interesting. I read the text. "While there is no generally accepted system of categorization of serial murderers, one of the most widespread is the division devised by the Holmes brothers, into visionary killers, missionary killers, hedonistic killers and killers driven by power and domination."

"That's right," I mumble. "I'm a missionary killer."

I read on.

"The selection of categories is based on the perpetrator's motive for committing a crime. Jozef Gurgul states that the research of numerous authors into the practices and mindsets of criminals show that it is virtually impossible to identify the perpetrator of a crime without establishing the motive."

Kristina's writing in bold capitals states: "REVENGE."
You've got that one right. Is this related to me or Stewart Bailey? I pick up
the piece of paper and look at the comparison in her table of notes.
Kristina states that his motive is jealousy and my motive, revenge.
Fucking bitch. She's referring to myself.

I sense a presence, drop the book on the table and turn around,
ready to attack. I let out a deep breath at the sight of Kristina.
"There's nobody here, but you need to change your lock first thing in
the morning."

"What a relief."

"Check if anything is missing or out of place."

Five minutes later she returns. "Everything seems fine."

"Come here."

She hesitates.

"Listen. I'll only say this once. Our situation is tiresome. If you
have any doubts, I'll leave and never return. I need you by my side,
Kristina, not under scrutiny all the time. You decide."

She avoids my gaze and stares at the table of profiling notes.

"It's not that simple. I'm being pulled in so many different
directions."

"You either believe my version of events or listen to that lunatic,
Inspector Canmore. We're not playing this game anymore. I don't
need this nonsense in my life. We don't need this kind of division."

Kristina sighs.

I wait.

"Fuck this crap!"

She flinches.

I walk towards the front door hoping for a response.

"Please, don't go, Jayden."

A wry smile passes across my face.

I turn around and stare for longer than necessary with that intense
gaze, wandering up and down her body. I penetrate her with my
eyes. We both know the outcome. Time seems to stand still, our
breathing, heavy. I watch her chest rise and fall. I feel the heaviness
in my groin. The atmosphere is ripe with sexual tension. She raises a
hand and wipes away beads of sweat accumulating on her forehead,
the expression on her face almost orgasmic, intense, as she rolls her
eyes up and over to the side. Nobody makes the first move. It is
like the moments, minutes, seconds before the ultimate reunion, each

waiting for the other one to take action. I break the equilibrium and walk forward, kiss her lips with such force, my hands wandering over those curves, pull at her clothes, eager to touch this beautiful woman's bare skin. She responds, takes hold of my hand and leads us towards the bedroom.

Our lovemaking is intense.

We reconcile.

Afterwards, I speak first.

"No more doubts?"

She nods. "I'll wrap up my profile. Stewart Bailey is the perpetrator in Annabel Taylor's murder with the motive of jealousy."

"Excellent. I want no more nonsense. If Inspector Canmore gets back in touch, ignore his accusations. I need you on my side or there's no point. I command loyalty from my subjects, Kristina."

She laughs. "I'll obey your every word."

"I love to see you happy."

"You're right. I'm far too serious for my own good."

"That's an understatement."

She shifts, straddles across my body, pinning both hands above my head. "I got the invitation for The Charity Ball plus one at the start of March. Do you want to come? You'll meet your nemesis in his own territory."

"How can I refuse? You're very persuasive." *I'll witness his death up close and personal. And what a perfect alibi.* "Your wish is my command."

"Solidarity, Jayden."

"We're unbreakable," I declare. "I'm away to get my bag out of the Noble." I lift Kristina off my body and lay her down on the bed. "Don't move."

She laughs, again.

I put on my clothes and rush down the stairs towards the vehicle. I press the button and the lights flicker on and off, lighting up the car park for a few moments. Just then, I am aware of the red Volvo out the corner of my eye. The same man sits in the driver seat. *Fuck sake!* I try to act normal. *The guy with the camera. He's followed me all the way from London. Oh God! Nottingham. SocialMisfit.* I wonder if this person took the key to Kristina's flat before I got here. Did he have a look inside? I am more than sure he is a retired cop. *Did Inspector Canmore organise this tail?* I smirk. *At least he will get to see SocialMisfit, the middleman behind his own murder. So, we are both following each other. Let's watch how this game of cat and mouse plays out. There can only be one winner and it's not Inspector Canmore.*

I lift the bag out of the Noble.

And return to the flat, muttering to myself, "The gloves are off. It's now time I interfere in your life, Inspector Canmore. There's no holding back."

****

We wake up late. I feel her lips brush mine. It is easy for Kristina to initiate a response. I turn on my side, wrap my arms around her body, pulling her close. We kiss, again. It can only lead to one outcome. The lust for this woman is insatiable. The love for this woman, inevitable. We cement that bond with intense, intimate lovemaking for the rest of the morning.

"What are your plans for today, Kristina?"

"Not sure?"

"I need to leave. We'll see each other in a few weeks' time at The Charity Ball."

"Are you certain you want to go to the event? It might be too awkward."

"Positive. I can handle Inspector Canmore even although he thinks I'm some kind of psychopathic killer."

She forces a nervous smile.

"There's nothing to worry about, Kristina. He's crazy. We must stick together."

"Agreed."

"Are you going to return the files to Superintendent Hunter?"

"Yes, I will box everything up and send the information back. We can draw a line under the Annabel Taylor murder. Inspector Canmore will organise the search at the cottage in Argyll. I don't care. As you said, there's nothing to find. I want to forget about this whole sordid affair."

"Let him play his games. He won't find anything, Kristina."

"I don't want to talk about this anymore. It's ruining our relationship. We need to move on. Inspector Canmore can do what he wants but not at our expense."

"Absolutely. I need to get up and head off. Shall I make us

something to eat first?"

"Thank you, Jayden. That would be nice."

I prepare the food.

The phone rings.

She rushes through to the hall.

The sound is on the loudspeaker.

"Kristina, how are you, my dear?"

"Clarissa. It's so nice to hear your voice. Yes, I'm fine."

"Do you want to meet? We can have lunch together."

"Jayden is here at the moment."

The old woman sighs.

"What about later on this afternoon?"

"Perfect, my dear. I will call round to the flat and pick you up."

"See you then."

"Bye for now."

I serve the poached eggs on toast and shout on Kristina, pour the coffee and wait until we settle before resuming our conversation.

"You two seem close at the moment."

"Clarissa is very supportive unlike my mother who judges my life all the time."

"Marion is quite a character."

Kristina rolls her eyes and changes the subject. "How is Charles and Carolyn?"

"Fine, as far as I know. Why don't we visit on your next trip to Scotland after The Charity Ball?"

"That would be fantastic."

"I spoke to the Reverend. Everything is much better now."

"He was very odd over New Year. I'm glad they're both well. I can't wait to go home."

I take hold of her hand across the table. "It feels good to be back on track."

She beams. "At last!"

"I need to leave now."

I pick up the bag from the bedroom. We say our goodbyes. Once outside, my mindset changes from romance to revenge. I start up the car and peer at the folder from SocialMisfit. I focus on the woman's pretty face. Inspector Canmore's new love interest? I will look online as soon as I get home to find out her name. She will be in the news archives. I pull out of the car park and focus on the five-hour trip back to Edinburgh, scheming and plotting my revenge before the final showdown at The Charity Ball. I notice the red Volvo in the distance but ignore my pursuer. Now I am aware of this idiot, I can deal with him, when and if the matter arises. In the meantime, I connect my second phone through bluetooth to the speaker in the car and phone SocialMisfit.

"Edward, how are you? Is everything okay?"

"Yes. It was a pleasure to meet you yesterday."

"Likewise. How can I help? I assume this is not a courtesy call."

"You're clever. I want to double check that everything will be in place to execute my nemesis."

"I've been in touch with Shoot To Kill. We're ready to go."

"Fantastic! And the surveillance on Inspector Canmore?"

"All in place. I'll get in contact every two days with updates."

"I also need one more favour."

"What?"

"I need you to set up a burglary."

"Of the target?"

"Yes. Search his home. Make it appear like a wider robbery. I want you to try and find a piece of jewellery. A ring. It's a gold wedding band with a recognisable inscription on the inside: Edward Scott. Take whatever else you want. I need that ring back."

"You're full of surprises."

"How much?"

"Another three thousand."

"Deal. If you find the ring, we can exchange the money through your contact in Edinburgh." *The gold band could be at his work and then I'll never get it back.* "I want this done as soon as possible."

"Fair enough."

"Speak soon."

The excitement is too much. The thought of getting my father's ring back after all this time is exhilarating, although, it may not even be in his house. One can only try. I had to give up Annabel Taylor's diamond ring in the name of justice. It does not compare. I can deal with that loss but not his ring. My father's gold band is a keepsake of my first kill and the dearest of all tokens. I spend the rest of the journey plotting my revenge. Inspector Nicholas Canmore deserves to die after all his interference in my life. There is just over two weeks to finalise the plans with SocialMisfit. I will receive his updates on my nemesis and proceed with caution. If Inspector Canmore causes any more immediate problems, I will kill his bitch. Everything is falling into place. The main goal is to have Kristina on my side. After all, we will be together, forever.

I arrive in Edinburgh before six o'clock.

The winter sun is low in the sky. I sit in the Noble for a while, watching day turn to night. The golden rays disappear behind the horizon over the Firth of Forth, the soft ripples of water glistening on the surface before the sky turns an ethereal shade of blue in contrast to the dark clouds. *Human behaviour is much like nature, full of dichotomies, fighting to find a balance between light and dark, good and evil, love and hate, myself and Kristina. What a strange phenomenon. My situation is ironic. A criminologist and a serial killer. But opposites attract. Am I making the right decisions for us? Does Inspector Canmore need to die? Aristotle is a firm believer that choices determine our fate.* "Yes! Never doubt your actions," I tell myself. *He's a liability and must die. My nemesis is a modern-day Macduff. It's only a matter of time before he finds out the truth.*

The bleep on the phone interrupts my thoughts.

It is a text from Kristina.

Are you home? Miss you already. See you the day before The Charity Ball. I will arrive on Friday. We can spend a long weekend together and visit your mother and Charles.

Just arrived home, parked the car and watching the sunset. See you in a few weeks. I'll book your flight.

Are you sure?

Positive.

We can now focus on building our relationship. Thank goodness all that profiling nonsense is over. I'll keep busy at work and meet up with Clarissa next week. The time will fly by.

Did you meet her today?

Yes.

What did she want to talk about?

Nothing much.

Clarissa doesn't like me, does she?

I'm not sure. She wanted to talk about our relationship, especially you. I closed down the conversation. I can't deal with any more negativity.

Good for you. All this nonsense about her sixth sense. It's a load of rubbish!

No, it's not. Her intentions are honourable.

I suppose. I adore you so much.

Likewise. Good night, Jayden.

This is a positive sign that Kristina refuses to listen to Clarissa Evans. Everything is back on track. I take my belongings out of the car and dump it in the hallway except for the file on Inspector Canmore. I search the news archives online and find out her name, Sally Walker. I watch the footage. She speaks about her ordeal the night I left Stewart Bailey's flat. Miss Walker was the person banging on the door along with another tenant, Brian Wallace. A clammy sweat develops on my forehead thinking about the narrow escape. Wiping the moisture away with the back of my hand, I focus on my plan of action for the next two weeks. I will receive updates from SocialMisfit on Inspector Canmore, the burglary and return [hopefully] of my father's wedding ring. And now, I have someone new to consider, Sally Walker. I may spare her life depending on Inspector Canmore's actions. *Choices determine our fate and the fate of your lady is in your hands, Canmore Macduff.* I smile, laughing at the new name for my nemesis. He is like Lord Macduff, Thane of Fife, the character in Shakespeare's play *Macbeth*, relentless in his pursuit for justice against a tyrannical force of nature like myself. But this story will end in Canmore's death and not mine.

All of a sudden, I am weary, the stress of the last two days taking its toll. I put on the heating, light the fire and intend to relax for the rest of the evening. I make some vegetable noodles and turn on the music player, pour a large glass of red wine and devour the food. Afterwards, I dose off. The words to the song register in my mind as I drift in and out of consciousness.

"… I'm burned out and wasted. I'm tired of pacing. I'm busy erasing, voices of the dead. Everything changes, and everyone's faceless. I want to replace this darkness in my head…"

"Go away," I mumble.

The music continues.

"… Have I been a sinner? A lover, a killer? Because the world I've discovered, it feels nothing like my home. I want to escape it or try to embrace it. I keep re-arranging everything I know…"

I jerk up at the sound of the phone.

Not now, I'm too sleepy.

"… Even fools they say can find a way out of the dark, of the dark…"

Answer the phone!

I open my eyes, reach into my pocket for the second mobile and connect to the caller. It can only be one person. In a sluggish voice, I say, "Hey there, SocialMisfit."

"The burglary takes place within the next half an hour."

I am now on high alert. "What? So soon?"

"Yes, we have a window of opportunity."

"You're efficient, that's for sure. Where's Canmore tonight?"

"He's having dinner with a lady friend in Bruntsfield at a restaurant called Bia Bistro. I have one informant there and another two on the way to his residence."

It must be Sally Walker.

"If the ring is there, will I have it back by tomorrow?"

"If all goes to plan. I'll arrange for the exchange to take place. Speak to you later."

He hangs up the phone.

The music finishes. "…Help me out of the dark."

"Piss off!" I shout to the lyricist. "It's my life. This is what I choose."

I go to the hall and rummage in the bag, pull out my usual attire and change. And then, I stop. *Stay at home. Don't risk being caught on CCTV in the vicinity. Don't go! Let Social Misfit's accomplices deal with the situation.* My advice is right. I need to stay away from Inspector Canmore, the restaurant and his home. I keep busy for the rest of the night, irritable, polish off a bottle of whisky, smoke an endless amount of cigarettes and pass out on the sofa until I wake up the next day, sluggish, hungover, with a dry mouth.

In a state of confusion, I sit up, rub my forehead with my fingers, trying to focus on the series of events from the previous night. *Social Misfit. The burglary. My father's ring.* I grab my phone from the table and check the messages. There are two texts from my partner in crime.

Mission complete.

Call to arrange the exchange.

I prepare a strong espresso. The caffeine clears my hazy mind. Only then, do I make the call to SocialMisfit.

"Edward, how are you today?"

"A bit worse for wear. Too much whisky last night."

"I hear Scotsmen like a dram or two," he says in a very bad Scottish accent.

I laugh.

"Let's get down to business. We have your item. Where would you like to meet for the exchange?"

I consider my state of mind and choose somewhere close. "The North Car Park at Leith Docks. Do you know the area?"

"No, but my contact will find the location."

"What time?"

"It's midday. Two o'clock? Does that give you enough time?"

"Yes."

"I'll dress in black running gear, baseball cap and a rucksack on my back."

"We'll find you. I plan to send the encrypted files of our surveillance on Inspector Canmore and the robbery in due course. We ransacked the house, took some electrical equipment, money and jewellery."

"Thank you."

"Our pleasure."

He disconnects the call.

My thoughts go into overdrive. I forget about my hangover. I make another coffee, my mind buzzing with excitement, eager to reclaim what is already mine. I take a shower, put on my clothes, pack the money in a brown envelope and place it in my rucksack. With a sly grin on my face, I look in the full-length mirror and announce, "I'm ready."

I leave the flat and take the lift to the ground floor. The doors open. A woman looks over in my direction, staring, as I walk towards the reception area.

She appears familiar.

"Good afternoon, Mr Scott," says the concierge.

"Hello, Michael. How are you today?"

"Very well, thank you."

"Is everything okay?" I say, shifting my gaze from him to the police officer.

"There's been a spate of burglaries in the area. The police are making routine inquiries to see if we have seen anything suspicious," he declares.

She speaks. "That's correct. Have you noticed anything suspicious, Mr Scott?"

"No, nothing... Constable... Inspector...?"

"Constable Peters. Police Scotland. We've met before."

"I remember. Quite a few years ago now."

She nods.

"I've been on a short trip to London. Got back last night about seven. Not ventured out since. I have nothing to report."

"That's correct," confirms Michael.

"Please get in touch if you see anything out of the ordinary." She hands us both a business card. "Thank you."

"I have one concern," says my concierge. "I've noticed a red Volvo lurking in our car park. I know it doesn't belong to any of the residents. Here is the number plate. You might want to speak to him," he declares, handing over the piece of paper.

"I'll do that now."

I stifle a smile.

He continues.

"You never know, that man might be hanging around our apartment block to check out the situation with the intent to burgle my residents. He's there at the moment. Can you check up on him?"

"Straight away."

She leaves the building.

"I'm heading out for a run. Catch you later, Michael."

"Have a good day, Mr Scott."

I see Constable Peters talk to the driver in the red Volvo and make my escape around the side of the building. I run the half-hour journey to help clear my mind. What a stroke of luck. On the orders of Inspector Canmore, he sends his Constable to my apartment block to ask questions, checking up on my whereabouts at the time of his burglary, and she ends up questioning Canmore's surveillance 'expert' whilst I make my getaway to pick up my father's ring stolen from his house.

Fucking genius!

I check the time.

Ten minutes left to run a mile. I increase my pace until I reach the car park. Puffing and panting, I slow down to catch my breath, pull the rucksack from my back, reach inside and retrieve the brown envelope. I spot a bench overlooking the dock, sit there and wait. It is not long before someone arrives.

"Nice day for a run, Edward Cooper."

"I agree," I say, without turning around.

I place the envelope on the seat. The woman leans over the back of the bench and picks it up. She leaves a small box in its place. I smell her scent. Our eyes never meet. I wait for a few minutes, turn around and there is nobody in the vicinity. SocialMisfit's contacts are professionals. I lift the box, eager to peer inside but wait. I keep it in my hand and sprint all the way home without stopping until I reach the Firth of Forth Apartments. I search the car park. The red Volvo is gone. As I rush towards the lift, Michael shouts in my direction.

"The person in the car left with Constable Peters."

"That's great. I'm sure it was nothing too serious."

"I'll phone and ask."

"Good idea."

"Thanks."

"I need to go. I'm late for a conference call."

"Catch up with you later, Mr Scott."

I wait. The lift remains on the fourth floor.

"Come on!" I say, tapping my foot on the ground. "Hurry up!"

As soon as it arrives, I press the button to my floor, time and time again. It does not make the doors close any faster. "Calm down," I tell myself. I get out of the lift, turn the key in the lock, push and slam the door shut. Taking a deep breath, I unclasp my hand to reveal the prize, make my way to the kitchen, put on the fan, light a cigarette and stare at the box for what seems like an eternity. *Open it!* I take a deep drag on the cigarette, exhale and open the lid.

I gasp.

Not one but two.

My father's gold band.

Annabel Taylor's diamond ring.

****

I sit and gaze at the tokens of death on the table. Two of my most personal kills are now back in my possession. I lean forward, pick up both rings, eyes wide, staring at his name on the inside of the gold band, look back and forth between the two, and focus on the solitary diamond. The seduction of its beauty and memories of the kill linger in my psyche. The fusion is one of homeostatic peace with these two objects. I take a deep, slow, breath. Nothing can beat the sense of omnipotence and euphoria that these memories evoke. Powerful. Potent. Penetrable. Ecstatic. Erotic. Energising. I blank out my surroundings, close my eyes, and revel in this catatonic state for a while.

BEEP BEEP, BEEP BEEP, BEEP BEEP.

My eyes flick open. The noise continues. It is SocialMisfit. My saviour and partner in crime. I answer the phone.
"Good afternoon, Edward."
"Hello. Thank you for the gift."
"I know you only wanted the one with the inscription. They were both in the box. I left it that way because you're such a good customer."
"You've no idea how much I appreciate your gesture. The diamond ring has so much sentimental value."
"My pleasure."
"What is the update on Canmore?"
"He returned home after his dinner date and must have got the shock of his life."
I laugh.
"Two police officers turned up an hour later, the house fitted with new locks and a surveillance camera but nothing else."
"It's too late for security."
"At least we completed the job."
"I can't thank you enough."
"No problem. I sent a few digital photographs of the burglary."
"I'll check that later."
"We also have arrangements in place to take out the target as he leaves The Charity Ball at the end of the night on Saturday, 3rd March."
I gasp. "Fantastic news!"
"Glad to be of help."

"Thank you very much."

"Have a good evening, Edward."

"Likewise."

I hang up the phone.

My plan is flawless so far. I check the email from SocialMisfit and scrutinise the images of the robbery and the two officers at the scene of the crime at Inspector Canmore's home. There is Constable Peters. Who is the other person? His face is familiar. I remember now. Jack? *Think, think, think!* Sergeant Jack Murray. The clever bastard at the interrogation about my father's disappearance just over seven years ago. He also conducted the search at the cottage in Argyll with his dogs. *I bet Murray leads the new search. I wonder when it takes place. Before or after Canmore's death? Either way, I need to leave that to fate and hope they find nothing. There is a large area to cover and my father's body is way off the beaten track.*

My senses are on high alert.

I need to be careful.

This trio of renegades must suspect my involvement in the robbery. Why else would Constable Peters snoop around so soon after the deed? However, I am one step ahead but need a contingency plan, just in case. I email SocialMisfit and attach my photograph.

I have one last favour to ask. I need some I.D. for Edward Cooper. Male. 30 years old. Passport and driving licence. As soon as possible. Can you arrange?

With a sense of urgency, I clear the flat of anything that might implicate my involvement, not just the robbery, but to any of my murders in the last seven years. I contemplate the technological proof and glance at my main computer. The memory on the hard drive is clean as I only ever use it for work issues. Tomorrow, on my way to the agency, I will take the laptop, my box of rings, money from the safe and keep these items in my deposit box at the bank. Once I get the new I.D. from SocialMisfit, I will set up a new account under Edward Cooper and syphon assets into this one in case of an emergency.

The email alert goes off on my phone.

I will have your I.D. complete within the next 48 hours and also add Edward Cooper to the official databases. If you prefer to deal in hard cash rather than bitcoin, I will arrange the exchange at the same place. The North Car Park at Leith Docks. This will cost £2,000.

Deal. We work well together SocialMisfit.

My pleasure. I'm here if you need anything else.

I will keep that in mind.

I experience a deep sense of satisfaction at my progress. It is necessary to have a contingency plan just in case something goes wrong. If it does, I need a quick getaway and money to survive. And, I will have a different identity. I like my choice of name— Edward Cooper. Part of my father and part of Kristina. Genius. The only issue out with my control is the new search in Argyll. I remember the documentary and take comfort because it is difficult to find a buried body, even with sniffer dogs. The scent of death travels underground, shifting with the changing seasons. My only saviour may be the bad weather on the west coast and the fact that my father's remains are on higher ground. I cross my fingers, muttering, "Please don't find anything."

I pause.

The red Volvo?

This is also an area of concern. I bet that old bastard took photographs of my rendezvous with SocialMisfit in Nottingham. I get up and peer out of the window. He is not there. I need to watch out for any other tails. At least Inspector Canmore and myself think alike, following each other before the ultimate showdown. At the moment, I have the upper hand but Inspector Canmore is adamant and trying to corrupt Kristina's mind. I recall her words from Inspector Canmore: "I'm bringing that psychopath down."

This game of cat and mouse is exciting.

I need to watch and wait for his next move.

"I'm ready for you, Canmore," I say out loud.

I blank out any other thoughts about my situation. Instead, I make a delicious meal of teriyaki noodles and settle down for the night. Before I head off to bed, I empty my safe, place the money in the side pocket of the laptop case and check my box of rings, ready to drop off at the bank.

I have a restless sleep until the alarm goes off the next morning. I am not sure whether to go to work. However, I need to catch up with my employees and live a normal life for a change. I want peace and quiet for the next few weeks until The Charity Ball. Once Kristina arrives we can also plan our trip home to see Charles and my mother. I reach over to the bedside table and pick up my phone.

I dial his number.

He answers.

"Hello, Jayden. How are you?"

"I'm fine, Charles. I called to say we'll come and visit you in a few weeks time. Is that okay?"

"Of course. Is everything all right with you and Kristina?"

"Yes. However, the search in Argyll will take place soon."

He sighs. "For the love of God, let's hope that they find nothing. I hate to imagine how this would affect your mother, Kristina and the consequences to your life, freedom and sanity."

"I can't think about that right now."

"We just need to wait, Jayden."

"Thank you for all your support. I couldn't get through this without you."

"I know, my boy. I am partly to blame for the situation."

"It's not your fault. It's all circumstance. Anyway, how is my mother? I've not spoken to her for ages."

"Loving village life."

"She belongs with you."

"This is true. Carolyn is out at the moment helping Mrs Cameron with the Spring bloom."

"I will call back later."

"Thanks. I'll tell Carolyn we spoke. I need to go, Jayden. I have a funeral service to conduct this morning."

"No problem. Take good care."

"You too. Goodbye."

I get out of bed, take a shower and potter about the kitchen for a while, thinking about the Reverend's funeral service, reliving the moment of Canmore's death over and over in my mind. To witness such an act of violence sends my pulse racing into overdrive. It is this adrenalin rush that lies at the heart of all my kills. Nothing compares. I put on my best suit, pick up the laptop case and leave the apartment.

I pass the concierge on the way out.

He waves. "Mr Scott, do you have a minute?"

"Yes."

"I spoke to Constable Peters about the man in the red Volvo."

"What did she say?"

"He was a police officer checking out the area."

"That's good to know."

"He looked more like a stalker than a policeman."

I laugh. "I'm not sure?"

He scratches his head.

"Anything else?"

"She seemed more interested in asking questions about you."

He has my full attention. "In what way?"

"Your whereabouts on Friday night. To make sure you never left the flat. Your visitors."

"And what did you tell the officer?"

"I confirmed, again, that you were here and told Constable Peters to mind her own business about your friends or ask you herself."

I chuckle. "Thanks."

"What a strange woman. There was a stalker in our car park and all she can do is ask personal questions about one of my residents. Perhaps, Constable Peters is a secret admirer." He chortles. "She's not your type though."

"Absolutely not! Have a good day, Michael."

He chuckles. "You too, Mr Scott."

Constable Peters is such an amateur. Silly cow.

I leave the building.

My drive to the city centre is unbearable. The amount of traffic, horrendous. I tap my fingers on the steering wheel, start, stop, sigh and do it all over again. This goes on for at least half an hour. I make a break down a side street and drive into the staff car park at the bank. I grab the laptop case, leave the Noble and walk to the front entrance.

"Good morning. How can I help?"

"I would like access to my safety deposit box."

"What's your name?"

"Jayden Edward Scott."

"One moment."

She makes a quick call on the pager.

A security guard arrives.

"If you follow our officer, he'll escort you to the area."

"Thank you."

I follow him through the security doors and get access to my deposit box. With a sense of relief, I get rid of the laptop case and slam the door shut. He waits. I follow him back to the main bank. As we go through the security doors, I begin to sweat, my hands tremble, my gut twists, nauseous, to the point I am almost sick.

I lean against the wall.

"Are you okay?" says the officer.

"Not really. Can I take a moment?"

He nods.

Through my heavy breathing, I assess the situation and declare, "I need to go back."

We head to the area with the safety deposit boxes. Once he leaves, I open the door and pull out the case. With trembling hands, my fingers grasp hold of the box from the side pocket and retrieve the keepsakes. I slam the door shut, take a deep breath, slide down the wall and sit on the floor. *It's a risk but I can't leave the rings here. I need to have them close, to relive my glorious kills.* I open the lid. One by one, I take out each piece of jewellery and Stewart Bailey's skull and crossbones keyring and slide them over my fingers on my left hand, admiring the different designs, seeing the faces of each of my victims.

BANG, BANG, BANG!

I snap out of my reverie.

"Are you okay, Mr Scott?" asks the security guard.

"I'm fine. I'll be out in a minute."

I put the rings and the keyring back in the box and tuck it into the inside pocket of my suit jacket. I exhale and open the door.

"Ready?"

"Yes, thanks."

I follow him back to the main bank, wait for the doors to open, and catch my breath as the fresh air gushes through the entrance, the sense of relief, immediate. The knot in my stomach disperses, calm, peaceful, the release of tension and the vice-like grip of emotion, disappearing. I stretch the muscles in my neck, my head moving in a circular motion as a last attempt to calm down. With a sense a relief, I stand on the steps and light a cigarette. I puzzle over my reaction to the angst of being apart from my keepsakes. I chuckle to myself. *Bloody idiot. They are now back where they belong. I must find a hiding place until all of this blows over.* I make my way to the back of the building, get into the Noble and call Kristina.

She answers.

"Hey sweetheart, how are you?" I ask.

"Good. I'm about to get ready and go to work."

I sigh. "Me too. I'm in the centre of Edinburgh at the bank and heading off to the agency."

"Are you okay?"

"Tired. I might head home and take it easy for the day. Jessica Logan takes care of the agency in my absence, so I don't need to be there all the time."

"Lucky for some. I suppose you're the boss."

"This is true."

She chuckles.

"I love to hear you laugh."

"I'm happy at the moment. At last, I believe everything will be fine."

"There was never any need for this drama."

"You're right, Jayden. Let's not talk about it anymore."

"Okay."

There is a mutual silence.

I break the momentum.

"I adore you more and more every day, Kristina Cooper."

"Likewise, Jayden Scott."

"See you in a few weeks."

"You too. I better get ready."

"Bye, Kristina."

She hangs up the phone.

I phone Jessica Logan and tell her I am tired after my trip to London and will catch up in a few days time. She reinforces that everything is fine. Now, I can focus on the task at hand and liaise with SocialMisfit to sort out the fake documents. I drive back to Leith and park the Noble. I check the time. It is just before midday. After a restless sleep the night before, I intend to relax for the rest of the day with no interruptions. I sneak past the concierge who is busy doing something on the computer and enter the apartment. I turn on the mute buttons on my mobile phones, pull out the plug to the landline, undress and flop down onto the bed. I wrap the duvet around my body, drift off to sleep and try to forget all about the drama of the last two months of my life.

Peaceful.

Dreamless.

Sleep.

When I wake up, the flat is quiet, dark, with no noise. I reach over to the bedside table and turn on the lamp, squinting my eyes to protect them from the sudden exposure of the bright light. I lift up my head and look around the room then relax back into the comforting pillow. I have no desire to know the time, no desire to get out of bed and no desire to check the messages on my phones. This precious time is mine to relax and gather my thoughts. I switch off the light and let my mind wander, for hours on end, reliving the happy times in my life: Charles, my mother, friends from school, Alex, Grant, Philip and Jacqueline and the day I met Kristina Cooper at her keynote speech. From time to time, sordid images creep into my psyche. I dismiss these dark thoughts and have only one woman on my mind, the lady I want to spend the rest of my life.

I sleep in peace until the next morning. Once awake, I stretch out and lie on my back, gazing up at the ceiling for a good length of time. *I wonder if SocialMisfit has been in touch? Are my fake documents ready? Do I have any messages from Kristina?* I check the time on my watch. It is nine thirty in the morning. I have been asleep, on and off, for the last twenty hours. Exhaustion. Rejuvenation. And now, ready to tackle the day. I get up, put on a pair of joggers, wander through to the living room and pick up both my mobile phones. I switch everything back on. There are no calls or texts from Kristina. There is one missed call and two messages from SocialMisfit.

Your documents are ready.

My associate will meet you today at the same place at twelve o'clock to make the exchange. Two thousand in cash.

I have several hours to get ready. I shower and put on my suit ready to go to work after the drop off. I check the flat to make sure I have everything, pick up the brown envelope with the money and pass the concierge at our reception.

"Have a good day, Mr Scott."

"You too, Michael."

I drive the Noble to the North Pier at Leith Docks and wait on the bench, wondering if I will see the messenger this time. I fantasise about the femme fatale—sexy, slim, tall, brunette. Ten minutes later, I am wary of a presence. My senses are on high alert. I smell this woman's scent and become aware of her light breathing just before she places a hand on my shoulder.

"Good afternoon, Mr Cooper."

I do not turn around. "Here's the money," I say, sliding the brown envelope across the bench.

She picks it up. "You seem different today. More polished?"

"I'm going to work."

"Very professional."

An elegant hand with slim fingers places the documents on the seat. My accomplice leans forward and whispers in my ear, "Here's your new identity. Have a good day, Edward Cooper."

I find it hard to control my erection and want to turn around to see this woman but refrain. I wait for several minutes, check the content, which all seems in order, get up off the bench, and look around the car park. She is gone. *Where is the messenger? Watching from a distance?* Her perfume still lingers in the air. I take a deep breath, revelling in the aftermath of her scent, shake my head and snap out of my fantasy. I tuck the documents into my suit pocket next to the box of keepsakes. There is no time to dwell on the mystery woman. I must go to work. But first, I have to go back to the apartment because I left my briefcase.

I take the short trip to the flat. On approaching the car park, I notice two police cars. *What's happening?* Wary, I enter the building. Michael rushes forward as soon as I walk through the door.

"I had to give them access to your apartment, Mr Scott. It's not my fault…"

"Slow down. What's going on?"

"Two officers have a warrant to search your flat."

"Who?"

"I'm not sure."

"Calm down and remember the names."

He pauses. "… Constable Peters and Inspector Canmore."

"I see."

"Why are they in your flat?"

"There's not anything to worry about."

"Are you sure?"

"Yes. I'm going to work. Please don't mention I was here."

"Okay, Mr Scott."

"Catch up when I get back."

He nods.

A devious smile passes across my face. My laptop is safe in the bank and the rings and fake documents in my jacket pocket.

I leave the building, knowing they will find nothing.

ABSOLUTELY NOTHING.

THE BREAKTHROUGH

"Very arrogant people, serial killers."
(Professor David Wilson)

Constable Peters searches Jayden Scott's flat. I sit on the sofa, looking at the images that Larry Parker left in my possession. I peer closer at his companion's face. Who is this man and why did Jayden Scott meet him at the National Justice Museum in Nottingham? I scrutinise the photographs, absorbing every detail of the rendezvous. There is an exchange going on but for what reason? Payment for burgling my house to get his keepsakes back? Why meet in person for such a small transaction? What else? Jayden Scott is a devious bastard, sneaking around the country, meeting up with dubious characters.

I shake my head and stop asking myself unanswerable questions.

Instead, I gaze at the close-up images of Kristina Cooper's work. Larry broke into the apartment and took some photographs. Not that I agree with his methods. She had a spare key under the flower pot to her flat in Lincoln. Larry got there before Jayden Scott's arrival. I can just make out the details comparing Stewart Bailey and Jayden Scott's motives for the Annabel Taylor murder. I contemplate her word: "REVENGE". Edward Scott: revenge for being a bad father. Annabel Taylor: revenge for being his father's mistress and hurting his mother. Stewart Bailey: revenge for being a scapegoat. What about Raymond Cartwright and Jake Driscoe? Revenge? For what reason? One ring is missing according to the autopsy report. Did he also take Cartwright's ring? Jayden Scott knew the owner of the Diamond Life casino. Larry checked with a receptionist called Crystal. For a long time, my prime suspect has been a regular gambler. She recalls his presence at a private function several months before Cartwright and Driscoe were both killed at the hangar near Dover almost three years ago. So… there may be five victims, four rings, and a missing silver skull and crossbones keyring belonging to Stewart Bailey.

"The flat is clean, Inspector Canmore."

"That's no surprise, Constable Peters."

"Shall we take the computer?"

"We won't find anything. There's a pattern here. The crime scenes are immaculate. He's not that stupid to keep incriminating evidence in his flat."

"I think you're right."

"I'm never wrong. Our best line of defence is his phone records, the search in Argyll and Kristina Cooper. That woman is a clever criminologist. She may be able to help locate the rings stolen from my flat, assuming he is the perpetrator. We need to find those keepsakes."

"Good idea. I'll finish the phone check in a few days."

"Are there any calls to Raymond Cartwright?"

"Yes, but not many."

"At least they were acquaintances."

"It would appear so and now he is also dead along with Jake Driscoe. I read about the paedophile ring and the gruesome death by fire. Horrific on both counts. It could be some kind of vigilante revenge."

I nod. "Perhaps? I want you to check the exact date of Cartwright and Driscoe's murder and determine if Jayden Scott was in London."

"Okay, Skipper. Anything else?"

"Take this photograph of Mr Scott's accomplice from Nottingham. See if you can identify him through facial recognition on our databases."

"Will do." She is about to leave and turns. "Do you think he organised the burglary at your house?"

"Yes. His meeting with the mystery man in Nottingham is not coincidental. I'm sure he staged the robbery and positive this is about the retrieval of the rings."

"You need to watch out, Inspector Canmore. He's a dangerous person. We both know that more than anyone."

"I understand."

"Be careful."

"Well done for organising the locksmith, new alarm system and the surveillance cameras at my home. It's a bit over the top!"

She laughs. "But a necessity. I'm going back to the station. Are you coming?"

"I'll stay here for a while."

"There's a safe we can't access."

"I can deal with that problem."

"See you later."

"Thanks, Peters."

I decide to call Jayden Scott to obtain the number for the safe. If not, I'll ask my men to come and break the goddam thing apart. The concierge said he had gone to work. I dial the agency.

"Can I speak to Mr Scott?"

"Who's calling?"

"Inspector Canmore. Police Scotland."

"One moment, please."

I hear several clicks, and then, his voice.

"Nice of you to get in touch. How can I help?"

"You must realise by now, I have a warrant to search your flat."

"I may have heard through the grapevine."

"I need the code for the safe. If you don't comply, I'll rip it out of the wall."

"Calm down. The number is 321456."

"How original."

He laughs. "I've nothing to hide, Inspector Canmore."

"I know there's nothing in the safe. You're not that stupid."

"Indeed."

Smug bastard, I think to myself.

And play one of my top cards.

"I have an officer looking into the deaths of Raymond Cartwright and Jake Driscoe." I hear a sharp intake of breath on the other end of the phone. "Do you know these men, Mr Scott?"

"Not sure?"

"You do 'indeed'. Raymond Cartwright's number is on your mobile records. A shady character just like you."

There is anger in his voice. "You're playing a dangerous game, Inspector Canmore."

"I'm only doing my job."

"Stay out of my life."

"Or what…?"

"You'll see."

"Have a good day, Mr Scott. I have a safe to check."

He slams down the phone.

As I suspect there are only a few useless documents and some spare cash. I sit down on the sofa, contemplate the circumstantial evidence, take out my notebook and write it all down. More than ever, the proof is overwhelming. If Peters finds out that Jayden Scott was in London when Raymond Cartwright and Jake Driscoe died, then I am more than sure I can add these two men to the list. He is a serial killer. My gut instinct is never wrong. I must warn Kristina Cooper. She is too close with Jayden Scott to seek the truth. I will speak to her when she attends The Charity Ball at the start of next month. In the meantime, it is a waiting game until more facts about the cases emerge. I need to back off for now. There is nothing to find. He is too clever, too devious and too deceptive.

What did he mean: "You'll see?"

My thoughts shift to Sally Walker.

I had a wonderful meal at the restaurant. She is all I want in a new relationship: intelligent, funny, charming, quirky and beautiful. We talked about my concerns related to Jayden Scott's involvement in Stewart Bailey's murder. It was such a relief to be able to speak to someone not connected to the case. The evening was everything I expected, and more, until I returned home to the chaotic scene in my house. I never even noticed the rings were missing until Sergeant Murray and Constable Peters did a thorough search of the premises. And then, it all fell into place. It could only involve one man and one man only. At that moment, I was more than sure that Jayden Scott had organised the burglary.

I think about Larry Parker following him and surmise that my prime suspect is doing the same thing. Not him directly but someone is watching my every move. Does the man in Nottingham have something to do with this scenario? My brow tightens, thinking back to the evening with Sally Walker, trying to remember if my subconscious mind recalls anything suspicious. No, nothing. With my attention on my date, I was caught off-guard. This is a worry. Sally may be in mortal danger if Jayden Scott knows about my new relationship. I must protect her from any potential harm. She is also a key witness that somebody else might have been in Stewart Bailey's flat on the night of his 'suicide'.

I call her mobile.

She answers.

"Hey! How are you? You've not been in touch for two days?"

"Not too good. I've been dealing with a burglary inquiry. Mine to be precise."

"What? Where? At your house?"

"Yes. When we were at the restaurant."

"How awful. What did they take?"

"It's complicated. Would you like to meet for lunch?"

"Sure."

"I will come and pick you up."

"Alright. Where are you?"

"I'm at Jayden Scott's flat."

She gasps. "The murderer?"

I laugh. "Potential murderer. I have a search warrant. We found nothing."

"Your burglary? Do you think he had...?"

I interrupt. "We can talk about this later."

"Okay."

"Bye for now."

I hang up the phone.

I take one last look around the flat and stare at the photograph of Charles McIntyre and Carolyn Scott. At some point in time in this investigation, I will speak to them both. They must know something. Apart from the recent harassment complaint by the Reverend to DCI Grace McFarlane, he has gone off the radar. Too quiet for an interfering man of God. I peer closer, looking into those divine eyes, wondering if they hold any secrets.

The startling noise makes my heart skip a beat.

It is the phone.

I pick it up. "Jayden Scott's residence."

"Who's that?" she declares.

"Inspector Nicholas Canmore of Police Scotland."

"Where the hell is Jayden?"

"Calm down, Dr Cooper."

"What's going on now?"

"He's at work. I have a warrant to search his premises."

"On what grounds?"

"Someone burgled my flat. I suspect your partner. Not directly, mind you. Two of the missing items from my house were his father's gold band and Annabel Taylor's diamond ring."

"This is ridiculous. Why won't you leave us alone?"

"I can't do that, Dr Cooper, until I uncover the truth."

"This is insane."

"No, he's insane. You're in danger."

"I'm not."

"Yes, you are, Kristina."

"NO, I'M NOT!"

"Are you going to listen for once?"

"No!" she says and slams down the phone.

"Well, that went just fine," I mumble to myself.

I will speak to her again when we meet at The Charity Ball. Until then, I need to keep Sally Walker safe. Jayden Scott may seek revenge for meddling in his life. Kristina Cooper will tell him about our conversation and his threatening tone is a serious consideration. This might get dangerous. It is necessary to take precautionary measures now Sally is part of this investigation. If anything happened to her, I would never forgive myself.

I make a hasty retreat.

As I walk out, the concierge says, "Thank goodness that's over. What a nonsense. Good riddance."

I stop and gaze in his direction.

"If you knew what I do about Jayden Scott…"

He sighs.

"What's the point. Goodbye."

I leave the building.

And get into my car.

I turn on the siren to help manoeuvre through the busy traffic and arrive at Sally's apartment half an hour later. I ring the buzzer. The latch unlocks. I make my way to the flat. She waits at the door. I embrace her petite frame and kiss her on the lips. One leads to another. We end up in bed rather than going to lunch. Several hours later, she lays her head on my shoulder and cuddles into my chest. We lie in that position until she breaks the silence.

"I like you, Nicholas Canmore."

"Likewise, but you can't stay here on your own anymore."

"Why?"

Despite the need for protocol, I tell her everything about Jayden

Scott, Edward Scott, Charles McIntyre, the cottage in Argyll, Annabel Taylor, Stewart Bailey, Raymond Cartwright, Jake Driscoe, the burglary and the rings.

She sits up, eyes wide, trembling. "Holy shit! This is almost unbelievable."

"It's the truth. He's a serial killer. All I have is circumstantial evidence. However, I'm close to solving this case. If I'm being followed, Jayden Scott knows about us. I fear you might be in danger."

"Where will I go?"

"Can you take time off work for a few weeks?"

"I suppose."

"Do you have relatives in the area?"

"My mother. I could stay there. She lives outside Edinburgh in a small village."

"It's only for a while. I have another search scheduled in Argyll to find his father's body at the beginning of next month. This time, we're not leaving until we recover the remains, and arrest the bastard for murder."

She nods.

"We'll move you during the night. It may take a few days to put the plan into action. I'll let you know when it's in place."

"I'm scared, Nicholas."

"You'll be fine. My officers will take care of everything and make sure nobody follows us."

"Thanks."

"In the meantime, I want to secure all access to this building. The front door is fine. The back one is broken. I'll phone Constable Peters to organise a new security system for the rear entrance and keys for the residents. Lock it at all times."

"Is this not too extreme?"

"No. I need to keep you safe, just in case."

"Can you stay tonight?"

"Yes, I'm finished work. Everything will be fine."

"Alright." She clasps my hand. "I trust you."

****

Several days pass. I never leave her side. The new lock is on the back door. The move takes place tomorrow night at midnight. As Sally packs a bag, I look at her with affection. The last two days seal our relationship. We both want to spend more time together after this comes to an end. I decide that she is safe enough in the flat and return to work. I must catch up with Constable Peters.

"I'll see you tonight after my shift at ten o'clock. There's an unmarked car monitoring the apartment for the rest of the day."

"Thanks, Nicholas."

I give her a lingering kiss on the lips and leave.

The drive helps to clear my mind and return to police mode. I have not spoken to Constable Peters in two days and wonder how she is getting on with the investigation? I plan to revisit all the evidence to determine if I have missed anything. What a task but I have the next ten hours free before I return and get Sally to safety. She is my main priority. Who knows how that deranged bastard will seek his revenge because I am pushing him to the limit? I suspect there is only so much Jayden Scott can take before he snaps.

I park the car in my space at the station, leave the vehicle and walk through the automatic doors with a sense of purpose. I stride up the stairs towards the incident room. To my surprise, Sergeant Murray and Constable Peters work together, both staring at the computer screen.

"Good morning."

They both look up.

"Hey, Skipper. You're back," announces Jack.

"What are you doing?"

"Dr Cooper returned the Annabel Taylor files. We're scrutinising the CCTV footage," declares Peters. "And, Jayden Scott was in London at the time of the Diamond Life Casino murders."

"Slow down. Start at the beginning."

She takes a deep breath. "I phoned the agency in Edinburgh. The receptionist put me through to a woman called Jessica Logan. I asked for the information related to his presence in London at the time of the Raymond Cartwright and Jake Driscoe murders. Miss Logan was reluctant at first, but I said we would get a warrant to search Jayden Scott's electronic diary and she complied."

"Excellent."

"And then I had another idea. I requested unlimited access to his account over the last seven years and she agreed. I will check out his appointments over the next few weeks."

"Well done. What about the CCTV footage?"

Peters continues. "I found something and called Jack to get a second opinion."

I stare at Sergeant Murray. "What?"

"We've made a possible link to connect Jayden Scott to Annabel Taylor's murder."

I race over to the computer. There is a blurry vision on the screen of a man with a baseball cap and black attire. I shift my head back, trying to focus on the facial features. "No way!"

"Yes!" he confirms. "The image was unrecognisable. Peters used some new software to enhance the clarity."

"No way!" I say again and slump down on the chair. "I'm speechless."

"It's definitely him, Skipper," says Jack.

"I agree," declares Peters.

"Without a doubt," I confirm. "Where is he lurking?"

Constable Peters zooms out of the close-up image of his face to reveal the name of the café. "The coffee shop is across the road from the pub where Annabel Taylor waited for someone on the night of her murder. There is no evidence to suggest our man in black left by the front door. I've checked all angles. He just disappears."

"Fire exit?" suggests Jack.

"Not sure? We can check it out," says Peters.

"I'll do that when I return to Sally's flat tonight."

"Thanks, Skipper."

"No problem. I scanned the footage many times and never noticed."

She beams. "I found him."

"Very well done."

Peters continues. "Jayden Scott wore the same clothes as he did when he met the guy in Nottingham. Larry Parker's photographs confirm this ritualistic dress code."

"This is a game changer," I say in disbelief. "Come to my office, both of you."

We leave and go to my room. I take out three glasses from the cabinet, find a bottle of brandy and pour a generous amount in each tumbler. We sit and stare at each other, not knowing how to proceed.

I am the first to speak.

"You have both done a fantastic job in my absence."

"Thanks," says Peters.

"What's our next move, Skipper?" says Jack.

"I need time to think."

They both wait in anticipation.

I continue to deliberate.

"We need to find more evidence over the next ten days before The Charity Ball and the search in Argyll."

"Do we keep the confirmation of the CCTV footage to ourselves for now?" declares Jack.

I nod.

"Until there's more concrete proof," says Peters.

"Yes, I need you to go through his phone records and electronic diary with no room for error. Check all contacts. You never know, there may well be more victims?"

"Do you think?" asks Jack.

"I'm not certain, but we're more than sure that he's responsible for the murder of his own father, Annabel Taylor and Stewart Bailey."

"We all agree on that point," says Peters.

"I never told you. Sally Walker is certain there was someone else in his flat on the night of his suicide. She felt cold air coming from the fire escape when she entered the apartment with her neighbour." I chuckle. "Once he kicked in the door."

"You think Jayden Scott was in Stewart Bailey's flat?" asks Peters.

"Yes."

"Christ almighty," says Jack. "I realise now why you want Sally moved. It's all planned for midnight. My team will escort her to safety."

"Good. Thanks for organising the lock at the back entrance, Peters."

"My pleasure."

"There are also the Diamond Life Casino murders to consider," declares Jack.

Constable Peters shivers. "Our suspect may well be a serial killer. It's unbelievably incredible."

"This is the perfect case to kick start your career," I say. "You have done an amazing job so far."

She blushes. "Thank you, Inspector Canmore."

"I think we need to ignore the casino murders for now. Jayden Scott phoned Raymond Cartwright on several occasions and was in London at the time of the execution. If there's a link, I will contact the Metropolitan Police in due course. First, we must focus on our victims: Edward Scott, Annabel Taylor and Stewart Bailey."

"The links are clear, Skipper. Jayden Scott is the one common thread running through all three fatalities," says Jack.

We nod in agreement.

"Jack, your team can move Sally Walker and conduct the search in Argyll. Constable Peters, you focus on the phone records and electronic diary. I will find out more about the person from Nottingham."

"I ran the facial recognition scan on the photographs from Larry Parker but nothing." She points her finger. "I left the images in that folder on your desk."

"Thanks, Peters."

"Why do you think they met in Nottingham?" asks Jack. "Does the mystery man have something to do with the robbery at your house?"

"I'm not sure yet. However, I have this gut instinct there's more to the meeting. What's that bastard planning?"

"Who knows?"

"Anyway, I will contact Nottingham Police to try and find out more information. They might know this person?"

"Good idea," says Peters.

"Let's get back to work. I'll see you tonight at the flat, Sergeant Murray."

He finishes his drink and gets up to leave. "Midnight, Skipper."

"Thanks."

Constable Peters returns to the incident room. I stay in my office, relax, and enjoy the calming effect of the brandy. I open the file from Larry Parker and review the photographs of Jayden Scott and the man from Nottingham. He looks like a shady character. Also, the black attire worn by my prime suspect is distinct in both the CCTV footage and these images. Constable Peters may be right. Is it some form of ritualistic dress code related to his devious acts? I pick up the phone and dial reception.

"Can you find the number and duty sergeant for Nottingham Police? I'll wait on the line."

"Of course, Sir," says the young officer. "One moment."

While I am on hold, I inspect the rest of Larry Parker's photographs. Jayden Scott left Nottingham and went to Kristina Cooper's flat in Lincoln. I look again at the images he took in her flat, squint my eyes and peer closer at the most interesting piece of information. The text is small. I can just make out her comparison profile between Stewart Bailey and Jayden Scott, the motive of jealousy and revenge in bold print next to each name. Therefore, she has her own suspicions but ignores the evidence. I suppose Annabel Taylor's ring found on the body of Stewart Bailey proves too much in Jayden Scott's favour.

The receptionist interrupts my thoughts.

"I have Sergeant Christopher Aitken on the line from Nottingham Police. I'll connect you."

"Thanks."

"Inspector Canmore. How can I help?"

"Will you take a look at several photographs of a young man under surveillance in your area? I can fax the images. You might be able to clarify his identification if known to the police."

"Yes, of course."

"What's your number? I will send the images now."

He recites the digits.

"Hang on." I tuck the phone under my chin, gather up the photographs and send the fax. "You should get them soon."

"Cheers. What's the story?"

"It's complicated."

He laughs. "Isn't it always?"

I listen to the machine in the background.

"That's the pictures coming through." Sergeant Aitken goes quiet for a few moments. "The man looks familiar. I'm positive he's a Dark Web operator but deals in legitimate goods, if that makes sense. I'll check with another few officers and let you know."

"The Dark Web?"

"Yeah, I think so."

"What does he trade?"

"Not sure. I'll try to get back to you by the end of this week."

"Thank you."

He hangs up the phone.

I scratch my head. "The Dark Web? What the hell is going on?"

All I can do is wait until Sergeant Aitken gets in touch. In the meantime, my team need to do a lot of work with an emphasis on Jayden Scott's electronic diary. I can leave that one with Constable Peters. Left to her own devices, she does a great job. I plan to spend the rest of the week with Sally and return to Edinburgh to rejoin the investigation. That gives us seven days until the search in Argyll. After that, father's body or not, I will bring that psychopath down based on our circumstantial evidence.

I devote the afternoon to sifting through the Edward Scott and Annabel Taylor files, again. I am going around in circles, but as seen with the CCTV footage, the proof is there waiting to emerge. At eight o'clock, I give up. Instead, I write down a few tasks to complete on my return:

Check with Constable Peters—electronic diary/phone records

Catch up with Sergeant Aitken (Dark Web?)

Contact Reverend Charles McIntyre for an informal chat

Speak to Kristina Cooper (The Charity Ball?)

An hour later, with a sense of satisfaction, I turn off the light and leave my office. I catch up with Constable Peters. I open the door to the incident room. She looks up from the screen, bleary eyes, tiresome, rubbing them with the back of her fingers.

"Go home, Peters. It's been a long day."

"Later. I'm sifting through Jayden Scott's electronic diary and will cross-reference with his phone records. I have a lot of people to consider, that's for sure." She picks up a piece of paper with a list of names, shaking it in the air. "And this is only the start."

"Best of luck. I'll catch up with you next week. Call if you need any advice. Sergeant Murray is also at the other end of the phone."

She yawns. "Will do."

"Good night, Peters."

"Bye."

I make a detour home, pack a bag and head towards Tollcross. I am vigilant, senses on high alert, checking in my rear-view mirror on many occasions. Nobody can follow us. I need to keep Sally safe from that lunatic. Perhaps, I am overly cautious, but she is worth the effort. I park the car and grab my bag. Jack can move the vehicle back to my house later. I check the time. It is ten o'clock. Two hours to wait until he arrives. First, I must satisfy my curiosity.

I walk towards Lothian Road. I stop outside the bar. Across the street is the café. It is still open but does not have many customers. I order a black coffee, sit in the same place as our psychopath and look over at the pub. *You're clever, Jayden Scott. What a fantastic vantage point. How did you know Annabel Taylor would be there at that moment and time, waiting on someone, your father perhaps, who was already missing, probably dead by your very own hand?* I answer my question. "Because you had access to her mobile phone, stolen on the night of her murder," I say, mumbling under my breath. "Such a devious bastard."

I sip my coffee, contemplate the situation, swivel around on the chair and see the sign next to the corridor leading to the toilets. I get up and go to the back of the building. There is an emergency exit. I push open the door, catching my breath as the crisp air brushes past my face. I stand in the alcove and look to the right. On the opposite side of the street is Annabel Taylor's house. *Now we know, Jayden Scott, now we know.*

I return to Tollcross and ring the buzzer.

Sally answers.

"It's Nicholas."

She clicks the button to unlatch the door. I bound up the stairs. Sally waits for my arrival. I take hold of her hand as we enter the flat. We stop in the corridor. She wraps her arms around my neck, clinging on tight, reluctant to let go.

"I'm glad you're back. What a long day stuck in this house on my own."

"Not for much longer. Jack and his team will be here soon."

She lets out a sigh of relief. "Thank you."

I dump my bag in the hallway and proceed to the living room.

"You all packed?"

"Yes. Drink? Coffee? Tea?"

I see a bottle of wine on the table and nod in that direction.

She laughs. "I'll get you a glass."

I walk towards the window and peek through the curtains. The street is quiet apart from a couple walking hand in hand along the road with their dog. *I'm glad she's moving to safety. Jayden Scott is a dangerous bastard. The sooner I arrest him, the better. It will be a relief once*

Sally is out of the area. And then, I can work with Sergeant Murray and Constable Peters to draw a line under this horrific case.

On edge, I jump at the sound of her voice.

"Here you go," she says.

I take the glass and swallow a large mouthful. "Thanks."

"Why are you so late?"

I am just about to tell her about the café. "Well... I've been busy at the office."

"Is everything okay? Any new developments?"

"A few but not much."

"What's wrong, Nicholas?"

"Nothing. It's been a long day."

"Are you certain?"

"Yes."

"Good."

"I'll stay with you until the end of the week."

"Really? That's fantastic news. Are you sure?"

"Positive."

I continue to stare out of the window.

"What's wrong?" she asks, again.

"Nothing! I'm waiting on Jack and his team."

She pats the cushion. "Please, sit down."

With reluctance, I move away from the window.

We sip our wine and wait.

Ten minutes later, the buzzer rings.

"Stay there." I get up and lift the intercom phone. "Hello."

"Hey, Skipper. We're ready to go."

With a sigh of relief, I push the button.

I meet him half way up the stairs. "I checked out the café tonight. I'm sure Jayden Scott left by the emergency exit. It leads to the side street across the road from Annabel Taylor's flat."

He runs his hands through his hair. "Bloody hell! This is out of control. First his father, then Annabel Taylor, possibly Stewart Bailey and those other two blokes in London. Who's next?"

We both stare at each other.

"I'm not insinuating...," he declares.

I interrupt. "You need to make sure we're not followed. If my name is a target on Jayden Scott's hit list, Sally could also be in danger."

"I understand, Skipper. My team are conducting a thorough check of the area before we leave. I also have three vehicles. One takes the lead, the other tails your car from behind. Nothing will get past our detection."

"Thank you. I'll get Sally. Meet you outside."

We lock up the flat and drive in unmarked cars to an isolated village fifteen miles from Edinburgh, just after midnight, through winding country roads, away from the potential threat of a serial killer.

****

Sally's mother is different. Eccentric but adorable. She leads a quiet existence in a small village. A colourful woman who likes to paint, tend to her brood of animals and barter with locals to exchange produce and logs for the fire. Despite the chill in the air, we spend the next few days meandering through the forests and vast hills surrounding the landscape. It stretches for miles, sheltering hidden lakes and reservoirs, sheep, cattle and country living. It is a welcome break from the hustle and bustle of the city. I almost forget about my duties as a policeman and fall in love with rural life. This is what I want for the future, both of us together, to share these intimate moments.

The week passes without incident.

On the last day, I roll over in bed, focusing on her delicate features. In my opinion, she is gorgeous. I could spend the rest of my life watching her sleep, so peaceful. My mobile rings, interrupting the moment.

"Good morning, Inspector Canmore."

"Hello, Constable Peters. How are you?"

She gushes. "You need to return, Skipper. I've found something significant."

I sit upright. "What?"

"I don't want to explain on the phone. It's about Jayden Scott. When are you coming back?"

"This afternoon… maybe tonight?"

"Come to the incident room as soon as you get here."

"Is it important enough that I leave now?"

"Yes. No. Please stay and enjoy your time off. You never have a proper break."

"Okay. I'll phone Sergeant Murray. We'll be there for six o'clock at the station."

She lets out a huge sigh. "Thanks, Skipper."

"See you later."

I need a lift back to the city and call Jack. He agrees to arrive at four thirty. I spend the last day with Sally and put the conversation with Peters to the back of my mind. We go out for a late lunch in the local pub.

"You seem a little distracted today, Nicholas?"

"Constable Peters phoned this morning when you were asleep and has found out something important about our case."

"What?"

"She wouldn't say." I look at my watch. "Jack is due to arrive in an hour. We'll meet her at the incident room at six."

"Sounds intriguing."

I reach over and take hold of her hand. "In the meantime, you stay here until I tell you it's safe to return."

She nods. "Please be careful."

"I will, don't you worry. I'll phone every day."

We leave the pub and wander up the country road back to her mother's cottage. With a sense of sadness, I pack my bag. Jack arrives on time. I hate leaving her alone, but know she is safe here, away from Tollcross.

I grasp hold of her hand and kiss her on the lips. "We'll see each other next Saturday. It's not long."

She smiles. "Take care."

"Everything will be fine."

"I trust you, Nicholas."

We share one last kiss before she lets go of my hand.

I climb into the car.

The drive home helps to get back into police mode. I leave a lover and return as a cop. Lost in my own thoughts, I stare out of the window, going over and over in my mind the conversation with Constable Peters.

"You okay, Skipper?"

"…Just thinking…"

"About Sally or the case?"

"The latter."

"Me too. I can't wait to find out."

It does not take long to drive the fifteen miles to the city centre but get stuck in busy traffic. We reach our destination at five thirty.

Jack turns off the engine. "Ready?"

"Absolutely."

We proceed to the incident room.

I open the door.

It is empty.

"We'll just need to wait," declares Jack.

I sit down, waiting, tapping my foot on the floor.

"Please stop doing that with your feet. It's annoying."

"Sorry."

He laughs.

"Is everything still okay for the search in Argyll next Saturday?"

"Yes, the team are in place along with our sniffer dogs, Blade and Lady. I took them both out of retirement. They are the best. We have the whole weekend to examine the surrounding area."

"Brilliant. I'm going back to see Sally on the morning of The Charity Ball. Call anytime with regular updates."

"Aye, aye, Skipper."

"His father's body could be anywhere, Jack. It's an extensive space to cover."

"If he had something to do with his disappearance, I don't think he would have gone far. Remember, he was there with his friends, and at the most, had one day to himself before he returned to Edinburgh."

"True."

I rub my head with my fingers to ease the pressure. "This is a mess but we're getting there."

He nods.

Just then, the door opens.

I stare at Peters with concern, the exhaustion evident: bloodshot eyes, tangles in her hair, the lethargy apparent in her demeanour. With enthusiasm, she says, "You're both back early? You said six o'clock?"

"We're keen to learn about the new developments," declares Jack.

"I have a lot to tell you both."

"Are you okay, Constable Peters?" I say. "You look awful."

She brushes a hand through her hair. "I've been working day and night since you left, living in this office for the last five days."

"That's not good practice." I am just about to reprimand her for this insane behaviour. "Peters..."

She interrupts. "You're not going to believe what I've found." She sits down, takes a deep breath and continues. "You know I was cross-checking Jayden Scott's electronic diary, meetings, business trips and phone records over the last seven years."

"Yes," we say in unison.

"I checked out most people. They are still alive and kicking, albeit four on the list."

I glance at Sergeant Murray, raising an eyebrow.

"Two died of natural causes, one of cancer and the other had a heart attack."

"What about the other people?" asks Jack.

She proceeds. "Martin Harris and Luiz Rodriguez. They were both Jayden Scott's business acquaintances. The first from New York and the other, Brasilia."

She stops, the nervous energy all too clear.

"And?" says Jack.

"After a little more research, I found out that Jayden Scott was a silent partner in Harris's software business albeit with controversial dealings in China. Luiz Rodriguez was a business tycoon in Brasilia with an extensive distribution company. Both were victims of a brutal crime."

"What?" I ask.

"Tell us," says Jack.

She breathes. "I spoke to the officers involved. I'm waiting on the files to arrive from both police departments across two countries. However, there were no witnesses and no forensic evidence. The murders remain unsolved."

"How did they die?" I ask.

She turns an ashen shade of white. "Both men died by a single cut to the throat, left on the street in their own pool of blood, just like Annabel Taylor."

"Oh, my fucking God!" shouts Jack.

"Unbelievable," I declare.

She starts to cry. "I'm exhausted."

I have no room for pity. "Peters, pull yourself together."

"Give the girl a break, Skipper." Jack gets up and puts a

reassuring arm around her shoulder. "You've done well, Constable Peters. You must go home and rest."

She nods. "Soon."

"Now," he declares. "We can take it from here. Don't come back until you feel better."

"The files are being sent from New York and Brasilia to my email address mid-week. I'll come back then." She gets up and puts on her coat. "Thanks, Jack."

I see her out of the building. "Sorry, for my outburst. Well done. You're a credit to the force. Go home and recover."

"Will do."

I pinch her cheek with my thumb and forefinger like a protective father does towards a vulnerable child.

She wipes a tear from her eye.

"It's overwhelming."

"Take care, Peters."

I watch her drive out of the station car park.

My mind is in turmoil as I race back up the stairs. What a breakthrough. There is no doubt anymore that he is a serial killer, but we need physical proof. Jack has to find his father's body before an arrest can happen. However, the circumstantial evidence is mounting up. I stop at the top of the staircase and retrieve my mobile. I dial the number. The call gets rejected. Kristina Cooper has blocked my number. I will call her work later. I must speak to Dr Cooper in confidence before The Charity Ball. *Silly woman.* I grab the bottle of brandy and two glasses from my office and proceed to the incident room.

"I'm lost for words," declares Jack.

I pour us both a drink.

"Unbelievable. We now suspect him of four additional murders on top of our three."

The tumblers clink together. "Cheers."

"Shall we arrest him, Skipper?"

"Not yet. Can we wait until after the search in Argyll?"

"Agreed."

"We still have to check out the files on Harris and Rodriguez."

He nods.

"You also need to find his father's body. No pressure."

He laughs. "Let's keep our fingers crossed."

"The net is closing in on that lunatic, Jack."

"There's no doubt."

"I tried to phone Kristina Cooper. She blocked my number. I must warn her as soon as possible."

"Do you think? She might pass on the information."

"True. We can wait until after the search is complete."

"Good idea."

"Another drink?"

"No, thanks. If I do, I need to ditch the car."

I pour one for myself. "I'll stick around for a while and make a few phone calls."

"It's Saturday night, Skipper. Get yourself home."

"In a while."

He gets up to leave. "Keep me updated on your progress."

"As always."

He slaps my back. "Don't stay too late."

I roll my eyes.

"Bye for now."

I am alone in the incident room and take my glass and bottle of brandy back to the office. I pour another drink, sit down on my chair and gaze at the list.

Check with Constable Peters—electronic diary/phone records
Catch up with Sergeant Aitken (Dark Web?)
Contact Reverend Charles McIntyre
Speak to Kristina Cooper (The Charity Ball?)

I can certainly cross off the first one. I am still in shock. My young officer did a fantastic job of uncovering the facts. She is a credit to our department. I ponder over the other three points. I will phone Sergeant Aitken to see if he is around. Jack is right. Charles McIntyre and Kristina Cooper are out of bounds until we conduct the search in Argyll. I dial the number. It rings out. I notice the reroute until a voice answers the phone.

"Nottingham Police. How can I help?"

"Could I speak to Sergeant Aitken, please?"

"He's away on business and returns to work on Thursday. Do you want to leave him a message?"

"Will you ask him to get in touch with Inspector Nicholas

Canmore at Police Scotland?"

"I'll pass on the request. Anything else?"

"That's everything."

"Thanks for the call. Goodbye."

Damn! This is frustrating.

As there is nothing more to do, I finish my drink, grab my bag and depart. There is a slight drizzle in the night air. It helps clear my mind. With each step, I get closer to home and cannot wait to sleep in my own bed. I approach the residence, chuckling at the amount of security Constable Peters ordered for my house. I wave at the camera, take out my key, open and shut the door, switch it off and reset the alarm.

After spending the week with Sally, my house seems agonisingly quiet. I love her company, but it is not safe for her to stay in Edinburgh, that much I know. I make a light snack and sit in my char in the study, thinking about the new turn of events. The case appears to have come to a standstill until Constable Peters receives the files from New York and Brasilia, Sergeant Aitken returns my call and Jack conducts the search in Argyll. In the meantime, I spend the next few days between my home and the office, waiting, contemplating the body of evidence against the foulest person I have ever met in my life.

Two days before The Charity Ball, Constable Peters texts to say she will return to work the following day. When I enter the incident room at nine o'clock on Friday morning, she is already at her desk.

"Good to have you here, young lady."

"It's great to be back," she says with a smile. All traces of fatigue have gone. "I'm ready to continue with a vengeance."

"Such dedication," I reply.

"I have the files on Martin Harris and Luiz Rodriguez. Take a look at the crime scene photographs."

I walk over to the desk and peer over her shoulder.

"Compare those images to Annabel Taylor." One after another, she clicks on the three pictures. "It's the same modus operandi. The slit on the neck is the same length. All left to die in the street. Annabel Taylor in front of her home, Martin Harris outside a bar in New York and Luiz Rodriguez in the red-light district of Brasilia. In my opinion, these people were killed by the same person."

"I agree, Peters."

"And, I cross-checked Jayden Scott's diary with the dates of the murders. He was in New York and Brasilia at the time."

"Were there any items of jewellery missing?"

"Yes."

"Check this out!" She enlarges the images. "On each of the victims' finger there's an indent but no rings, just like Annabel Taylor."

Speechless, I sit down on the chair next to Constable Peters.

"I've been working on this since five o'clock this morning."

"Well done, but no more nonsense. You must leave early today."

She grimaces, watching for my reaction. "I have to cover the reception until six."

"Fair enough."

My young officer smiles. "I'll write up the report on both cases."

"Thanks, Peters. Can you call Sergeant Murray and update him on our progress?"

"Of course. What are your plans over the next few days?"

"There's nothing more I can do. I'm waiting for information on our mystery man in Nottingham from Sergeant Aitken. I'll also sort out the circumstantial evidence into one folder."

"Good idea." She pauses, then continues. "I often doubted your suspicions about Jayden Scott."

I laugh. "Me too on occasion, but don't tell anyone."

She chuckles. "You're a great detective and a fantastic boss."

"Thanks." I stand up to leave. "Now get on with your work."

Constable Peters gestures with a salute.

I head up to my office and spend the rest of the day sorting out the files. It is good to have it all in one place, ready to start the criminal proceedings. With the additional evidence, the case is stronger than ever before. There are a few loose ends to tie up. I still need to talk to Kristina Cooper and Reverend Charles McIntyre and find out the identity of the mystery man in Nottingham.

I pick up my phone and call Sergeant Aitken.

Again, it goes through to the reception. The operator states that he is elsewhere on another business trip. "Please ask Sergeant Aitken to contact Inspector Canmore at Police Scotland as soon as possible," I say, leaving no time for him to reply before hanging up.

"Bloody useless."

I also call Sally Walker.

In contrast, she answers straight away.

"Hi, Nicholas. How are you?"

"Good."

"When can I come home?"

"Early next week, perhaps."

"That's fantastic news. My mother is insufferable at times."

I laugh, thinking about her eccentric ways.

"It's not funny."

"Sorry."

"I miss you," she declares.

"See you tomorrow morning. Remember, I have to attend The Charity Ball in the evening."

"I can't wait to meet again."

"I'll call you later on tonight."

"Alright."

She hangs up the phone.

"I miss you too," I say to myself.

It is nine o'clock. I want to go home. I have an early start in the morning. After I visit Sally, there are pre-drinks and speeches at The Charity Ball from three and dinner at seven. I hope to talk to Dr Cooper about Jayden Scott without giving away too much detail. I shut down the computer, lock up and leave the office. At that moment, my mobile phone rings.

"Hey, Jack. How are you?"

"Not bad."

"Did Constable Peters call about the new developments?"

"Yes. There's no doubt anymore, Skipper. He's a serial killer."

"That's for sure."

"We plan to leave now for Glencoe. I booked the team into the local hotel. We can work around the clock for the whole weekend. I aim to start at first light tomorrow. I'll find that body, Skipper."

"Let's hope so, Jack."

"I need to go and pack up our kit."

"Best of luck. I'll call you later. Remember, I have to visit Sally in the morning and go to The Charity Ball late afternoon and evening but will have access to your calls and messages."

"Okay, Skipper. Be vigilante. Make sure you're not followed."

"I know the drill, Jack."

"Good night. Get yourself home."

"I'm just about to leave. Although, I must admit, I'm a bit apprehensive about tomorrow. You must find that body, Jack. This is seven years of hard work."

"I understand. It's make or break time."

"Speak to you later."

He ends the call.

I proceed down the stairs.

In the background, I hear the faint sound of a phone.

It rings out.

"It's probably not mine," I mumble to myself.

****

"This is Inspector Canmore of Police Scotland. I'm not available right now. Please leave a message after the tone."

BBBBBBBBEEEEEEEPPPPPPP.

"This is Sergeant Aitken of Nottingham Police. While I have been away, my team investigated the photographs you sent. His name is SocialMisfit. He is an elusive Dark Web operator known in our area. This man is a dangerous individual and deals in firearms. I repeat. Extremely dangerous."

8

SHOOT TO KILL

Saturday, 3rd March

It is the morning of The Charity Ball. Kristina is asleep. We met at the airport last night, our evening spent full of intimacy. I get out of bed, pull on a pair of joggers and sneak into the closet. My keepsakes are like a magnet, the attraction, inseparable. I reach into my suit pocket and retrieve the second mobile phone and box of rings. I pull open the lid and stare at the tokens of death with a sense of relief they are all together again. I peek around the corner. She is still sleeping. I put the box back into my pocket, sit on the chair and check the message from SocialMisfit.

I read it with nervous excitement.

The plan is in place for tonight. Shoot To Kill is already in Edinburgh. He will set up and wait for the target to leave The Charity Ball from the Balmoral Hotel at the end of the night.

I reply.

Perfect.

Kristina stirs.
I freeze.
"What are you doing?" she says.
"Just sending a message. Go back to sleep. It's still early."
She snuggles into the pillow and appears to drift off.

I wait until she is asleep and head towards the kitchen to make some coffee. I turn on the fan, light a cigarette, inhale the smoke deep into my lungs and watch the coffee, drip, drip, drip, into my favourite cup. Today is not a day to rest. Tonight, my nemesis will die from a bullet straight through his goddam brain. *Interfering bastard.* Kristina mentioned that Inspector Canmore called on several occasions. She blocked his number. Clever woman. I do not need any hassle leading up to the kill. I must admit, SocialMisfit has exceeded all my expectations. He is an astute businessman despite his appearance. I suppose he dresses in a baseball cap and hoodie, baggy jeans and a prominent swagger to portray a public persona but underneath he is an intelligent individual with a genius, criminal mind.

Several minutes later, I pick up the drink, smell the rich aroma and take a sip. I go to the living area and get my other mobile phone. The sun rises over the Firth of Forth. I take my coffee onto the balcony and switch on the outdoor heater, light another cigarette and contemplate life. Before I picked Kristina up from the airport, I went to the bank to retrieve the contents of the safety deposit box and stashed my laptop in my new 4x4 car. I parked it in a secure site not far from the apartment, ready for my escape, if necessary. I have the fake I.D. and lots of spare money. With help from SocialMisfit, I syphoned off most of my accounts and made significant investments in cryptocurrency under Edward Cooper's name. My contingency plan is in place. And now, I think about the search in Argyll. I wonder when it takes place? It must be soon? No doubt, Inspector Canmore will mention this at some point in time today.

I have another niggle on my mind.

Jessica Logan.

Something is not right. She said the police wanted access to my schedule in London, several years ago, and Constable Peters threatened her with a warrant if she did not comply. The dates coincide with the deaths of Raymond Cartwright and Jake Driscoe. *However, there's no proof and no evidence of my involvement.* Jessica told her the information but ever since then, she looks guilty, stares for longer than necessary in my direction, wondering if I know anything. *What has she done?* I can call later and ask outright. In the meantime, I want to enjoy the day with my criminologist. We plan to go to The Charity Ball around five o'clock to listen to a few speakers and attend the dinner at seven. Inspector Canmore will get the shock of his life at my presence. He has tried his best to harass Kristina but if we stick together, all will be fine. I take a drag of my cigarette, close my eyes and soak up the early morning rays of light. I feel at peace with the world. Everything is in place. I have control over my own destiny and ready to kill anyone who stands in my way.

A devious smile passes across my face.

Just then, my phone rings.

"Good morning, Charles. How are you today?"

"Not too great. Carolyn is not well."

"Why? What's wrong?"

"This is all too much."

"What?"

"Did you know the search takes place in Argyll over the weekend?"

"No! Why did you not call?"

"We only found out yesterday. I have been busy looking after your mother, Jayden. It brings back a lot of bad memories, the accusations against you, your father's disappearance and the abuse."

"What a shame."

"They better not find your father's body. This will destroy her if she ever finds out you had anything to do with his death."

"It's a worry, but it's now or never."

"May the Lord have mercy on us all."

"Pray to your God, Charles."

"I'm sorry. That's out of the question. Not in this case. I can pray for you, although not to HIM on your behalf."

"I understand."

"I need to go and check on Carolyn."

"We'll see you in a few days."

"Hopefully," he says. "If they find anything, I'm sure you'll be the first to know."

I shift in my chair. "I hope not."

"Goodbye, Jayden."

He hangs up the phone.

I tap my fingers on the table, anxious about the result. However, Inspector Canmore will never live to hear the tale. What a pity. Either way, I am ready for the outcome. I need to stay vigilant. How can I keep up-to-date on the events in Argyll? I think for a moment and pick up my mobile to call our gardener.

"Hello," he says.

"Henry, it's Jayden Scott."

"Hey, Squire. Is everything okay?"

"Yes, just a quick chat to ask you to check the garden over the weekend. The winter is nearly over, anyway."

"I returned to work last week."

"Fantastic."

"Anything else?"

"Can you keep an eye on the police and report back?"

"What police?"

"There's another search of the grounds over the next few days."

"What a joke! After all this time?"

"Yes." I laugh. "The police are sure my father's remains are somewhere near our land. I am the main suspect."

"I've never heard such nonsense. Bloody lunatics."

"My mother is at the end of her tether with all this harassment."

"You can count on my help, Squire. I'll keep you informed. I'm just heading off now with Misty."

"Great."

"Heal, boy," he shouts.

I listen to Misty bark in the background. The clever dog that smelled the scent of death in the boot of my car when I arrived at the cottage over seven years ago. He also came tantalisingly close to revealing my hiding place with the dead body of my father in the wheelbarrow when I hid in the prickly gorse bushes at the edge of the forest.

"He's a clever mutt."

"The best. Talk later, Squire."

"Goodbye."

As I disconnect the call, I relax. Henry is my eyes and ears over the next few days. Genius. Any sign of trouble and I will put my plan into action. I think about leaving Kristina behind and dismiss the thought from my mind. I have more important plans for the day. At least I can monitor the course of events in Argyll and let SocialMisfit and Shoot To Kill deal with Inspector Canmore.

With a sense of satisfaction, I decide to make us breakfast. But first, I phone the agency to speak to Jessica Logan. There is no answer. I will call her later to find out what she is hiding. In the meantime, I prepare some food: bacon, eggs, toast and orange juice, arrange the plates on the tray and take it through to the bedroom.

"Good morning, Dr Cooper."

She stirs.

"Breakfast time!"

Kristina lifts her head off the pillow. I see her nostrils twitch before she opens her eyes. "Something smells nice."

I place the tray on the dresser, straddle her body, my knees bent on each side, lean closer and whisper, "A special treat for my special lady."

"How thoughtful."

"Sit up."

She laughs. "Woof, woof."

"You're not funny."

She rolls her eyes, wraps the sheet across her breasts, tucking the rim under her arms. I get the tray and we share an intimate breakfast, talk, laugh, flirt, tease. I clear the dishes and head back to the bedroom.

"You okay, my darling?"

"Fine."

I lean forward and kiss her lips.

Kristina responds.

There is no need for any words. The chemistry between us is undeniable. She is like a diamond. My unbreakable, solid, mesmerisingly beautiful, cubic crystalline. I lose myself in our lovemaking. It is a place full of pleasurable torment. I drown in her musky scent: serious, sensual, vibrant, youthful, complex, all the traits I adore. As we come to a climactic end, I whisper in her ear, "You, my diamond life are a rare symbol of beauty, forever more."

"I love you, Jayden Scott."

"Likewise." I wrap my arms around her body. "No matter what, we'll never be apart Kristina, ever."

I think about her declaration of love. We spend most of the day in bed. It is the first time she has ever spoken these words. In my mind, we now have an unbreakable bond. Nothing can come between us, not even Inspector Nicholas Canmore.

She interrupts my thoughts.

"We need to get up."

"Say it, again."

"What?"

I stare into her eyes, waiting for an answer. "Well...?"

"I said those words in the heat of the moment."

"Did you mean it?"

She pauses. "Yes, I do love you, Jayden."

"You *are* my life, Kristina."

She nods, stroking the side of my face and changes the subject. "You must deal with Inspector Canmore today. He keeps calling my phone for some odd reason."

I sigh.

"We have to talk about this, Jayden."

"Okay, okay. Let's speak to him at The Charity Ball. We must stick together, Kristina."

"Agreed."

"The search takes place in Argyll this weekend."

"How did you find out?"

"Charles called this morning. This harassment is making my mother ill."

"Poor woman. Are we still going to visit?"

"Yes, we leave on Monday."

"I hope all this doubt will be over by then."

"What doubt?" I declare. "I'm innocent, Kristina. This is nothing more than a manhunt. One that has gone on for seven fucking years with no evidence to back up that lunatic's claims."

"Calm down."

"Let's get the weekend out of the way and go home. We can relax with my mother and Charles."

She smiles. "Deal."

Kristina is the first to take a shower. I leave her alone, for now, and ring Jessica Logan. The receptionist confirms she is in the office, but the call returns to the main desk. I insist, "Please try again. It's urgent."

Miss Logan answers.

"Mr Scott, how can I help?"

"I'll get straight to the point. You must tell the truth."

"What's wrong?"

"You're hiding something."

"I'm not sure what you mean?"

"We've known each other a long time. You seem uneasy. What's going on?"

"Well…"

"Yes?"

"You know I had to confirm whether you were in London a few years ago."

"I do."

"I also had to give Police Scotland access to your electronic diary over the last seven years."

What the fuck! "Why did you not say anything?"

"I was scared."

"Scared of what?"

"Your reaction."

I am about to blow a fuse but take a deep breath and exhale. "Jessica, don't do that again without my permission."

"Sorry."

"Why on earth do they want access to my schedule?"

"Not sure?"

"Is it my diary or does that include emails?"

"Just the diary."

I let out a long, deep, audible breath.

"Honestly, there's nothing else, Mr Scott."

"Don't worry. I need to go and get ready for The Charity Ball. Remember, I'm away next week with Dr Cooper."

"Have a fantastic break."

"Thanks. Can you ask Richard McKenzie to take charge of the Edinburgh agency in my absence?"

"That's my job?"

"Just do it, Miss Logan. I will also call him later if I have time."

She sighs.

"Goodbye."

Fuck! Fuck! Fuck!

I go into the kitchen, pour a large glass of wine, get one for Kristina and take them back to the bedroom. She is still in the shower. Why does Police Scotland want to check my diary over the last seven years? I take a generous mouthful. Sure enough, there is Raymond Cartwright and Jake Driscoe. Anything else? *Oh no!* My initial meetings with Martin Harris and Luiz Rodriguez are in that diary. The sleazy bastards I killed in New York and Brasilia. Will the police establish the connection? Surely not? I imagine it takes a lot of work to piece together the clues, different types of people, other countries, but the same modus operandi as my father and Annabel Taylor. I groan and convince myself there is no point in worrying about information the police may never find. Besides, there is no evidence of my involvement to my father's disappearance, not yet anyway, Stewart Bailey is the prime suspect on the Annabel Taylor murder, the London duo died in a different manner, and hopefully, they never make the connection to the other two scumbags from New York and Brasilia.

I take the box of rings out of the suit pocket. My fingers touch the precious metal, reliving each one in turn. My body stirs. In a trance-like state, I create a scenario, standing on the steps of the Balmoral Hotel, search for the shooter, seeing the bullet in slow motion as it finds the target straight through his head. The scene is on replay, repeating over and over again in my mind. Oblivious, I notice her voice and turn around.

"What are you doing?"

I clamp the lid shut.

"What's in there?" she asks.

I try to regain some kind of composure and reply, "None of your business. It's a secret, for you, later."

"You're full of surprises." Kristina leans forward and wraps her arms over my shoulders and presses into my body. "Do you want more?" she says, before kissing my lips.

"We should get ready."

"You're right, Jayden. Go for a shower."

I have the box in my hand. As she turns away, I go into the closet and put it back into my jacket pocket. I have to be more careful. Now, I need to present her with a gift. I can slip out at The Charity Ball to buy a piece of jewellery. I decide on a ring. Not like the emerald one I bought when we first met, but a delicate piece with a precision-cut diamond to celebrate our unbreakable bond.

"Hurry up, Jayden!"

"Just choosing my suit." I pick out one made of merino wool and close the cupboard door. "This okay?"

"Lovely."

I go for my shower and try to focus on the task at hand rather than Jessica Logan's admission of betrayal, my box of keepsakes and the near miss with Kristina. The day will soon be over. Nicholas Canmore will die. We can leave for a break and spend time with my mother and Charles. Upbeat, I return to the bedroom. As usual, I am ready first and put on a tie to compliment her attire. I like to watch Kristina add all the final touches: hair, makeup, outfit, perfume. Her chiffon dress is chalky white with a shimmering glow, subtle sparkles emanating from the folds in the light fabric.

"What do you think?"

"Beautiful."

"Ready, Mr Scott?"

"Absolutely, Dr Cooper."

****

The taxi stops outside the Balmoral Hotel. I take our coats to the cloakroom and put the ticket in my wallet. We have several hours before dinner and listen to a few speakers from different charities around the world such as homelessness, mental health, abuse and domestic violence to name a few. We follow the crowds of supporters and decide upon the talk from a children's charity at home and abroad. It is a reminder of Raymond Cartwright and Jake Driscoe. There are always scumbags in society waiting to exploit the vulnerable. That is why I killed them both. The information is emotive, the images, harrowing. Kristina slips her hand into mine and rests her head on my shoulder.

"This is awful. However, the charities provide a safe haven for these children. Should we choose one and both support the cause?"

"Yes, that's a great idea."

"We can go to some other talks and decide together."

As we leave, a voice shouts, "Dr Cooper."

I turn. He walks in our direction and stops. His hand rests upon Kristina's shoulder, lingering for too long. I wrap my arm around her waist in a sign of territorial possession.

"Superintendent Hunter. Nice to see you again," she declares.

"You too. Thank you for the box files. At least we have drawn a line under the death of Annabel Taylor."

She looks over in my direction, then shifts her gaze back to him. "It's an interesting case. Stewart Bailey remains the main suspect with the motive of jealousy. Besides, one has to consider his suicide and the retrieval of his ex-partners ring."

"I had no doubt," he replies.

Superintendent Hunter stares in my direction.

"This is Jayden Scott," she declares.

He shakes my hand. "I believe we have met before at Dr Cooper's keynote speech. You're also the focus of Inspector Nicholas Canmore's inquiry."

"That's correct, but…"

She interrupts. "It's not the appropriate time for this discussion."

I change the subject. "Kristina, I need to go out for a while. Can you stay with Superintendent Hunter?"

"Why?"

I wink. "It's a secret. I must go to the jewellers and sort out a few minor details."

Realisation passes across her face from our earlier conversation. "Don't be too long."

I kiss her on the lips. "See you soon."

I quicken my pace and leave the venue, grab a glass of champagne off the tray in the foyer and gulp it down before leaving the building. There is a jewellery shop around the corner from the hotel. This is an expensive mistake. I need to get rid of the trinket box from my closet and find another hiding place. I open the door and enter the premises, waste no time on the purchase and ask the vendor for help.

"I want a diamond ring. Silver. I have a budget of two thousand pounds."

He raises an eyebrow.

"It's for someone special in my life."

His eyes glimmer. "What you need to consider is the reflection, refraction and dispersion. The more expensive cut absorbs and reflects the colourful spears of light from deep within the gemstone."

"That's interesting."

"Here, look at this one." He picks up an oval shaped diamond ring. "The dispersion of light acts like nature's prism, the symmetry of the cut in precise equilibrium to produce such optimum brilliance."

"It's perfect."

He beams. "This is my personal favourite."

I decide on his recommendation at a cost of three and half thousand pounds.

"You have made a magnificent choice," he declares. "I'll wrap this in a beautiful box."

"Thank you."

I pay on my credit card and leave the shop. I place the gift in my jacket pocket and want to give it to Kristina at the hotel. It will be an intimate moment, one we can remember and cherish. My groin twitches. I want her more with each passing day and will never tire of her body. I arrive at the entrance of the building. My phone rings. It is not a recognisable number. I rush over to a quiet alcove at the reception and answer the call.

"Hello, this is Jayden Scott."

"Hey, Squire. It's Henry."

"What's happening?"

"I'm at the cottage. There are several officers and two dogs searching the surrounding area. One great big muckle beast called Blade and a spaniel named Lady. They were here when I arrived and went in the direction of the forest this morning."

"Thanks for the update."

"It's the same guy as the last time. Sergeant Jack Murray. I checked the warrant and his I.D."

"That's no surprise."

"I'll monitor the team on my way home. There are echoes of clanking metal coming from the wood. What's that I wonder?"

"Not sure?"

"I'm away to find out," he says with conviction.

I laugh. "You're doing a great job."

"I'm doing this for Carolyn."

"Thanks, Henry."

"I have to go. Misty has disappeared. It's all that noise up in the hills. He's a nosy bugger, my dog."

"You take care. I appreciate the effort. Don't speak to my mother. She's too ill at the moment. I'll phone her on your behalf."

"No problem, Squire."

He disconnects the call.

I will just need to wait on the next installment.

Content with the snippets of information, I take another glass of champagne from the tray in the foyer and search for Kristina. I head back to the previous room. She is not there. I notice the venue for Police Scotland and the charity support the force provides for its officers, families and victims of crime. Unable to find them in any of the presentations, I check the various bars in the hotel. As I approach the Whisky Bar, Kristina stands in the corner of the pub with Superintendent Hunter and Inspector Canmore.

For fuck sake, I can't leave her alone for five minutes.

I order a double malt and proceed with caution. Both men attract attention, appearing to argue, but I cannot hear the conversation until I get closer to the trio.

I wait and listen.

"What a load of bullshit!" cries Inspector Canmore. "Stewart Bailey is an innocent man."

"Keep your voice down. That's an order," says Superintendent Hunter.

"To hell with your orders."

"Take control of yourself."

I move forward, staring at Inspector Canmore.

He glares back.

Kristina takes hold of my hand.

With a look of shock on his face, he says, "What the hell is he doing here?"

"Stop being rude," replies Superintendent Hunter. "Dr Cooper and Mr Scott are our guests."

He laughs. "This just gets even better."

"I think you need to leave," declares Kristina.

No! No! No! He has to stay until the end of the night.

"I'm not going anywhere. I want to attend the dinner."

Stand your ground, Inspector Canmore.

He points in my direction. "And you're on my hit list."

I smirk. *No, you're on mine.*

"That's enough, Inspector Canmore," demands Hunter.

"What's the point."

My nemesis walks forward, knocking my shoulder as he passes and leaves the company. Canmore makes his way towards the bar. I watch his every move. He orders a large bottle of water, fills the glass, gulps down the contents and pours another. He reaches for his phone, perches on the stool and concentrates on the conversation.

Sergeant Jack Murray, perhaps? It's not like Inspector Canmore to lose control?

"What was that all about?" I ask.

"Inspector Canmore insists that Stewart Bailey is innocent of the Annabel Taylor murder but refuses to say why?" Kristina continues. "He said, and I quote: 'I will reveal everything in a few days.'"

Holy shit! He's close to a breakthrough.

With conviction, I declare, "That man is caught in a time loop and can't let go of the past." I stare at Superintendent Hunter. "Do you know another search team are at my cottage in Argyll to try and find the buried remains of my father at this very moment?"

"I had no idea."

"Both officers and sniffer dogs."

"I have no control over these decisions. Not this time."

"Inspector Canmore is a lunatic," I say.

"There's method in his madness," he replies.

I shrug my shoulders. "You know him better than we do, however, that doesn't excuse his incessant behaviour when there's no reason to conduct the search again."

"This is true. I'll go and check up on him."

Superintendent Hunter proceeds to the bar.

"What else did he say, Kristina?"

"Nothing much. I think he's under a lot of pressure."

"That's not our problem. The sooner we're out of here the better."

"Just ignore Inspector Canmore."

"Let's have another drink but not here."

She loops her arm through mine.

I lead the way.

Hunter has a hand on Canmore's shoulder and both men appear deep in conversation. I catch them staring in my direction as we leave the bar. Kristina heads off to the bathroom. I sit down on a comfortable sofa in the quiet area of the foyer and contemplate the situation. *Now I know there's something going on. It looks like he's confiding in Superintendent Hunter. Canmore never loses control. He must be on the brink of a breakthrough. The strain, pressure, long working hours are all in vain. After his death, I need to fine tune my plans just in case they find my father's body. If necessary, I have to contact Richard McKenzie and transfer the title of the deeds into his name for both of the agencies. One thing I'm not doing is leaving Kristina Cooper behind. Wherever I go, she comes too, willingly or not. She's mine. We made a promise never to be apart.*

This experience adds to the excitement about Inspector Canmore's imminent death. I suspect the dinner will be over by ten. I can only imagine the chaos to follow. The more I think about his murder, the adrenalin returns. And when that happens, I am unable to control the euphoria and hedonistic pleasure of the moment. I am more than aware of my erection. I watch my criminologist return from the bathroom and notice her every move, the flow of the material caressing Kristina's body, revealing her natural curves with each stride. My beautiful lady smiles, knows my mind, seeing the reaction she provokes.

"That familiar look of lust," she declares.

I laugh. "I can't help myself."

My arm stretches out across the top of the sofa.

She sits down.

I flag down a passing waiter. "A bottle of your finest champagne."

"Coming right up."

I take hold of her hand.

"What's the occasion, Mr Scott?"

"I have a gift for you."

"I'm intrigued."

The waiter returns and pours the sparkling liquid.

"To us," I say.

"To us," she replies.

The crystal glasses clink together.

I take the present out of my suit pocket. "This is for you."

"Thank you. It's in a different box?"

"I had to make more of an effort."

Kristina peels off the wrapping paper to reveal the velvet box. Her eyes stare in awe when she peers inside and gasps. "Oh my goodness! How wonderful." She takes out the diamond ring, places it on the palm of her hand, staring at the crystalline structure. "I love the oval shape. Look how the cut reflects the light. This is insanely beautiful."

"Put it on now."

"Which finger?"

"Your fourth digit on your left hand.

Her eyes widen in shock. "A perfect fit. That's my wedding finger?"

"Don't worry, it's not an engagement ring but a declaration of the strength of our bond, our friendship and our love."

She lets out a sigh of relief. "Unbreakable, Jayden."

"Promise?"

"Promise!"

We spend our time together until the dinner, drink champagne, relishing our unbreakable bond. I want to take this image of beauty home and make love to her all night.

But first, we have a date with death.

****

We leave the foyer five minutes before the dinner. Kristina is tipsy and picks up a glass of champagne from the tray at the entrance to the dining hall.

"Take it easy, Dr Cooper."

"I'll be fine once I eat something."

I laugh. "Fair enough."

I also get another drink.

We see the round table for Police Scotland. I count eight people including Superintendent Hunter and Inspector Canmore. So, ten in total. We have the last two seats, opposite but far enough away from my nemesis. He looks more in control. Superintendent Hunter sits beside Kristina on her right and on my left, a mystery woman talks to a man in the next seat. I look at the card. DCI Grace McFarlane. I knock back my drink. *Fuck! I recognise the name. That's the person who allowed Canmore to reopen my father's case.* I feel uneasy in this setting and chuckle to myself. *A psychotic serial killer surrounded by senior members of Police Scotland. You couldn't make it up!*

I snap out of my reverie.

Kristina speaks to Superintendent Hunter.

I lean sideways, listening.

"Inspector Canmore is fine. I'm not sure what happened? He seems on edge but wouldn't say why?"

I let out a huge sigh of relief.

"What about the search at the cottage?" she asks.

"That's classified information, Dr Cooper."

"Sorry."

I interrupt. "Don't even think about that scenario. I keep telling you, there's nothing to find."

Hunter relents. "Mr Scott is right. There's no evidence so far according to Sergeant Murray."

With a sly grin, I peer over at Inspector Canmore.

He gestures back with a forceful smile.

That is why Canmore is out of control. He is under pressure to locate my father's body. What other evidence does that modern-day Macduff have to carry out an arrest? Either way, that bastard will do it sooner rather than later. I have to be ready. With a heavy heart, I stare at Kristina. I need her in my life. When the time comes, she must decide, or I will make that choice for us both.

She leans closer. "You're quiet."

"This is not my scene."

"I understand. It will soon be over."

"It's taking ages to serve the food." I check out the menu. "There are five courses."

"Great! I'm starving."

I laugh.

"Try to relax and enjoy the evening, Jayden."

"Perhaps."

At that moment, my mobile rings. "Do you mind? This is urgent."

"No, but don't be too long."

I rush out of the room and find a quiet area in the hotel. I manage to swipe the phone before it rings out.

"How are you?"

"All good, Squire. I want to update you on the day's events."

"Continue."

"I went to find Misty on my way home. My dog joined the team and helped with the search."

For fuck sake. Not again. Bloody interfering mutt!

"What was the noise?"

"I saw the officers banging on metal poles. These are used to vent the ground. It releases the scent of death from the depths of the soil. I had a good chat with Sergeant Murray about this very concept."

"How interesting, Henry."

"They've not found anything."

"That's because there's nothing to find."

"Sorry, I wasn't implying…."

"I know."

"It's getting dark. Sergeant Murray stopped the search and plan to come back tomorrow. On the last day, the weather is set to change."

"In what way?"

"Bloody rain." He laughs. "Typical of the west coast."

"Phone with any other news. I can let my mother know the search is nearly over."

"Will do, Squire."

"Thanks, Henry."

I close the call.

The weather could end up in my favour, washing away any scent of death those vent poles release. Perhaps our creator is on my side after all and has sympathy for the devil. I chuckle, enjoying this devilish status. With an evil smile on my face, I rejoin the table.

"Good news?" she asks.

"Very good news."

"What?"

I tell the truth for a change. "Henry, our gardener at the cottage in Argyll called to say the search will end tomorrow. After that, we can move on from this nonsense."

She squeezes my hand. "That's fantastic." We both look over at Inspector Canmore who watches our every move. "He looks pissed off."

"Who cares, Kristina. Let's get tonight over and done with and start afresh."

She nods in agreement.

The meal is delicious: soup, fish, lamb, dessert and coffee. I try to avoid any contact with DCI McFarlane. However, this woman starts a conversation when Kristina goes to the bathroom.

She glances at my name tag. "Mr Scott?"

"Yes."

"I don't recognise you from the task force."

"I'm a loose end."

She laughs.

"I came here with Dr Cooper. She's a criminologist and works as a profiler for the Metropolitan Police and Police Scotland."

"What an interesting job."

"Kristina helped solve the Annabel Taylor murder."

She thinks for a moment. "Superintendent Hunter's case?"

I nod.

"At least that's one less to consider," she declares. "We're under pressure to perform, resolve and close down these old crimes."

"I hear Inspector Canmore is also working on a cold case."

"Yes, I believe it's going well so far." She stares over in his direction. "I need to catch up with him. We've not spoken since the complaint."

"What complaint?"

"From a man of God, of all people."

"Really?"

"This character had a lot to say about Inspector Canmore."

How hilarious. "What?"

"That's confidential information."

"Spoilsport!"

"Do you know each other?"

"Yes, we're very good friends."

"Ask him later."

I laugh. "Absolutely."

She chuckles.

"Good luck with the case."

"Thanks."

Our conversation continues.

"What do you do?"

"Advertising, investments, dodgy deals, self-made millionaire."

"You're funny."

"I try my best."

She looks at the time. "I have to leave. Busy day tomorrow. It was nice to meet you." She shakes my hand. "Goodbye, Mr Scott."

"Goodbye."

DCI McFarlane touches the hand of a serial killer. This action sends my senses into overdrive. I take in a deep breath, lose myself in my own perverse imagination, fantasising about that special moment.

"Are you ready to go, Jayden?"

"What? Yes."

As the crowds of people leave the dining room, we all congregate at the cloakroom, chat, waiting in line for our coats. Inspector Canmore is ahead in the queue. *I can't miss his execution and need to stay close. I've dreamed of this moment on many occasions.* I take hold of Kristina's hand, making sure we proceed to the front. We end up next to him as he hands over the ticket. He looks over at Kristina, ignoring my presence.

"Dr Cooper, I'm sorry about earlier."

"No problem."

"I would like to talk to you and get your expert opinion on a few matters. I promise, I'll back off with the accusations."

"Perhaps."

"Thank you. Have a good evening."

He puts on his coat and leaves.

"Why did you agree?" I ask.

"To avoid another scene."

"Clever girl."

We get our coats and head out into the foyer. It is busy. I see Inspector Canmore through the sea of bodies, and then, lose sight of him. I hold on to her hand and manoeuvre through the crowd. Superintendent Hunter is next to Kristina, both jostling for space. In anticipation, my nervous excitement is evident, the clammy secretion transforming into beads of sweat on my forehead and upper lip, pulse racing, dry mouth.

We walk through the doors.

At last, the cold air hits my face. I shiver due to the interaction of the heat from my nervous sweat and low temperature outside. The pressure is almost unbearable. I take in a deep breath. And watch his every move. Inspector Canmore stops on the stairs to answer his phone as people bypass his position. Now is the time. I stare out into the night and wonder about the hiding place of Shoot To Kill, pointing the gun at his target. The front of the hotel swathes in hazy light. It is almost ethereal. The moments tick by in unison with the beat of my heart.

Just then, everything happens in slow motion.

We walk down the steps.

Kristina is in the middle. Marcus Hunter stands to her right. I am on the left. We approach Inspector Canmore. He moves the phone from the side of his face to body level to disconnect the call, loses his grip, knees buckle as he bends down to catch the device. It is enough of a gap. As he clutches it in his hands, Superintendent Hunter is behind him and takes a bullet straight to the head.

The blood spatters.

I stare at Kristina.

She touches the specks of red liquid on her face.

And looks down, screaming at the sight.

Marcus Hunter drops to the ground.

Inspector Canmore shouts, "Get down!"

Panic ensues.

Some people follow his orders, others flee the scene in all different directions. I pull Kristina down next to Marcus Hunter's body on the steps. She shakes, uncontrollably.

"We're going to die, Jayden."

"No, we're not."

"I love you," she declares.

"I love you, too, Kristina."

"Please, God. Don't let us die."

I dare to look up.

People are still in a crouching position except for Inspector Canmore. He stands on the stairs, staring up at the buildings across the street. *Do it now, Shoot To Kill. End this bastard's life. PLEASE.*

I wait.

It never comes.

The moment passes.

Sirens wail in the distance, becoming louder and louder with each moment. The area is soon swarming with police and ambulance. It is too late. Marcus Hunter is dead. An unfortunate victim in a deadly game of cat and mouse. Once it is safe, I take Kristina out of harm's reach and watch from the sidelines. An officer takes our statement.

"We need to leave. There's nothing more we can do," I declare.

"Wait here."

Kristina lets go of my hand.

I follow.

She walks towards the crime scene. "Inspector Canmore!"

He turns around.

"I'm sorry for your loss."

I lurk in the background.

Canmore leans over the tape and whispers in her ear.

Kristina shakes her head.

He storms off.

I grasp hold of her arm. "What did he say?"

"He said: "Tell him I know that bullet killed the wrong man." With a nervous gesture, she twirls the diamond ring on her finger. "I take it he means you."

"I've fucking had enough of this bullshit."

I turn to leave.

"Don't go." Tears trickle down her cheeks, diluting the specks of blood, drip, drip, drip, onto her white dress. It stains her innocence. My beautiful criminologist is a victim of beauty. I wipe away the blood-stained tears leaving a trail of streak marks across her face and say, "We're unbreakable."

I hail a taxi.

Kristina goes into shock.

In a trance-like state, she lays her head on my shoulder all the way home with a blank stare on her face. I grip her arm and help Kristina up to the apartment. There is no need to explain as the concierge is on a break. Once inside, I slip off her coat, bend down and remove her shoes, take hold of her hand and lead the way to the bathroom. I need to consume this distraught image of beauty. I put on the shower and dispose of her dress. She unclips her bra and steps out of her underwear as I pull them down over her legs.

My erection is solid.

I take off my clothes.

We stand under the water. I wipe away the last remnants of blood from my lover's face and wash her hair. This sexual ritual is even more stimulating than a night with Koko Kanu or the beautiful Italian escort, Caterina.

"Are you okay?"

She nods.

"You're in shock."

"It all happened so quick."

"Poor man. Such a tragedy."

I wrap my arms around her torso, pulling her close.

I wait for her to react.

She complies.

I take full advantage of her vulnerability. My imagination goes into overdrive as I enter her body: the kill, Hunter's dead body, the red spatter, her face, the blood-stained tears dripping onto her white dress, our desire, my victim of beauty. I never want it to end, to relish in this euphoric pleasure for the rest of our lives, drowning in a sea of unimaginable deadly lust.

9

BANDS OF GOLD

"Gold is the corpse of value."
(Neal Stephenson)

My eyes open.

The next morning, I look over and Jayden is fast asleep. The pain in my head is severe, banging away at my forehead, travelling down the back of my neck. I press my fingers and massage the top of my brow. I am living in a permanent nightmare. Since I met Jayden Edward Scott at my keynote speech, the last four months of my life has gone from one drama to another. Who do I believe? Inspector Canmore or Jayden Scott? Was that bullet meant for him and not Marcus Hunter? Either way, this may not end well. Inspector Canmore is obsessive, and Jayden Scott is either a brilliant sociopathic liar, or he is telling the truth.

No wonder my headache is so bad.

I pull the sheet over my face to block out the light and drift off to sleep. Sometime later, I awake to his hand caressing my skin. He spoons into my back, wanting more, pressing his body into mine.

"Good morning, Kristina."

"I have a sore head, Jayden."

He stops.

"Can you find some headache tablets?"

"Of course," he says, getting out of bed.

I laugh. "You seem to have a constant erection."

"That's because I love your body."

"I need that medication first."

Jayden grabs a pair of joggers and hops forward. He puts in each leg as he makes his way to the bedroom door. "I'll be back in a minute."

I hear him in the kitchen, the noise, unbearable.

"I'm making coffee. Do you want one?"

"Can I have peppermint tea? Sweeten it with honey."

"Okay."

Several minutes pass and he appears with a glass of fizzy water. "I only have soluble tablets."

"I don't care as long as it gets rid of this headache." I gulp down the contents and hand back the tumbler. "Thanks."

I lay my head down on the pillow, close my eyes, waiting for the pain to subside. Ten minutes later he returns and puts my cup of tea down on the unit by the bed.

"Sit up." He plumps up the pillows and rests my head on the soft surface. "Better?"

"Yes."

I reach over and get the herbal tea and breathe in the fresh smell of mint and honey before blowing on the hot liquid to cool it down. I take a small sip. "Beautiful."

"How's your headache?"

I wrinkle my forehead. "Slightly better."

"Good."

We sit in bed, silent, not saying a word for a while.

He is the first to speak.

"What a night!"

"I still can't comprehend the situation, Jayden."

"Who on earth would want to shoot Marcus Hunter?"

"I don't know. I'm trying to remember the exact details. It's all a blur in my mind."

"Me too."

"Do you think Inspector Canmore is insane? He implied the bullet was meant for him and that you're involved."

"Speculation from a madman. Why would I do that anyway? We have our differences because he's obsessed with my life. However, I would never plan to kill anyone. Now that's insane."

She nods.

"We need to get away for a while. He won't find anything in Argyll. Perhaps that's tipping him over the edge."

"Maybe you're right."

"His conduct at The Charity Ball was out of order."

"This is true."

"I don't want to talk about him anymore, Kristina. It's tedious."

"Shall we watch the news for an update on Marcus Hunter?"

"Not now. It's still too raw."

"Later?"

"Okay. Finish your tea."

"Thanks, Jayden."

"For what?"

"Dealing with this so well. I do think about Inspector Canmore's accusations, but then you appear normal when we're together. I can only surmise he's the mad one."

He laughs. "I am normal, Dr Cooper."

"No, you're not. You have an abnormal sex drive."

He bursts out laughing.

Jayden slips under the covers at the bottom of the bed and pulls on my legs until I disappear and reappear into his embrace. He is a considerate lover, seeking satisfaction from my pleasure. We make love on and off until late afternoon and fall asleep. The sound of his ringtone wakes us both up.

He groans.

I see him fumble for his phone on the side table.

"Hello."

Lip synching, he says, "Our gardener, Henry."

"Turn on the speaker," I whisper.

He presses the button.

"Hey, Squire. The police are still in the forest. There's nothing more to report."

"That's no surprise."

"It's been raining all day. They're going around in circles."

"Leave them alone, Henry."

"I will. How's your mother?"

"She's fine. I plan to visit her tomorrow."

"Send Carolyn my best wishes for a speedy recovery."

"Of course. Thanks for your help."

"Enjoy the rest of your day, Squire."

Jayden ends the call.

"That search is a bloody nonsense. I'm not even going to comment," he declares. "Enough is enough."

"I agree. I look forward to seeing your mother and Charles tomorrow. It is peaceful when we go home."

"We can set off early in the morning if you want?"

"Great."

He looks at the time. "It's four o'clock. Are you hungry?"

"Starving."

"I'll get us some food. What do you fancy?"

"You choose."

"There's a small supermarket at the start of Leith. I want to walk. I need some fresh air."

"Take your time, Jayden. There's no rush."

I watch as he dresses in casual clothes, sweatshirt, running pants, trainers and a black baseball cap. Despite all the false accusations, I am so lucky to have him in my life. I realise now he would never lie. Jayden Edward Scott, my childhood friend and lover is charming, funny, romantic, handsome, protective, and everything I want and more. We can get through this together. I stare at the diamond ring. Our bond is unbreakable.

"I've never seen you dress like that before?"

"It's my day off, hence the outfit."

"It looks comfortable."

"I truly feel at home in these clothes."

"Come over here."

He flops down on the bed.

I pull off his hat and give him a smouldering kiss.

"Let's continue later, Dr Cooper."

I laugh. "Get going!"

He smooths out his clothes and puts on the cap.

"I do love you."

He winks and rolls his eyes.

Jayden leaves the flat. I think about his unusual choice of attire. It appears familiar? I slip on his old t-shirt and some underwear. I turn on the television in the bedroom and listen to the report on Marcus Hunter. The tape cordons off the crime scene and forensic specialists in white coveralls and masks examine the area across the street. The camera zooms up to an empty building and potential hiding place of the killer. As the news coverage continues, I take a peek in his top drawer. Socks! I proceed to the closet and run my fingers over the merino wool suits, smell his shirts, and breathe in his distinct scent. There is a protrusion in one of his pockets. I put my hand inside and lift out the object. It is the box where he hid my diamond ring. I shake it and there is still something there. Did he buy another gift?

"It must be a surprise," I mumble to myself.

I replace it and continue to watch the television.

Several minutes later, curious, I rush to the closet and retrieve the box. *Take a look!* With excitement, I open the lid, staring at the contents. I empty the jewellery onto the bed and count out six rings of all different shapes and sizes. There is also a silver skull and crossbones keyring. I study each in more detail and pick up the gold band which looks like a wedding ring, looking at the distinct etchings on the surface. I am about to put it back down and notice the engravement and the name of Edward Scott inside.

"His father's ring," I say out loud.

I drop it on the cover.

Just then, I remember the blurry image of the man dressed in black with the baseball cap in the café on the CCTV footage for the Annabel Taylor murder.

My mouth is dry.

I try to swallow.

And shake my head trying to comprehend the situation.

I also recall snippets of conversation with Inspector Canmore:

"I know this is awkward because of your involvement with Jayden Scott. I'll get straight to the point. I think he killed his father, Annabel Taylor and Stewart Bailey."

"It's the rings."

"I found his father's wedding band in the hallway of his family home seven years ago. And now, Annabel Taylor's ring turns up in Stewart Bailey's pocket."

"You're involved with the wrong man and could be in mortal danger because of the Taylor profile. Be careful."

"Someone burgled my flat. I suspect Mr Scott planned the robbery. Not directly, mind you. Two of the missing items were his father's gold band and Annabel Taylor's ring."

My face turns pale.

I focus on the diamond ring. It must belong to Annabel Taylor. My stomach churns. I caught him the other day obsessing over these tokens of death. These are keepsakes of a psychotic serial killer. The lies, betrayal, denial, and more lies. My ring? Where did it come from? I shout at the top of my voice, "You're a fucking lying bastard!"

My gut lurches.

I run to the bathroom and just get there on time, convulsing, again and again, ridding myself of his lies. I feel dirty, the scent of his touch on mine, the stench of a devious killer. Tears flow down my cheeks. I become almost hysterical, leaning on the toilet for support, limp body on bended knees, muttering to myself in a delirious state.

Time is timeless.

Until reality bites.

I come to my senses.

"I need to get out of here… NOW!"

My survival instinct is on high alert albeit one of confusion. I run to the bedroom, grab the rings off the bed and put them in the box. I return the keepsakes to his jacket pocket. *What am I doing? This is evidence.* As I take the container back out, my fingertips brush across another object. I stare at the mobile phone, switch it on, waiting for the display screen and click on the messages. *I don't have time! Do it later!* I ignore my own advice. There is a dialogue between two people called SocialMisfit and Edward Cooper. I read through the thread and drop to my knees.

Tears well up in my eyes.

Unbelievable.

I find my mobile phone, dash through to the kitchen and grab his car keys. *It's time to go.* I run out of the door and press the button on the lift. It goes down before it comes up. It might be him. I sprint towards the stairwell, bound down the stairs, and continue until I reach the basement. I stop. Which way? There is a fire exit. I burst through the doors and set off the alarm. I am at the back of the building and see the car park. I glance around the corner. All is clear. The ground hurts my bare feet. Ignoring the pain, I dash towards the Noble, point the key and hear the automatic locks before the lights appear and disappear. I throw the items on the passenger seat. Just as I am about to start the car, I see him walk into the building. I duck down, wait, praying for him to pass. I peek out of the window. The noise of the alarm stops as he enters the complex. I watch for a few moments to make sure he is truly gone. With a sigh of relief, I start up the Noble and drive onto the main road, not knowing where I am going, but keep on driving until I park at the waterfront overlooking the Firth of Forth.

The shock is all too much.

I break down, shake, crying uncontrollably for a life that was all a lie, pray for his victims and have a tremendous amount of guilt for the death of Superintendent Hunter, respect for Inspector Nicholas Canmore and devastation for his mother and Reverend Charles McIntyre.

I sit and cry, and cry, and cry.

Until there are no more tears left.

Searching the interior of the car, I notice a pack of cigarettes and lighter in the small compartment beside the gear stick. I remember my university days when I was a social smoker and light one up. I feel nauseous at first but enjoy the sensation with each inhalation and roll down the window, deciding on my next move. I pick up my phone and call Inspector Canmore. It rings out. I do it again, and again and again. There is no answer and no voicemail. I search for the station number.

I make the most important call of my life.

"Can I speak to Inspector Nicholas Canmore?"

"He's not here at the moment."

"Ask him to call Kristina Cooper? It's urgent."

"Does he have your number?"

"Yes, but I blocked him."

"Pardon?"

"Can you pass on the message?"

"Yes."

I end the call and unblock his number.

"Where do I go?"

I light another cigarette and get out of the car, laughing at my lack of clothes, oblivious of the cold. I only have on his t-shirt and a pair of knickers. I blow the smoke up into the night air. As daylight fades, I can see the new Queensferry Crossing bridge which connects Edinburgh to Fife, stare at the light reflecting off the sweeping cables, shimmering in the distance and catch sight of my diamond ring. I am more than sure he bought this when he left The Charity Ball to cover up his death-box-blunder at the flat.

I finish the cigarette and stub it out on top of a bin next to the car, get into the Noble and pick up his phone. There is nothing else apart from a few calls to the same number and the message thread between

SocialMisfit and Edward Cooper. I laugh at his alias although it is not funny. It says a lot about his sociopathic state of mind. His father's forename and my surname. Speechless, I read it again to double check my interpretation due to my confusion. There is no doubt he planned to kill Inspector Canmore. I look at the timescale of the exchange. This has been going on for months. *You're a sick bastard.* I throw it back on the seat and light another cigarette.

I drive, heading toward my destination.

Night creeps over the sky. It starts to rain, relentlessly. As I proceed towards the quieter country roads, my concentration levels rise and the headache returns, beating on the top of my skull. To make matters worse, I am not used to his car. The windscreen wipers are on full. I crawl along at a slow pace. The journey seems to last for hours, the rain, unforgiving, just like my tears.

I reach my destiny.

And drive through the quiet village.

I hear the anger of thunder, witness the flashes of lightning overhead, the rain falling with such force. I take a left turn, continue up the driveway and park the Noble. With a huge sense of relief, I get out of the car. My bare feet hit the ground. I run towards the manse and push on the handle. It does not open. Losing control, I lift the metal knocker and bang on the door like a madwoman, over and over again. I stand on the doorstep, half naked, soaking wet, wait, the tears on my face merging with the rainwater.

A key turns in the lock.

It opens.

Reverend McIntyre and Jayden's mother stare in awe.

I reach out.

He moves forward.

I collapse in his arms.

****

I wake up. It is pitch black. I breathe in the familiar scent of the old room, touch the soft covers, brush my hand over the bedspread and smell the freshness on the cotton-white nightdress. The last thing I remember is falling into the arms of Reverend Charles McIntyre on the doorstep of the manse. I am safe now, but a rush of emotion overcomes my very soul, pining for a man I despise. My whole life is a mess. Jayden Scott is a liar. The worst kind of predator: charming, charismatic, romantic, deadly. Not unlike his description of Ted Bundy at my keynote speech. I am such a fool. I remove the blankets and get out of bed. The carpet caresses the bottom of my sore feet. I limp towards the window, take hold of the drapes and pull open each in turn. I stagger back as the burst of morning sunlight enters the bedroom. *At least it has stopped raining.* I peer out. The Noble is in the driveway. Shaking, my hands reach up to my forehead in a gesture of disbelief at my situation. "Why?" I mumble. "Why, why, why?"

I refuse to torture my mind with such questions. It is not the right time. Instead, I search around the room for my mobile, but no, it is not here. *It must be in the Noble.* I walk towards the bedroom door, turn the handle and make my way down the wooden staircase, look left, then right, there is nobody there. I spot a pair of wellingtons at the front entrance, slip my feet into each boot and chuckle at the sight. A white cotton nightdress and green boots. Disgustingly charming. I leave the house and proceed to the car. The key is still in the ignition. My phone, his mobile and the box of rings, wait, in the same place to scrutinise in more detail.

I sit down and close the door, press the button to unwind the window and light a cigarette, blowing out a small plume of smoke. I run my fingers over the interior, touching parts of my psychotic lover's life. When I am ready, I pick up my phone. It is seven o'clock in the morning. There are six missed calls, four texts and two voicemails: one from Jayden Scott and the other from Inspector Nicholas Canmore. With nervous excitement, I take another draw of my cigarette and read the messages from Jayden first.

Where are you?

What's going on in that beautiful mind? You need to come home, Kristina. I want back my box of rings. They mean as much as you do. And, you're mine. I will hunt you down. Remember, we're unbreakable.

I shiver, stare at the diamond ring on my finger and continue.

Where have you gone?

I'm coming to get you.

I click on the voicemail and put on the speaker, lay it on the dashboard and listen, smoking my cigarette.

Dr Cooper, this is Inspector Nicholas Canmore. Are you okay? Please call back at your convenience. We must talk.

I will call Inspector Canmore soon. He should be up first thing on a Monday morning dealing with the death of Superintendent Hunter and the search in Argyll. I need to speak to him before I talk to Charles and Carolyn. They must be sick with worry. What do I say? "Sorry, your son is a serial killer." I stretch the muscles in my shoulders to release the tension, bend my head forward and turn from left to right, right to left.

The second message plays.

If you go to the police, I will kill you.

The tone in his voice is beyond sinister.

I try to control the nausea and put out the cigarette.

"What is my next move?" I ask myself.

I pick up the phone and press the call button.

It rings out.

But not quite.

He yawns. "Dr Cooper. You're up early. How can I help?"

I am lost for words.

"Hello."

Silence.

"Hello," he repeats. "Are you there?"

"I'm here, Inspector Canmore."

"Is something wrong?"

"I drove to Reverend McIntyre's home last night."

"And...?"

"I came alone."

"Where is Mr Scott?"

"I don't know."

"What's happened?"

His prompt is enough.

"I found his box of rings," I blurt out. "Jayden arranged your murder. His name is SocialMisfit. Shoot To Kill. Something must have gone wrong because Superintendent Hunter died. The Noble. I stole his car. Edward Cooper..."

"Slow down. I'm confused."

I begin to cry.

More alert, he says, "Calm down and start again."

I continue. "You were right. Jayden Scott is a psychotic serial killer. He murdered so many people. I found the box of rings."

"How many?"

"Six and a silver skull and crossbones keyring."

He goes silent.

"What's wrong?"

"Edward Cooper, Annabel Taylor, Raymond Cartwright, Jake Driscoe, Martin Harris, Luiz Rodriguez and Stewart Bailey but he had no time to retrieve that keepsake and took the key to the fire escape."

"This is insane."

He interrupts. "Put those keepsakes in a safe place. Stay right there. I'm coming to see you."

I put the box of rings and mobile into my nightdress pocket. "Thanks."

"I'll be with you before ten."

I stop crying and pull myself together.

"Have you said anything to Charles and Carolyn?"

"Not yet."

"Don't. Wait until I arrive."

"Okay."

He hangs up the phone.

I replay Jayden's message over and over again.

If you go to the police, I will kill you. If you go to the police, I will kill you. If you go to the police, I will kill you. If you go to the police, I will kill you. If you go to the police, I will kill you.

I have done what he said not to do and called his nemesis. *I'm not scared of you, Jayden Scott.* With a newfound strength of courage, I light another cigarette and call his mobile.

He answers straight away. "Hello, Kristina."

"Jayden..."

He shouts. "Where are you?"

"I can't tell you."

"I'll hunt you down. I want you back and my box of rings. I don't give a shit about anything else."

"You're delusional," I say, blowing out a plume of smoke.

"Are you smoking?"

"One of your cigarettes."

He sighs. "Come home, Kristina. We can work it out."

"Are you insane? I just found out my partner is a serial killer?"

"This is true."

Anger wells up inside. "All the fucking lies, Jayden. Why?"

"Because I love you."

"What a lunatic. And you have the audacity to use an Edward Cooper pseudonym."

He laughs.

"It's not funny."

"Hilarious."

"Is that your father and Annabel Taylor's rings in your box?"

"Yes, I have no need to lie anymore."

"I'm such a bloody idiot."

"But a beautiful one."

"Did you kill Stewart Bailey?"

"Yes."

"What about the other tokens of death?"

"You must work that out, Dr Cooper."

"You're a smug bastard." I play my trump card. "I called Inspector Canmore. I'm meeting up with him soon to unravel your web of lies."

"You did what?" He laughs. "Don't phone again."

And disconnects the call.

My confidence dissipates at that moment.

What have I done?

Just then, I hear a noise on the gravel.

It is the Reverend.

I stub out the cigarette and get out of the car.

"What on earth are you doing out here?"

"I needed to check my messages."

"What's happened, Kristina?"

"I can't say, Charles. Inspector Canmore is on his way. I need to speak to him first."

"What's going on?" he bellows.

"It's Jayden…"

He looks back at the house. "Let's go to the church," he says, taking hold of my arm. "I don't want to disturb Carolyn. She's been up all night worried about you."

We approach the front entrance.

I stop.

"I can't tell you, Charles. It will break your heart."

"I already know, Kristina."

"What?"

He tugs on my hand as we walk up the aisle and stops at the altar. "Sit down."

I obey his command. "Know what?" I say in disbelief.

"I witnessed his confession at New Year when I came down to the church. He spoke to *my* God asking for redemption."

"For what? Are we talking about the same thing?"

"He killed his own father."

I put my hands on my face. "Charles, there's more…"

"What do you mean?"

"He's murdered at least seven people."

The Reverend staggers back, banging into the pulpit and holds onto the bannister. He is in shock, ashen white, trembling, mouth agape before coming to his senses. "Hold on a minute," he bellows. "What proof do you have to make such an allegation?"

"It's a long story, Charles. Can we wait until Inspector Canmore arrives?"

"NO! NOW!"

I tell him everything that happened over the last four months: my keynote speech, Jayden's unexpected arrival at my hotel, Inspector Canmore's obsessive allegations about his father, Annabel Taylor, Stewart Bailey, the search in Argyll over the weekend, the box of rings, his second phone, SocialMisfit, Edward Cooper, his foiled plan to kill Inspector Canmore, the death of Superintendent Hunter and messages he sent this morning but not the call I made.

That was stupid.

I take the box out of my pocket and open the lid.

He looks inside and takes out Edward Scott's wedding band. "Carolyn has one with the same engraving."

He replaces the ring.

I snap it shut.

"I'm sorry, Charles. This must be such a shock."

"That's an understatement. Does Jayden know where you are? You're in mortal danger."

"No."

He drops to his knees and looks up at the cross. "This is my responsibility, Lord." He turns in my direction, his face flush, eyes welling up with tears. "I've known since New Year. Only about his father. I chose to support him when I should have gone to the police. What a bloody fool."

I get up and lay a hand on his shoulder. "It's not your fault, Charles."

"Yes, it is mine."

"No, it's not."

"Why did I not say anything?"

"Because Jayden Scott is a master manipulator."

"We both realise that now. He buried his father near the cottage in Argyll."

"You need to tell Inspector Canmore."

He nods. "This will destroy Carolyn and ruin my reputation."

"It will destroy us all."

I sit down next to him and we wrap our arms around each other, sitting on the floor of the church, cry, pray, trying to console one another.

Sometime later, the Reverend breaks the silence.

"No wonder you were in such a state last night."

"I remember nothing after I collapsed at your front door."

"I took you upstairs and Carolyn put you to bed. She stayed with you most of the night and never slept until the early hours of the morning."

"Thank you, Charles."

He squeezes my hand.

"What do we do now?" I ask.

"We both need to speak to Inspector Canmore. What time does he arrive?"

"About ten o'clock."

He looks at his watch. "It's nine thirty."

"Let's go back to the house and get ready." He chuckles. "Nice outfit, Kristina."

I smirk.

We look at each other and burst out giggling, unable to stop, finding this one of the most amusing moments of our lives. The more he snorts, the more I laugh and the more I laugh, the more he finds it hilarious. Tears stream down our faces, a mixture of shock, trauma, grief, disbelief at our ridiculous situation as we sit on the floor laughing about my attire.

The church doors open.

I slip the box of rings into the pocket of the nightdress.

"What's so funny?" she declares, staring in wonder.

We get up off the floor and brush down our clothes.

"Just sharing a funny moment, my dear," says the Reverend.

She walks up the aisle. "Are you better today, Kristina? I've been worried about you."

"Much better, Mrs Scott."

She corrects my mistake. "Stewart. Remember, I changed back to my maiden name."

"Sorry, Carolyn."

She smiles. "Glad to see you up and about. Jayden called. He's concerned about your state of mind. I told him you're here."

"You did what?" yells the Reverend.

I notice the shock in her wide eyes at his reaction.

"It's okay, Charles," I insist.

"Why are you shouting?" she declares. "My son cares about his girlfriend."

His face reddens.

I take hold of his arm and make up a lie. "I'll call Jayden later and talk to him."

"Thank you, Kristina," says Carolyn, staring at the Reverend.

"Let's go back to the house," he announces.

We leave the church, walk up the hill towards the manse and hear a car coming up the driveway. We stop, waiting for it to drive around the corner. Whoever is in the vehicle parks next to the Noble.

"It must be Jayden," declares Carolyn, quickening her pace.

We proceed with caution.

Someone gets out of the car.

"What are you doing here, Inspector Canmore?" asks Carolyn.

He stares in our direction. The Reverend shakes his head, waiting, pleading with a lingering look not to say anything about her son.

"I have to talk to Dr Cooper about an important case, Mrs Scott."

****

I leave them in the vestibule and rush upstairs to change my clothes, kick off the wellington boots, place the box of rings and mobile phones on top of the dressing table, pull the nightdress over my head and realise I have nothing else to wear. I sit on the edge of the bed, wondering how my life is so incredulously insane in such a short period of time. I wrap the cover around my naked body, alone, sad, staring into empty space, in need of support. I want to call my parents but do not have the energy to face my mother's questions.

I decide to phone Clarissa Evans.

She answers.

"Kristina, how are you?"

"Awful."

"What's wrong, my dear?"

I start to cry, unable to speak.

"Kristina?"

"I... sorry... I've had an argument with Jayden."

"About what?"

"He's a liar."

"I had a bad feeling about that man. He made my skin crawl. It's my sixth sense. Tell me, Kristina."

"The situation is complicated. Can I ring you back in a few days? I need time to calm down."

"We could chat now if you want?"

"I must go and talk to a police officer."

"The police? What's happened?"

"Jayden... he... he's a murderer."

"What!?"

I blurt out. "Not just one person. He's killed so many people, Clarissa."

She gasps. "Are you sure?"

"Yes. I know this sounds insane. He's…. he's a serial killer."

"I'm not sure what to say?"

I start to cry.

"I did try and speak to you about him when we met for lunch. You refused to listen and shut down our conversation."

"I know."

"My goodness. This is unbelievable. How awful for you, my dear. Where are you now? Are you safe?"

"Yes."

"What can I do to help?"

"I'll need your support when I come home."

"Of course. I'll always be here for you, Kristina."

"I need to go now."

"Call anytime."

I nod my head.

"I love you like my own daughter."

"Thank you."

"Goodbye, my darling."

She disconnects the line.

I wipe away the tears with the back of my hand.

And gaze around the room, noticing some clothes on the chair. I rifle through the pile, find an old sweater and a pair of trousers. The bottom half is too big. I have no choice. *Did Carolyn leave them last night? Charity donations, perhaps?* Mrs Scott is a lovely person. I fear her reaction when she finds out about her only son. Poor woman. She deserves better. I tuck the box of rings and Jayden's mobile phone into the deep recess of the front pockets.

I make my way downstairs. Reverend McIntyre and Inspector Canmore wait in the sitting room and Carolyn is in the kitchen making refreshments. They both stare in pity as I enter the room.

"Are you okay?" asks Inspector Canmore.

"No. I have no choice but to continue."

"You're a brave lady, Dr Cooper."

I shake my head. "I'm an idiot."

"Likewise," announces the Reverend.

"It's a good idea not to dwell on the past and work together to find that psychopath," says Inspector Canmore.

We nod in agreement.

Carolyn enters the room with a tray. "Here's the tea," she

declares. "How can we help you, Inspector Canmore?"

"No offence. This is a private matter between me and Dr Cooper."

She looks at him with anger.

The Reverend interrupts. "Let's leave them alone, Carolyn. Besides, you have a meeting about the Spring Fair this morning."

She agrees.

They both leave the room.

We let out a huge sigh of relief.

"Charles said you told him everything. Not his mother."

"That's right. We agreed to speak to her after our talk. I'm not sure when? She needs to know the truth. The Reverend will deal with the fallout."

"Poor man."

"Please stop treating us with such pity, Inspector Canmore."

"Sorry."

I roll my eyes.

He changes his tone and gets down to business. I tell him everything and hand over the box of rings as well as Jayden's mobile phone. He appears in shock as he reads the messages between SocialMisfit and Edward Cooper, the plan to murder him after The Charity Ball, Shoot To Kill, the robbery at his house, surveillance, fake I.D., meetings at Leith Docks to pick up the documents and the untimely death of his colleague.

"Jayden Scott planned my murder at The Charity Ball for a while," he says in disbelief. "At least we know his new name. However, I suspect he'll get another alias."

"I never even suspected he led a double life."

"He's a clever bastard. And there are his dealings with SocialMisfit."

"Who is this man?"

"A Dark Web operator from Nottingham. Jayden Scott met up with him before he returned to see you in Lincoln on his last visit. One of my connections, Larry Parker, followed him from London to Nottingham and from there to Lincoln and back to Edinburgh."

"What?"

"I'm sorry. It's the truth." He shudders. "I got a chilling voice message from Sergeant Aitken from Nottingham Police on Friday night about SocialMisfit saying he was a dangerous individual. I never got the information until Sunday morning. As a result, Superintendent Hunter died for no reason. If only I had received the call."

Now it is my turn to pity him. "Don't go there," I say. "Nobody could predict this scenario."

"Perhaps. I knew something was not right."

"His death is not your fault."

"But..."

"Stop torturing yourself. We've all made mistakes."

He puts the evidence into plastic bags and snaps out of his guilt-ridden mood. "Thank you very much for retrieving the phone and the box of rings. This is the first piece of physical evidence to connect Jayden Scott to possibly seven murders, Superintendent Hunter's death and his ever expanding web of lies."

I nod. "Do you have any further proof, Inspector Canmore?"

He puts a briefcase on the coffee table and clicks it open.

I wait in anticipation.

He hands over some photographs. "The search in Argyll pinpoints a half-mile radius we need to excavate."

"His father's body?"

"Yes."

"Reverend McIntyre mentioned Jayden's confession at New Year. Edward Scott is near the cottage, somewhere. It's not an easy task. I spoke to my superior officer, DCI McFarlane, on my way here. She agreed to provide the resources to complete a thorough search. Sergeant Murray will conduct another one at the weekend. He's back in Edinburgh just now."

"What about the Reverend for withholding evidence?"

"I'm not sure, Dr Cooper. Let's focus on the facts at the moment. You're both victims of his manipulative behaviour."

His words are brutal.

Are we victims?

I answer my own question.

"Please do not use that word, Inspector Canmore. We are people involved in a deadly tale of murder and revenge. Not anymore. We're not victims but survivors."

"Sorry."

"Thank you. What else?"

"My colleague, Constable Peters, pieced together the list of casualties. She tracked down another man in New York called Martin Harris and Luiz Rodriguez from Brazil with the same modus operandi as Annabel Taylor."

"A slit to the throat?"

"Yes."

"My goodness."

"We're not sure of Jayden Scott's involvement with two other men, Raymond Cartwright and Jake Driscoe. Someone shot and burned the bodies in a hangar near Dover. It could be about revenge. Vigilante driven, perhaps. They were both nasty individuals."

"I'll review the case and assess whether this links to his modus operandi. Serial murderers do change the way they kill in certain situations. We can determine his motive for the crime rather than the way the people died. If there's a connection, I'll find the link."

"Thank you."

"Do you think he killed his father in the same manner as Annabel Taylor and the two men in New York and Brasilia?"

"There's no doubt."

He hands over more photographs. "Forensics revealed the same serration on the knife edge matches the cuts on the throats of Annabel Taylor, Martin Harris and Luiz Rodriguez."

I stare at the images. "So, there's a weapon?"

"Yes."

"Interesting ritual. I wonder where he keeps the blade?"

"Not sure? Jayden Scott is a devious killer, Dr Cooper."

I inhale and exhale. "What now?"

"I sent a team of police officers to his flat this morning after your call. He's not there. We found no further evidence of his crimes. He must have the murder weapon in his possession."

My hand reaches to my throat. "Very dangerous."

"I don't suspect he'll come to the manse, Dr Cooper."

"I can only remain here for so long. Will you pick up my belongings? I ran out of his flat without any clothes. I'll get them when I return to Edinburgh."

"Yes, when are you coming back?"

"I'm not sure. I need to stay here for a few days and support Charles with Carolyn. It will break her heart."

"Horrendous task. Police Scotland have trained counsellors to help with these situations."

"We need to deal with this ourselves."

"Good luck."

"Inspector Canmore, one more thing."

"Yes?"

"I phoned Jayden this morning."

"You did what?"

"He knows I arranged to meet you."

"That's not good."

"It was stupid.

"Does he know you're at the manse?"

"No. Yes. I never told him. Jayden called the house. Carolyn mentioned I was here."

He groans.

"Sorry."

"What's done is done. I'll organise round-the-clock surveillance on the house until you return to Edinburgh."

I take hold of his hand.

He smiles. "We'll keep you safe, Dr Cooper."

"Thank you very much."

"I need to get back to the station. There's a lot to do. It's necessary to go public with the information. You have to tell Carolyn today."

"We will."

"Stay in touch by phone. I'll sort the security before the end of the day."

"Thank you, again."

"My pleasure."

"I want to help with the investigation when I return to Edinburgh. Not just the profile."

"I could do with your assistance, Dr Cooper. We need to track him down and you know more about this lunatic than anyone."

I feel hurt by his 'lunatic' remark. The last twelve hours seem like a foggy haze of events and my mind is still to digest all this new information about the man I love—loved, still love but hate, want yet despise. I see Inspector Canmore to the front entrance and watch him leave down the driveway, close the door and turn the key in the lock. Just then, Charles shouts from the kitchen, "Kristina!"

I enter the room.

He walks forward. "Are you okay?"

"Yes. No. I'm not sure. It's all too much."

He wraps a protective arm around my shoulders. "What did you say?"

"I told Inspector Canmore everything. The search in Argyll will resume next week. The police linked him to several other victims. He has left his flat in Edinburgh. I'll help with the case when I return in a few days." I struggle to continue. "He's... Jayden is on the run, Charles."

"He knows you're at my home, Kristina."

"Inspector Canmore is going to arrange 24-hour surveillance on the house by the end of the day."

"Thank God! However, we must keep all the doors and windows locked, just in case."

"Agreed. Where's Carolyn?"

"She went away to her meeting about the Spring Fair."

"We need to tell her today, Charles."

He nods in agreement. "I let Carolyn leave to get her out of the way. I will go and meet her to make sure she gets home safe and sound."

"Good idea."

"I'll speak to her when we return. I would appreciate your help over the next few days." He sighs. "After that, I have to deal with the aftermath on my own."

"Inspector Canmore said there are professional counsellors in the police force who can also offer assistance."

"I think she might need that help in the long run, Kristina."

"We will *all* need further support."

He nods, appreciating the comment.

"Thank you. You're always a pillar of strength, Charles."

"I'm a man of God. There's no other way to behave. No matter the severity of the situation. That is the purpose of my life."

I nod in agreement.

"You must be exhausted, Kristina." He puts some white powder in a glass and fills it up with water. "It's a sleeping aid. You need to rest."

I hesitate, then gulp down the contents.

I squeeze his hand and head upstairs.

Exhaustion takes hold of my mind and body.

I throw off the over-sized clothes.
Drowsy, I fall asleep.

10

ENTRAPMENT

"It's my will. There's no other way."
(Salison Jose das Gracas)

I lurk in the grounds of the manse, watching the events unfold. And think back over the last twenty-four hours in the life of a serial killer. The shock. Treachery. Betrayal. By the woman I love. I returned home, dumped the bags of shopping in the kitchen and heard music on the television in the bedroom.

"...And every time, every time you go. It's like a knife, that cuts right through my soul. Only love can hurt like this..."

I looked forward to the night with Kristina and our trip to visit Reverend McIntyre and my mother to get away from the memories of the previous evening at The Charity Ball. Although it did not go to plan, I knew there would be another time and place to take revenge on my nemesis. I marched towards the bedroom and burst through the door with a smile on my face.
The room was empty.
"Kristina!"
Silence apart from the music.
"Where are you?"
Nothing but the melody.
"...Only love can hurt like this. It must have been a deadly kiss..."
I searched the whole flat in a delirious state, knowing something was wrong. I went back into the bedroom and noticed her bags, clothes, shoes and makeup. Everything was still there. I called her mobile number. No response from within the apartment. Just then, my eyes focused on the closet door. Ajar. I raced towards the

cupboard and checked the suit for my box of rings and illegitimate phone.

They were gone.

Kristina had taken my precious tokens and mobile with the correspondence between myself and SocialMisfit, evidence to the robbery, Shoot To Kill and my false I.D., putting an end to Edward Cooper.

In shock, I sat down on the edge of the bed.

"She's found out about my secret life," I mumbled to myself.

"...Only love can hurt like this. Your kisses burning to my skin..."

I ignored the music and got up and raced out the front door, bound down the stairs and said to Michael, "Have you seen Dr Cooper?"

"No," he replied.

"Why did the alarm go off?"

"The fire exit at the back of the building. I never saw anyone. It must be a malfunction."

I ran outside and noticed the empty space in the parking lot. Kristina had taken the Noble. *For fuck sake! Where's she gone? The police?* I had to leave the flat. With a sense of nervous excitement, I went up and packed several cases. It was time to put my plan into action.

I contacted SocialMisfit to warn him of the situation without giving away too much detail. He seemed unconcerned about the nature of his identity and said he was an elusive character with regards to the police. They would never find him. My partner in crime also apologised for the mistake with Shoot To Kill. I told him what happened with Inspector Canmore's phone on the steps of the Balmoral Hotel, creating enough of a diversion as the bullet travelled towards the target but missed by a split second and hit Superintendent Hunter.

"That was a stroke of luck for Nicholas Canmore," he declared. "I can give you back part of the payment due to our error."

"That's not necessary but I need a new identity. Edward Cooper no longer exists."

He seemed puzzled. "Why?"

"Don't ask. What a bloody nightmare."

"Who are you today?"

I laughed. "Edward Stewart. My father's first name and my mother's maiden name."

"It will be ready in a few days. No need for any payment. It's on the house. You're a good client."

"Thanks."

"We'll use the same courier but a different pick-up point."

My groin stirred, remembering her scent. "Perfect."

"Keep in touch, Edward, or whoever you are?"

I chuckled.

He disconnected the phone.

Once I recovered from the shock, I also called my solicitor to transfer both the agencies and my flat in Edinburgh and London to Richard McKenzie. The Noble was of no use anymore. However, I knew these were only materialistic possessions and did not matter. What mattered was getting Kristina Cooper back. I decided to text her once I was safely out of the vicinity. When it was time to leave, I did a last-minute check of the flat, stared around at the familiar setting with a sense of sadness, turned and left.

On leaving the elevator, I saw Michael at the reception.

"Are you going on a business trip, Mr Scott?"

"Yes."

He looked at the amount of luggage and raised an eyebrow.

"I'll be away for a while."

"You take care," he said.

"You're a good man, Michael."

"Thank you."

I took my wallet out of my jacket and handed over several hundred pounds. "Thanks for your service over the years."

He smiled. "My pleasure."

"Goodbye, Michael."

"Goodbye," Mr Scott.

I left the building.

And walked the half a mile to pick up the 4x4, paid for in a secure parking lot. I pressed on the key to open the car, placed the luggage in the back seat, checked the case of money and left. I had a few days to wait on my identification and booked into a hotel on the outskirts of Edinburgh under the name of Edward Stewart.

I settled into my new residence and turned on the television, restless, waiting on the news footage that would expose my sordid life, but it never came. *Where is Kristina?* I ordered room service: steak, salad, bread and a vintage bottle of red wine. I chuckled to myself, lifted my glass in the air and said, "Just like old times, Edward Scott." More relaxed in the safety of the hotel, I turned on my mobile phone and texted Kristina.

Where are you?

What's going on in that beautiful mind? You need to come home, Kristina. I want back my box of rings. They mean as much as you do. And, you're mine. I will hunt you down. Remember, we're unbreakable.

I waited and finished the bottle of wine. After two hours, I gave up on a reply. I ventured out onto the private balcony and lit a cigarette, drawing in a huge amount of smoke into my lungs. *Where the fuck is Kristina?* I sent another two messages.

Where have you gone?

I'm coming to get you.

Pacing back and forth, I took another drag, waiting on a reply. But again, it never came. More and more agitated, I left a voice message.

If you go to the police, I will kill you.

I got ready for bed and stared at the phone. I knew it was a dangerous move to keep it switched on. I had to wait. She could be my downfall. It was a chance I had to take. I fell asleep. The noise of the ringtone disrupted my sleep at seven o'clock in the morning.

I grabbed the mobile.

"Hello, Kristina."

"Jayden…"

"Where are you?" I shouted.

"I'm not telling you."

"I'll hunt you down. I want you back and my box of rings. I don't give a shit about anything else."

"You're delusional," she said.

I hear a long exhale.

"Are you smoking?" I asked.

"One of your cigarettes."

I sighed. "Come home, Kristina. We can work it out."

"Are you insane? I just found out my partner is a serial killer?"

"This is true."

She raised her voice. "All the fucking lies, Jayden. Why?"

"Because I love you."

"You're a lunatic. And you have the audacity to use an Edward Cooper pseudonym."

I laughed.

"It's not funny."

"Hilarious."

"Is that your father and Annabel Taylor's rings in your box?"

"Yes, I have no need to lie anymore."

"I'm such a bloody idiot."

"But a beautiful one."

"Did you kill Stewart Bailey?"

"Yes."

"And what about the other tokens of death?"

"You'll have to work that out, Dr Cooper."

"You're a smug bastard," she said in a defiant tone. "I called Inspector Canmore. I'm meeting up with him soon to unravel your web of lies."

"You did what?" I laughed. "Don't phone again."

I disconnected the call. She clearly had not spoken to the police at that time. Where was she hiding? I got up and had a shower, pondering over her defiant attitude. It fuelled my sexual desire for that woman. I tried to contain myself, but it was hard. I wanted her more than ever before. I contemplated the scenario. She was in the Noble, smoking my cigarettes, somewhere quiet, very quiet.

It took a while to work out.

I grabbed my phone and pressed the contact.

My mother answered.

"Jayden, what's going on?"

"What do you mean?"

"Kristina arrived here last night in your car with hardly any clothes on and no shoes, knocking on the door, standing in the pouring rain."

"We had an argument. Have you spoken to her yet?"

"No, she's asleep in her room."

No, she's not. I just spoke to her.

"Are you coming to get Kristina?"

Oh yes, I am. "I'll wait until she's ready to come home."

"I need to go and find Charles. We can speak to her today and ring you back."

"Thanks."

"Are you okay, Jayden?"

"Yes, it was just a stupid argument. We'll be fine."

"Thank goodness."

"Goodbye."

I disconnected the call and dismantled the mobile.

I had a quick breakfast, packed up and left the hotel, bought another phone and made my way to the manse. I called SocialMisfit to give him my new number.

"I'll be in touch soon about the other documents," he said.

"Thanks."

"I also have the rest of the information from the tail on Inspector Canmore."

"And?"

"He visited his girlfriend in a village just outside Edinburgh on the morning of The Charity Ball."

"She's not in the flat at Tollcross?"

"Nope."

"Send the address."

"I'll do that once we finish this call."

"Okay."

"Anything else I can do?"

"Not at the moment."

"Catch you, Edward Stewart."

Well, well, well, Miss Walker. That's interesting.

Several minutes later, the text message with Sally Walker's information landed in my inbox. I took a quick glance whilst driving. The remote village was less than an hour from Edinburgh. I dismissed the information and focused on the task at hand.

On the journey home, all I could think about was the reunion with Kristina, even if that meant using force. I found a hardware shop in one of the larger towns and bought rope, zip ties and silk scarves to use as a gag. How I would get her from the house, I had no idea, but

I needed to try. I parked the 4X4 in a small lane about a mile from the back of the Reverend's home to reclaim my possession.

****

And now, I lurk in the grounds of the manse in my black attire, bordering on the edge of insanity, the hunter stalking his prey. An insane fury radiates from my eyes the more I think about Kristina Cooper's betrayal. I watch the events unfold. First, the arrival and departure of Inspector Canmore. Next, my mother walks towards some unknown destination, perhaps a church meeting. And finally, Reverend McIntyre leaves the house and locks the front door behind him. The time has come. Kristina must be alone in the house. It is now or never. I watch until the Reverend is out of sight and make my way round to the back of the building. I turn and push on the handle. The door is locked. Frantically searching for another entrance, I notice several small windows at the base of the building that lead to the cellar. They are just big enough for my frame. I prise one of them open to its full tilt, crawl through the space until my arms and body point at the floor and my feet disappear through the window. I fall to the ground and take the full weight on my hands. Rolling over in agony, I wait until the pain subsides.

I have no plan.

But I am not leaving without Kristina Cooper.

I stand up and brush off the dust. The basement is dark and damp. I switch on a small torch and proceed to the cellar door. I turn the handle. It opens. I climb up the stairs towards another exit. It leads into the kitchen. I take a look around and notice the sleeping powder next to an empty glass. The house is abnormally quiet. I sneak upstairs and knock on the bedroom door. There is no answer. I knock again, listen to her groan, and then, nothing. I enter the room, lock it from the inside and put the key in my pocket. I stare at her beautiful features. She is fast asleep. I sit on the edge of the bed, pick up one arm and let it drop back down onto the covers.

I think about the sleeping powder in the kitchen and the empty glass. Perfect. At least now, I will not have to use force. This is the best-case scenario. She has made my task much easier.

The situation is intense.

I run my fingers over her face. So delicate. So beautiful. So treacherously defiant. I pull back the covers to reveal her naked body. I respond to this beauty of nature, knowing we should leave. However, the temptation is overwhelming. It is her own fault. I undress and lie down, stroking her gentle skin from head to torso with my fingertips. I notice the diamond ring on her finger. She has not taken it off yet. I interpret this action as a symbol of love and loyalty.

She stirs.

I lean forward and caress her face with my hand.

"Kristina, I love you."

"I love you but also despise you," she says in a drug-induced state.

Her arms wrap around my neck.

I kiss her soft lips, fusing to become one.

It is euphoric. I never thought I would see her again let alone touch her beautiful body. Kristina Cooper is mine. My fingers slide between her thighs, gently caressing the folds of skin. She appears lifeless and unresponsive. I own this image of beauty and enter her body, having absolute control over the situation. This fuels my uncontrollable desire until I can bear it no longer.

My heavy breathing subsides.

I stare at her innocent features.

And release, savouring every movement.

Just then, Kristina becomes conscious for a moment, flicking open her eyes, stares in disbelief before falling back into a deep sleep. She mutters away to herself, laughing at the absurdity of the situation and says, "It's only a nightmare."

I get out of bed and put on my clothes.

I hear the front door slam and the Reverend says to my mother he is going to check on Kristina. I fumble to retrieve the key from my pocket, turn the lock just on time, and hide behind the side of the wardrobe.

He enters the room and whispers, "Are you awake?"

There is no response.

"Don't worry, my sweet girl. I'm away to tell Carolyn everything about her twisted excuse of a son."

Furious, I am about to confront him but stop.

He leaves.

Tell her what? About my secret life? That I killed her husband, my father, adulterer and abuser, the mistress, Annabel Taylor or her stupid ex-partner, Stewart Bailey, take your pick between Raymond Cartwright and Jake Driscoe, putrid paedophiles or the greedy bastard, Martin Harris and wife beater, Luiz Rodriguez. My mother clearly does not know I am a cold-blooded killer. She would not have said Kristina was at the house. Carolyn will understand more than anyone, taking into consideration the vile nature of the people I murdered. However, the truth may destroy my mother. That is not my concern anymore, neither Reverend McIntyre nor Edward Scott's wife. They are all traitors. I stare at Kristina and think, *You're the biggest traitor of all.* I walk towards the bed and stare at her neck. My hand lingers over the knife in the sheath around my waist. Just then, I hear a blood-curdling shriek from downstairs. I sneak out the room and listen to the hysteria from the landing on the third floor.

"No!" she shouts. "I don't believe you."

"Calm down, Carolyn."

"No, I won't calm down," she screams at the top of her voice.

The door to the sitting room opens.

"Come back," he bellows.

"Let go of my fucking arm."

"Take control of yourself, Carolyn."

"I was a bad mother. This is all my bloody fault."

This is bad. She never swears.

I peek over the side of the bannister. She cries uncontrollably and crumples to the floor. The Reverend sits down next to my mother, cradling her in his arms. "I'm here, Carolyn. I'm here for you, my love. Your son is an evil man. We're not to blame for his actions."

She sobs like a child, the sound echoing up the stairs.

I have no remorse.

Carolyn Scott gave birth to this killer.

With the taste of disgust in my mouth, I wait for her to stop crying. Charles lifts up my mother, takes her to the second floor and closes the bedroom door. I continue to listen to her pathetic sobbing and wait until there is no sound. I let out a sigh of relief. It is time to go. I head back to the room and lift up the garments lying on the floor. I dress Kristina's limp body with the over-sized clothes but leave her mobile phone. There are no shoes. I lift her off the bed, sit her up and bend down. She flops over my left shoulder. I step towards the door and prepare to leave this life behind. I sneak down the stairs and enter the kitchen, pick up the sleeping powder, just in case I need it later, unlock the rear door, and walk through the grounds to the car hidden between two trees on an overgrown track at the back of the manse. She is heavy. A mile later, I slump her into the front seat of the 4X4, the relief, immense.

I lean against the vehicle, light a cigarette and contemplate my next move. I have no need for the gag or the zip ties, not just yet. She has to comply. I do not want to hurt the one person I love. With a sense of satisfaction she is back in my possession, I need to return to Edinburgh to pick up my new I.D. I also have some unfinished business with Inspector Canmore. Earlier, when I spoke to SocialMisfit, he sent a text with the pick-up point for my new documents and Sally Walker's details. I now have the address on my mobile phone. I will pay her a visit. A farewell present for Inspector Nicholas Canmore.

A sly grin passes across my face.

He ruined my life.

I must return the favour.

Taking the last drag of my cigarette straight into my lungs, I prepare to give up my childhood village. I will have to leave everything I own. It is time to start a new life with Kristina Cooper away from all this drama. I drive back to Edinburgh and park in a secluded spot near the rendezvous to pick up my documents the following day. Kristina is still fast asleep. I secure the car from the inside out. I did not rest well the previous night at the hotel and fall into a deep sleep.

Sometime later, in the early hours of the morning, I awake to hysterical screams and the frantic noise of the door handle. I stare over in her direction and say, "Stop it."

Kristina continues

I grab her arm with a forceful grip. "STOP!"

She freezes.

"That's better."

Kristina rubs the temples with her fingers. "What am I doing here?" she says in a state of confusion, trembling, uncontrollably.

"I came to see you at the manse."

"I dreamt…"

"That wasn't a dream."

She convulses and lifts her hand towards her mouth.

I smile.

A look of disgust passes across her face as she wraps her arms around her body. My criminologist turns and spits in my eye. "You fucking bastard."

I wipe it away.

Kristina lunges forward, clenches her fists and hits my chest.

I take hold of her hands. "Calm down."

"That is the ultimate act of violation."

"You were a willing participant and declared your love."

"This is insane."

"Totally."

"What is your plan now that you're not only a serial killer but a rapist and a kidnapper."

"We need to talk away from here. I want to explain."

"Explain what?" she screams.

"Why I did, what I do."

"Please, let me go, Jayden."

"No, remember our bond is unbreakable."

"Solid," she declares in a sarcastic tone, twirling the diamond ring.

I gaze at her hand.

"Did this belong to one of your victims?"

"Of course not. I bought that on the day of The Charity Ball."

"To cover up your faux pas with the box of rings?"

"Yes, but I wanted to buy you a gift. It cost a lot of money."

"I don't care."

"You do and that is why you're still wearing my ring."

She sighs. "What now master manipulator?"

I laugh. "I have a few things to deal with in Edinburgh. After that we're going on a trip."

"Where?"

"I'm not sure. The west coast, perhaps?"

I see her contemplate the situation.

"Did Inspector Canmore mention anything about the investigation at the cottage?"

She shakes her head.

"I know you're lying," I say, reaching for the knife.

She retracts in fear. "Sergeant Murray cordoned off an area of half a mile. The search resumes at the weekend."

"He's a clever bastard. Either way, my web of lies are now out in the open by him, you, both. There's no police there at the moment?"

"Not as far as I know."

"Then we might stop for the night and head deeper into the heart of Argyll tomorrow. We need to disappear for a while."

She changes the subject. "Can I see your knife?"

I take it out of the sheath.

"So, that's the weapon of choice."

"It's beautiful, don't you think?"

She stares at the blade, nodding in approval.

It is an intimate moment.

I move closer.

Kristina flinches back.

"Don't ever be scared. I'll never hurt you."

She relaxes.

I kiss her lips, lingering, wanting more.

She tries to resist.

My hands wander up the inside of her sweater.

"Please stop, Jayden."

"Why?"

"This is not right. You're insane."

"Sorry, it's easy to get carried away."

She forces a smile.

"I want everything to return to normal. You must behave and not try to escape. Promise?"

"Promise."

"I have to meet a few people, book somewhere remote to stay in Argyll and stock up on provisions for our trip."

"Great plan, Jayden Scott."

"Thank you, Dr Cooper."

She smirks.

"I need you to hold out your hands in front of you."

"Why?"

"Just do it, Kristina, or I will use force."

She complies.

I take the zip ties out of the compartment and tighten the plastic on her wrists. I do the same with her ankles and tie a gag over her mouth. Her eyes widen in horror. I stroke her hair and say, "It's only for a few hours. Don't struggle. It will become tighter and cut into your skin."

She nods.

I check the area. There is nobody around. I help her into the boot of the car and slam the door shut. With a sense of relief that she is out of sight, I make my way to the meeting place to collect the documents. I sit on a bench overlooking The Firth of Forth. This drop off is free. I insisted that SocialMisfit keep the money for the mix-up with Shoot To Kill. My courier arrives ten minutes later. I sense her presence from behind. The woman places the documents on the seat. I take in a deep breath and pick up the envelope.

"Nice doing business again," she declares.

I stand up and turn around.

This femme fatale is sultry in a masculine kind of way. Her dress code and short-cropped hair, messy but stylish. I enter her with my dark, piercing, eyes. She stares back, enjoys the moment, her pupils dilating due to the intensity of the situation.

"Likewise," I declare.

Without another word, she walks off, gets into a car and leaves.

My sexual desire is on high alert as I walk back to the 4X4. I think about Kristina in the back of the boot. Once we settle in a different area, we can lose ourselves in a world of intimacy. But first, I have to make the trip to the address of a certain young lady. On the way there, I pick up a bite to eat. I check the local papers. There is nothing about my crimes. Not yet, but there will be shortly. We need to leave Edinburgh as soon as possible. It does not take long to find the village. I drive past the house. There is no activity or any police cars, anywhere.

Why would there be any extra security?

Sally Walker is safe here, is she not?

"No," I reply, to my own question.

I wait.

In the meantime, I search the internet for a remote cottage in the highlands. I spot the perfect place in the middle of nowhere next to a loch. The path leads down to an old pier. I notice the reflection of the wooden structure rippling in the water. The surrounding area is full of thick woodland stretching far into the distance.

The seclusion is perfect.

I ring the number and ask to rent it for a month.

"You're in luck. At this time of year we're not busy."

"Good. I can pay in cash."

The man gives directions to his home to drop off the money and pick up the key. With a sense of excitement, I end the call. Our time there together will allow us to talk, plan our future and decide where we want to start a new life. I light a cigarette and gaze into the wing mirror, scratching the growth on my chin. I need a new image. I may as well grow a beard and might shave off my hair. I blow the smoke out of the window and notice some activity at the house, see her wander down the path, swinging a basket in her hand as she turns onto the country road.

I stub out the cigarette and leave the car.

Striding at a fast pace, I catch up with my target.

I lay my hand on Sally Walker's shoulder and swipe the knife clean across her throat. She stumbles forward, her free hand reaching for her neck, hesitates for a moment, and drops to the ground. I watch the eggs tumble out of the basket and smash, mingling with the stream of blood gushing from the wound in her neck.

I look at her with disgust.

Turn and walk away.

****

I stop in a quiet spot outside Edinburgh. The nature of the kill still fresh in my mind. What makes it even more enjoyable is the connection to Inspector Canmore. Now he will experience the devastation of life, love and loss. Fortunately, I have my woman back. The after-kill-lust is overwhelming. However, the sexual release will have to wait but the heaviness in my groin is hard to ignore. I am exhausted and need to sleep. But first, I light a cigarette, walk to the mobile van at the other end of the layby, order two coffees and return to the 4X4. I check the time. It is midday. I tap a large amount of sleeping powder into the coffee, so I do not have to worry about Kristina trying to escape when I fall asleep. I decide to let her out but not for long.

I open the boot of the car.

She squints her eyes.

I cut the ties, take off the gag, help her back into the vehicle, lock it from the inside out and put the key in my trouser pocket.

"Where did you go?"

"I had to deal with unfinished business."

"What?"

"Nothing important."

"Tell me, Jayden."

I stare at her in a threatening manner. "NO!"

She heeds my warning. "What are we going to do now?"

"I've booked us a cottage for the next month in a remote place in the highlands."

"A month? I have no clothes or possessions. This is insane."

"We have each other. That's all we need."

She has a drink of coffee.

"I'm exhausted," I declare.

She clasps hold of my hand. "Why don't we both go to sleep together and carry on with our journey later."

"Maybe."

Kristina moves closer. "I do love you, Jayden."

"I know you do."

She takes another drink and finishes the contents.

I close my eyes as she strokes my hair. The arousal is evident in my groin. I need her body to clear the sexual frustration of the kill. She allows a passionate kiss. I push the button and the seat reclines to the back of the 4X4, the tint of the windows blocking the view to the inside of the car. Kristina unzips my trousers and pulls them down over my knees. She takes off her trousers and climbs on top, my erection waiting to enter her beautiful body. As she slides down onto my shaft, the sensation is indescribable. It is a romantic moment despite our bizarre predicament. Kristina grinds into my groin, slowing down as time elapses. I feel her muscles tighten and release the killing power of a serial murderer into her body. In a state of confusion, she drapes forward and kisses my lips.

"I am so tired," she declares.

I lift Kristina off. She falls into the seat, clasping hold of an object in her hand before it drops to the ground. Her eyes close. I bend down and pick up the keys. *You're a silly woman. She planned to escape. I need to keep an eye on her every move.* I put on her trousers and replace the ties and gag, open the door and check the layby. There is one more car apart from the mobile van at the other end. I wait until the vehicle leaves and lock her up in the boot. I get back in the 4X4 and fall asleep, not having to worry about anything or anyone. I have done everything for today, and much, much, more.

Sometime later, I open my eyes. The fading sun settles behind the clouds. I note the time. It is seven o'clock. I check out the destination of the rented accommodation on the map, my finger following the single track route for miles on end. The road is too dangerous to drive at night. Therefore, I plan to stay over at our own cottage, only if it is safe and leave early in the morning. I light a cigarette and watch the sunset between the showers. A rainbow lights up the sky, the arc of colours fuse together, providing promise and hope for the future.

Before leaving busy civilisation, I stop to buy provisions, enough to last for several weeks. With bag loads of food, I return to the vehicle and rearrange my luggage in the back of the 4x4 to make room for the shopping. Despite Kristina's continual attempts to escape, I know she will accept our situation through time. At the moment, she is in shock and denial. I must shield her from the outside world, the news about my life and the recent death of Sally Walker. That might tip her over the edge. She has a volatile state of mind. I reach over and take the whisky out of the bag. I light a cigarette, open the window and drink straight from the bottle. The alcohol calms my thoughts. I people watch in the bustling car park and notice a small child with a red balloon. He laughs and lets go of the string. It floats up in the air. The father and son point up at the balloon drifting in the breeze, flying higher in the sky until it becomes a tiny speck in the distance.

I smile.

It is a precious occasion to witness.

There are no happy childhood memories with Edward Scott.

The moment passes.

I take another slug of whisky and light a cigarette. *That's enough. I must get us to our destination.* I proceed on our journey to the west coast. As twilight fades to night, the mountainous structures overlooking Glencoe come into view. I drive through the winding road towards the cottage. I stop at the top of the hill. All is dark and quiet apart from the glare of the moon, casting eerie shadows across the glen. I continue and park the 4X4 at the rear of the building. I pick up the flashlight from the back seat and open the boot. She flinches from the light. I cut the ties on her wrists and ankles. My hand reaches out, gripping her arm.

"Get out of the car. Don't try to escape this time."

Kristina follows my instructions.

Despite my warning, she tries to struggle from my grip. I hold on tighter as we make our way along the path towards the rear of the cottage. I take the key from the shelf on top of the door and try to find the lock. I drop the torch. My criminologist seizes the opportunity and grabs it before cracking it across my head. I flinch. My hand grips the back of my skull. In an almost insane act of violence, she smashes it over my head, again and again. I fall to the ground. I see her out the corner of my eye running towards the car. She pulls on the handle. It does not open. The key is in my pocket. Less than coherent, I raise my head in the air, try to refocus, blink my eyes open and shut until my vision returns to normal. She runs away from the cottage, over the gate and along a path leading to the forest.

I call out her name. "KRISTINA, COME BACK!"

The light of the torch vanishes.

I continue to pursue her through the wood and try to ignore the pain from the cracks to the skull. The thin tendrils of tree branches also whip into my face and body, stinging, showing no mercy. I refuse to give up. She can never escape. I need her in my life more than ever. Kristina is all I have left.

I close in on my target.

She stops to catch a breath and looks around. I am not far behind, running like a predator hunting its prey. She has no more energy left to escape and gives up like a defeated animal accepting its fate. We stare at each other, breathe heavily, in and out, in and out, gasping for air.

I see the cuts on her feet.

And blood oozes from the injuries to my head.

DRIP... DRIP... DRIP.

She drops to her knees and stares at the knife in my hand.

"Don't do it, Jayden. Please..."

"I warned you, Kristina. Not to try and escape."

I crouch down.

The blade rests on the thin layer of skin around her throat.

What the fuck am I doing?

Tears trickle down her face. "STOP!" she screams. "I'm pregnant with our child."

ABOUT THE AUTHOR

Marshall Hughes is a marketing lecturer in Scotland. Areas of expertise include how the work environment enhances or constrains creativity/innovation within the advertising sector as well as a fascination with the tantalising, creative minds that generate and produce inspirational ideas, products, services and media campaigns. Academic life aside, the author lives in a beautiful town with its gorgeous beaches and tranquil setting on the east coast of Scotland. The inspiration and motivation behind the compelling story transpires from his experiences, psychological challenges of life and somewhat morbid fascination with the darker side of human nature.

Printed in Great Britain
by Amazon